NEVER

NEVER

JOEL F. JOHNSON

ARBITRARY PRESS

New York

Published by Arbitrary Press

ISBN 978-1-958762-04-2

Typesetting services by BOOKOW.COM

To William, Henry, and Amelia

CHAPTER 1

I didn't know her given name. Never met her husband or any of her siblings. I knew only one story from her childhood: that as a girl of no more than seven, she visited her grandfather on the new Macon Road, where he worked on a chain gang clearing brush. Her mother carried a basket to the men, and they sat together in the shade, the men in their bib overalls and leg irons. The guard sat a few yards off, a white boy in his teens. He rested the twelve-gauge on his lap as he ate her mother's pimento cheese and Saltines. One of the shackled men, teasing her, pretended to catch at her leg. She laughed and darted away, knowing that he could not chase her in his heavy chains. Her mother scolded her for that.

I didn't know any of her friends other than the women she climbed the hill with before work. Like her, some wore their uniforms, a cotton dress of soft gray with white trim at the collar and rolled sleeves. Others wore their own clothes, loose cotton print dresses, some with check or floral patterns, and they carried their uniforms in paper grocery bags. They trudged up the hill in flip-flops, the asphalt already getting warm beneath their feet though the sun was still climbing through the pines.

We called her Bit. That's how she introduced herself to my mother before I was born, when Bit was in her mid-twenties and my mother, just two years out of college, was setting up house for the first time. My parents grew up in southern Georgia, in a small town where my grandfather on my mother's side managed the peanut mill. They married not long after the war and moved to LaSalle, a textile manufacturing town sixty miles north, where my father opened a woodworking shop. My mother was looking for help. An acquaintance from church introduced her to Bit, and she responded to Bit's poise. Bit knew how to hold herself, back straight, chin tilted, in a way that conveyed her dignity. Whether she inherited her good posture or adopted the stance to protect herself in an environment of perpetual insult, I do not know.

Her favorite drink was ice water; her favorite color yellow. She cooked without consulting recipes. Hid her use of snuff. Her palms felt soft and cool. She pulled her hair straight back, exposing a tall forehead, and she tied it behind her head in wiry, woven strands, sometimes adding a thin ribbon. Her pronounced cheekbones and strong jaw gave her face a sculpted quality. She often complained that her feet and legs hurt her, which I thought comical, a small cruelty I now regret. The varicose veins twisted in knots on her calves.

A tall woman with a wide back, Bit climbed our hill in the morning, vacuumed, swept, changed sheets, folded laundry, fixed dinner, and washed dishes, then went back down the hill in the late afternoon, caught a bus home, and did her own housework in the evening. She did what she had to do. She came to our house five days a week, early enough to fix my breakfast and late enough to leave our supper on the stove.

I knew where she lived because sometimes my mother would drive her home, with me up front, and Bit in back. Bit always rode in back—like all the maids who worked in my neighborhood. She lived in Baker Bottom with her daughter, Emma G, on a rutted clay road lined by shotgun shacks. Once, I went inside Bit's shack, but I'll save that story for later.

Bit's husband was killed in a car crash in 1946. Six weeks later, she gave birth to Emma G, and not long after, my sister Allyn was born. Bit had planned to leave her infant daughter with her husband's extended family while she worked, but after her husband died, she wanted to keep her daughter close. She approached my mother with what seemed like an outrageous idea, and my mother, unsure of her maternal skills and desperate for Bit's help, agreed to it. My father objected, but my mother got her way. So, for four days a week, Bit brought her infant daughter to our house and looked after the two babies together.

This solution, meant to be temporary, lasted almost until my sister entered kindergarten. My father never liked it. It embarrassed him to have a brown child under his roof. My mother, on the other hand, loved it. Bit may have been helping her but my mother also helped Bit. Bit lived on next-to-nothing, and she hated that she had to sleep with her infant child in the backroom of her mother-in-law's house. Somehow, my mother persuaded my father to buy Bit her own shack, a decidedly humble place in which she could cook her own meals, sleep in her own room, and raise Emma G as she saw fit.

My father saw himself as Bit's savior because he had given her a house, but my mother felt otherwise. She learned to care for Allyn by watching Bit breast feed and change diapers. For a few meaningful years, while my father was off at work and I was not yet on the scene, they raised their daughters together, the two of them alone in our house with their baby girls.

My mother never left Allyn at Bit's house. That would have been illegal under Georgia state law. In the late forties, Rosa Parks had not yet refused to surrender her seat, and the Georgia legislature had not yet decided to add the Confederate stars and bars to the state flag. Once Allyn started school, the girls saw less of one another, but Allyn continued to think of Emma G as her first friend. She took pride in her interracial friendship, just as I am perversely proud of my mid-century birthday (June 30, 1950). Whether throwing left-handed or having red hair or learning to swim before we can walk, each of us can find some minor trait or circumstance that separates us from the crowd. For Allyn, her friendship with Emma G counted as one of those things.

All this feels like it happened a hundred years ago. I would remember less of it if not for Allyn. "Hey, Little," she says when she calls. Of all the people on this planet, only Allyn still calls me Little. I was named after my father, who was called Big Morris, or Big M. I was to be Little Morris, but my mother dropped the "Morris."

"Hey yourself," I say.

"More snow, I see." Allyn pities me, the poor southerner trapped in arctic New England. Allyn lives with her husband in Texas. I have lived in Massachusetts for more than forty years.

We discuss the weather, our spouses, our children. Then Allyn says, "I assume you've been following the brouhaha in LaSalle." She is indulging in a bit of irony. We both know that she reads the LaSalle paper online, and I do not. She feels obligated to keep me up to date on events in a place I have not visited or thought much about in years. Allyn stays in touch with our various cousins down there. I don't. I keep my childhood encased in glass.

"Let me guess," I say. "Someone has proposed taking down Sweet Papa."

It pleases me to catch Allyn by surprise. "You mean you have been following it?" she asks.

I laugh. "A lucky guess. If they are taking down the Confederate monuments in Richmond, they are taking them down everywhere. It's inevitable that someone would complain about ours." The granite figure stands guard in LaSalle's Courthouse Square, the butt of his musket resting at his foot, a canteen hanging from the strap across his shoulder. The absurd name came from my father, who insisted that his great grandfather, a Confederate veteran, served as the model for the statue. When my father came up with this whopper, complete with the name 'Sweet Papa,' and when I fell for it, we were playing our standard roles. I should have known better. Whenever we passed the square, my father would call out, "Y'all pay your respects to Sweet Papa!" I always laughed because I doubted that we were related, but still, I wondered.

"I hope they don't plan to crush him up," I say to Allyn.

"Not to worry. They'll find a spot for him out in the cemetery somewhere," Allyn says, "But that leaves a big hole in the center of town. They may rename the square, and if they can find the money, they are even talking about putting up a new monument, something to commemorate the mass arrest."

"That I cannot believe," I say. "I spend my entire life either hiding where I'm from or making excuses for that day, and now they want to commemorate it?"

"The Reverend Timothy Butters Memorial Square."

Tim Butters. I remember the jolt of his handshake, his ferocious smile, his brown bald head, and how his horn-rimmed glasses reflected the lectern light. I feel a brief surge of nostalgia, surely a symptom of my advanced years, and I manage to say, "That would be nice, a memorial to Tim Butters."

"Tim Butters is only the half of it. Memorials don't come cheap. They are having a fundraiser at his old church with a guest speaker. You won't believe this. The speaker is Dr. Emogene Harrison."

"I don't know who that is."

"I think you do. It's Emma G, Bit's daughter." I am so taken aback by this news that I miss some of what Allyn is telling me, until she says, "I'm worried about what she's going to say. I mean, she's a former professor of sociology or something like that, and it's a memorial to Tim Butters, so you know she's going to talk about civil rights. Her mother was a maid, our maid. Emma G is going to talk about that. She's going to talk about us: you, me, Mama and Daddy. She's going to talk about how we treated her and Bit."

"What is that supposed to mean? We loved Bit, and Mama let Emma G come and play at our house. You two were friends."

"A friend I couldn't go see. A friend who wore my old clothes."

"Those were just the times. We were nice to Bit. Daddy gave her a house, for crying out loud. She was part of the family."

"I don't think Emma G is going to say that. They are going to be talking about what happened in Courthouse Square. Do you really think she's going to stand up and talk about how sweet we were to her mother?"

"Well, it's true. Look, no one can find fault with the way we treated Bit. We loved her, and she loved us. End of story."

Allyn doesn't answer.

"Are you going to go?" I ask.

"To the fundraiser? I'll send a check for fifty dollars, but I'm not planning a trip. They are going to need more than fifty bucks, though. You're the one who should go. Mama would have gone."

Allyn excels at manipulating me. If she suggests my mother would have gone, she knows I'll feel compelled to go myself. In my private pantheon, my mother serves as an ideal for me, and I often measure myself against her elevated image. Like most children, I always thought I occupied the center of our family's planetary system. My mother revolved around me as the introverted moon that governed my father's extroverted tides. She often kept her own counsel, but she read a lot and thought about things and spoke in a quiet way that commanded my attention. I resemble her both by nature and by choice.

My other role model swept our floors. She came to our house every day, fed me my bottle as an infant, held my hand at the curb, crushed crackers into my soft-boiled eggs. Bit commanded a vital place in our home, mother figure and servant, confidant and cook, a stranger I thought I knew.

CHAPTER 2

I have an old photograph of Bit holding me as a baby. She sits in an aluminum chair with me in the crook of her arm, a bottle in hand, sunlight and leaf shade thrown across our figures. The contrast's all wrong. I look like a slash of whiteness with an open mouth, and Bit's face appears so dark as to be almost featureless but for a dab of light on her forehead. Her strong jaw and the bones of her cheeks, which seemed to elevate and enliven her eyes, are obscured. Nevertheless, I often considered framing that picture and putting it on my desk. What stopped me was the thought that someone who doesn't know me might see the image as a parody of mammy and child. All I see is Bit holding me in her lap. I don't want anyone to make a caricature of a person I knew and loved.

An early memory. I am looking up at Bit as sweat from her hair runs in a glistening trail down her cheek. She scowls as she demands, "Why you have to be this way, Little?" Not so much asking the question as requiring of me an answer.

It hurts my neck to tilt my head so far. "Not next to me," I say. "Behind me. You have to walk behind me."

I imagined that all my classmates were watching us, which cannot be true, of course. The other students had no reason to stay inside as I walked home, but it felt that way, like the school was watching me and laughing, so I made her walk behind me. I wanted them to see that I could walk home alone, and that my family's maid just happened to follow behind. On a different day, Bit would have stopped outside the grocery store and sent me inside to buy Popsicles, orange for her and grape for me, but not that day. I marched ahead, my shirt sticking to my back, and Bit trudged behind, resenting the incline.

At the top of the hill, we turned off onto a narrow road called Private Drive that wound its way through enormous oaks and magnolias and uncut grass past an old, abandoned house. No one could see us back there, so I relented when Bit said, "Let's rest before I give out." She sat on an ancient wrought iron bench in the shade, mopping her glowing face. I poked around the bench, kicking at rocks and sticks, studying the ground where there was nothing to be found. "It is some kind of hot," she complained. "You hot?"

"No," I said.

"I can see you is," she said, "just by looking at your cheeks. You feel all right?"

"I'm fine," I said. I had made that walk plenty of times, but I was prone to migraine headaches, a condition I inherited from my mother. My episodes were not nearly as powerful as hers were. She would retreat to her bed for three days at a time. Mine lasted just an hour or so, a constricted pain in one eye along with a bout of nausea. In my first years of school, I walked home with Allyn, but once she went off to junior high, I climbed the hill alone. That went fine until one day, crossing the bridge at Cuttawa Creek, I saw the sun flash on the water in brilliant, jabbing light. As I climbed the hill, the pain in my eye grew intense. By the top of the hill, I was nauseated. Sick and confused, I turned onto Private Drive and wandered off the narrow leaf-strewn road into the dense shade beneath a magnolia. I crawled beneath the tree and vomited over the dried leathery leaves, then fell asleep on the hard, root-braided ground and did not wake until I heard a neighbor's maid calling my name. She was part of a small search party Bit had organized when I was late coming home from school. I sat up, a low branch across my chest, and saw her looking at me through the parted leaves.

Bit carried me home that day. I was too tired to resist. My mother, worried sick, insisted that, from then on, if she could not come pick me up, Bit would walk me home. I tried to talk her out of this humiliating plan but could not. So, there I was, the only boy in school who had to be walked home by his maid.

"Why you think you can't tell me how hot you is?" Bit demanded from her bench. "I don't want you getting sick on me."

"I'm not sick. I'm fine," I insisted.

"You weren't fine that day you crawled off the way you did. You scared your mama half to death."

"Wasn't my fault."

"Did I say it was your fault? Ain't nobody blaming you. Your mama just wants you looked after, that's all."

"I can look after myself. I'm big now."

Bit sniffed.

"You know what I mean," I said.

"I do. You know what else I know? That you don't want me walking you home from school. I could see that on your face the minute I got there. But I have to do like your mama tells me. She can't have you falling out the way you did."

"That was one time. I won't let it happen again."

"They ain't nothing you can do about it, honey. That's who you is. Your mama is the same way. You think she wants to be getting sick the way she does? If she could stop it, she would. Same as you."

My mother's headaches were the source of an odd rhythm in our family, the rise and fall of her episodes separating those days when we were a normal, busy household from those in which her door was closed, and silence smothered our world. I became expert at diagnosing the state of her aching head. Her eyes, cheerfully ironic when she was well, clouded over and turned inward, as if to read from a hidden page. She held herself very still, protecting her head. With the onset of those symptoms, I knew she would be leaving me, and Bit would take over. Bit was a good caregiver, but that did not keep me from worrying about my mother and longing for her attention. I sulked outside her door, waiting for the gloom to lift.

When one of my mother's headaches was reaching its peak, only Bit entered the sick room. She slipped off her flip-flops at the door and moved soundlessly from the bed to the bathroom and back. She emptied the throw-up bowl and brought a fresh, damp cloth for my mother's forehead, her voice a murmur, her words indistinct, though I struggled to hear.

"There is something else I want you to know," Bit said from her bench in the shade. "Look at me when I tell you this." She was pointing at me. "You can't be treating me the way you did back there, making me walk behind you like you did. That ain't no way to treat a person, especially not me. You hear?"

"I guess so," I said.

"I don't want you to guess so. I want you to know so."

"I didn't want them laughing at me."

"They weren't laughing at you. You always think people are laughing at you. Nobody is looking at you or thinking about you neither. They are thinking about themselves."

"Not Larry Williams," I said. Larry Williams ruled the playground at recess, an oversized kid with a braying laugh, a connoisseur of fart jokes.

"Larry Williams," Bit said, as if by simply repeating his name, she had dismissed the argument. She sat studying me, a restless pattern of shade playing across her face. With her hair pulled straight back, her strength seemed to gather in her chiseled cheeks and sharp eyes. "I tell you what," she said, "Suppose you meet me at the Piggly Wiggly? I don't reckon nothing is going to happen to you between the school and the Piggly Wiggly. You leave school by yourself, just like everybody else, then meet me at the store, and we'll walk up the hill together when won't nobody be looking at you. How about that?" Crisis solved.

I worried that Bit would tell my mother how I had treated her. I couldn't bear the thought of that. But Bit never told. She didn't need my mother's help to keep me in line. I knew I'd failed to understand and follow some elliptical code of conduct. I'd have to figure that out on my own.

CHAPTER 3

Y hometown has a notorious past. People remember an old article from *Newsweek,* or they've watched an episode about civil rights on *The American Experience.* When I was growing up, LaSalle, Georgia seemed benign to me. But if I try to express that now, people regard me with condescending smiles, as if I'm naïve or trying to hide something. I suppose my treatment of Bit that day, like the photograph of her feeding me my bottle, falls into the "things to hide" category.

My father possessed a remarkable ability to tell stories from his past in a matter-of-fact way, even if the story involved horrific details like clearing Japanese soldiers from a cave with a flamethrower, or worse, in what was supposed to be peacetime, watching a couple of acquaintances drag a corpse behind a car. I might try to brush off the past, but once I start thinking about it, I can't distance myself or put it aside. Allyn's call has unsettled me, stirring up old memories of Bit and my mother.

After that first day, Bit would meet me at the store, and we would climb the hill together. We didn't eat Popsicles though. Our walks were all business. Bit typically had a supper to fix before she could go home, and even when the weather cooled off, she didn't enjoy the extra exercise of walking up and down the hill. I may have been the first to rebel, but Bit came to resent those walks more than I did. And so we would climb the hill in silence, Bit self-absorbed and moody, grunting softly as she walked.

That changed when Jamie McAllister decided to walk from school with me. This must have been late November or early December. I don't remember inviting Jamie to my house. It would have been just like him to invite himself. In any case, he was walking with me when we found Bit waiting outside the Piggly Wiggly.

"Hey, Bit," he said, "Little and I are going inside for a pack of gum. Can we get you something?"

Bit laughed. "Ain't you sweet! No, thank you, Jamie. I'll wait for y'all out here." If Bit needed to get back to put a meatloaf in the oven, she didn't let on. I followed Jamie inside and watched him pay for the gum. The three of us walked up the hill together, each chewing a fresh stick of Juicy Fruit. That became the new routine. If my mother drove me home, Jamie rode with us, and on the days when Bit waited at the store, she seemed to look forward to seeing Jamie. Winter gave way to spring, and still Jamie walked with us, chatting as we climbed, commenting on the squirrels, on the abundance of acorns or lack thereof, speculating on the abandoned house, wondering who had lived there and why they left, describing his father's new car (a *Chev-ro-lay*, he announced, as if it were a French import), asking Bit which church she attended. When we got to my house, Bit fixed us a snack, peanut butter on Saltines or sandwiches of pineapple, mayonnaise and white bread trimmed of its crust. All the while Jamie chatted, telling us about the TV show he'd watched the night before, asking Bit where she'd learned to cook, commenting on our dog, expressing his preference for cats, assuring us he liked both, asking me if I had read *Tom Sawyer*. The school year ended, but our snack times continued. While Bit fixed supper and we sat at the table, Jamie talked as much to Bit as to me. He asked her what made self-rising flour rise, and he wondered whether the chickens we ate were hens only or roosters as well, and could one taste the difference? He asked what a cling peach clung to. Bit had to admit she didn't know.

When school started again and I entered fifth grade, my mother no longer insisted that Bit walk with me. Instead, I walked with Jamie, sometimes to his house, but more often to mine. Our house was larger, with a pool and a trampoline in the backyard. Allyn had her own room, and I had mine, and there was a third room, intended as a guest room, that we called the "sick room." When my mother had a headache, she retreated there, away from my father's snoring, our television set, and the window unit he kept at Hi Cool. The house was a long ranch, with a living room of polished brick floors and glass doors that opened out to a generously shaded yard. Floor-to-ceiling shelves held my mother's books, a framed watercolor of my grandmother's house, a nautilus shell, and a massive dictionary opened to a color plate of gemstones. For most of the summer, we left the doors open, and an overhead fan stirred the air, providing us with what my father called "self-cleaning ashtrays."

Allyn kept her door closed, which intrigued Jamie. She was younger than his sister, Julia, closer in age to the two of us, a mystery we could almost solve. Once, when Allyn happened to leave her door open, he stepped inside. "We're not supposed to go in there," I told him. But Jamie had to look. He peeked in her closet and flipped through the book beside her bed. He inspected her stuffed tiger perched on its mound of pillows, a trophy my father had brought home from Atlanta. Allyn had a "portable" turntable (it must have weighed twenty pounds) and a metal box of forty-fives. Jamie flipped through them, studying the titles, trying to decipher her world. One of her favorites was Ray Charles singing "What'd I Say?" a song that appalled my father. Ray moaning back and forth with his Raelettes was not something Big M wanted his adolescent daughter to hear.

My father brought home the money that paid for everything in that house, every chair, book, pillow, and pot. We were not rich, but Big M did well, and providing for his family pleased him. That he loved us went without saying, and so it was never said. When we were younger, he liked to roughhouse, not hug. On my mother's birthdays, he handed over cash without the sappy card. Wrapped gifts were rare. "Words are easy," he told me one evening when we were sitting by the pool. "People can say anything. It's the work you do for others that counts. You want to know how I feel about this family? Look around you."

Jamie's house was on the far side of school, closer to downtown. His father was our minister, and the Presbyterian church provided his family with a small but respectable place, with a functional kitchen, three adequate bedrooms, and a fenced yard just large enough to hold a swing set Jamie never used. Jamie's mother kept plastic slipcovers over the furniture in the living room. A cheap painting of a cheerful stream hung over the couch. End tables guarded either side of the couch with dragonware vases, hideous and fragile, the scaly dragons writhing upwards, souvenirs from Reverend McAllister's time in occupied Japan. We had a maid; Jamie's family did not. But Jamie's house was neater than ours. Three magazines, *Look, Life,* and *Time,* lay on the coffee table in perfect strata, each spine one inch from the next. The carpet kept the pattern of Carol McAllister's even strokes with the vacuum. The kitchen looked unused.

Reverend McAllister's study might have been a converted closet, sandwiched between the bedrooms, barely large enough for the reverend's desk, lamp, and chair. Shelves of books lined the walls with titles like *Destiny and Choice, Either/Or, Lanterns on the Levee, Ivanhoe, Roughing It, Thus Spoke Zarathustra,* and, of course, *Collected Sermons.* I pitied Jamie for his cramped, pool-less yard, but his father's study evoked awe, a place of mysterious and scholarly work. My mother belonged to the Book-of-the-Month Club, but she did not study her books as the reverend did his. This library was a place of serious purpose, an intimate sanctuary where a man toiled in silence.

Lunch was the only meal I ate regularly at Jamie's house, typically peanut butter and jelly. If the reverend ate with us, we held hands and recited a blessing before the meal. This small ritual did not strike me as odd—I knew his profession required the saying of grace—but holding hands made me uncomfortable. Who holds hands just to eat peanut butter and jelly? No one in my family. The McAllisters hugged and kissed. The Nickersons did not.

Jamie regularly spent the night at our house, sleeping on an army cot in my room. Eventually, his mother decided she had to reciprocate, or maybe the reverend decided it was time to get to know me better. In any case, Jamie invited me to have dinner and spend the night.

When I arrived, Jamie took me in to say hello to his father, who was seated at his desk behind a sturdy black typewriter. The study contained no chairs other than his own, so we stood before him, like soldiers reporting to a commanding officer. Reverend McAllister was a tall, once-dark Scot, whose hair turned white at an early age, though his thick eyebrows remained a peppery black. His crest of snowy hair and his keen blue eyes intimidated me, but his smile was genuine.

I didn't trust grownup smiles. I knew my nickname amused most adults, and I suspected them of laughing at me. Not the reverend. His face communicated a surprising measure of respect, his gaze a frank appraisal of my character. "I'm so happy you could join us this evening," he said. "It seems like Jamie is at your house all the time these days, and I'm glad we can return the favor."

"Thank you for having me," I answered, remembering my manners.

"What are you working on?" Jamie asked his father.

"Just another sermon. Nothing special."

"Can I look?" Jamie moved around the desk toward the paper stacked beside the typewriter.

His father put his hand on the stack. "Not yet," he said. "When I have something worth showing you, I'll let you read it. This one isn't ready for the critics yet." That stack of pages stirred my curiosity. I had sat through any number of the reverend's sermons, eager for each to end, never paying attention to a word he said. But a sermon he would not let us see had interest. The keys of the big Royal stood erect and proud, and beside the typewriter lay a well-worn Bible, together with an ashtray, an old-fashioned fountain pen and bottled ink, and one or two open books taken down from the reverend's shelves. Why these books and not others? How did he decide what to say and where to begin? As if reading my thoughts, Jamie's father turned one of his books around and pushed it toward me. "This is Dickens," he said. "He writes so well you almost don't notice how angry he is. A good trick to learn for a man in my profession. Have you read him?"

I laughed before I realized he was serious. "No sir," I said.

"Well, you should," he said, "Maybe try *A Tale of Two Cities*. You'd like it, I think." He tilted his head, his upper lip slightly curled. "You do enjoy reading about people having their heads removed, I hope?"

"Yes sir," I said, "I mean I guess so."

His eyes fell back to the page in his typewriter. "Oh," he said, discovering something there. He crossed it out. "I'm afraid," he said, rolling the typewriter carriage up, then down, "this is going to require more work. I'll see you two at dinner."

Jamie took me into his room. I had been there before, but this time, he put his finger to his lips and led me to his small closet. With me standing behind him in the room, he got down on his hands and knees and showed me a small gate hook and eye on the closet's back wall. He flashed me a wicked smile, unlatched the hook, and opened a vent that led into the closet of his sister's room. We could hear her talking on the telephone. I crouched and listened.

Julia McAllister was everything Allyn aspired to be, outgoing and glamorous, a cheerleader in an era when being a cheerleader meant everything. She wore her hair poufed into a hairspray lacquered dome, like Jackie Kennedy. She called me "little Little" but said it in a way that made me feel like I was in on the joke. I was attracted to her brilliant eyes and infectious laugh, and I was not the only one. My mother said she was lively, but my father said she was trouble. On the far side of Jamie's closet, we could hear her saying, "I can't believe she's still dating him. Have you seen the bruises on her arm from where he pinches her? It's gross." Jamie's shoulders shook with exaggerated, silent laughter, and he covered the vent again.

We found Carol McAllister in the kitchen, arms crossed, watching a pot on the stove. She seemed to be waiting to see what happened next. "Little Morris!" she called out, slightly startled, "We're delighted to have you!" She was tall and pretty, with red hair and pale skin. Her skin was so thin and white that I could see one of the veins on her forehead, a faint, rounded thread of blue that ascended into her hairline. She had the nervous eyes of a sparrow. I had heard my mother say that every talk with Carol McAllister felt like an interruption of some other conversation.

Julia blew past us in a hurry, startling her mother. "I'm gone!" she called.

Her mother turned. "Don't be ..."

"I won't!" Julia answered, and the door closed behind her. Jamie's mother shook her head, cleared her throat, looked at me, then at the stove, uncertain.

Jamie and I took seats at the kitchen table. Carol asked how my mother was but paid no attention to my answer. She washed her hands, placed a pan on the stove, and rested her slender fingers inside the pan to feel it as it warmed. "Have either of you ever fried bacon before?" she asked. I gave Jamie a quick look. Everyone knows how to fry bacon. Bit did it every day. The pan grew suddenly hot, and she snatched her hand way. She wrestled with the package of bacon, pulling at the plastic wrapping, then slashing it with a carving knife. When she dropped the bacon into the pan, which was now much too hot, the fat hissed and spattered. Instead of turning down the heat, she went to the sink to wash her hands again. A thread of white smoke rose and curled along the ceiling. Reverend McAllister called from down the hall, "How's it going? Everything under control?"

"Everything's fine," Carol called back, an edge in her voice. "It's just this silly bacon. I don't know..." She shook the pan hard, slopping grease onto the stove. It ignited into a finger of pale yellow flame. Jumping back, she emitted a single, sharp "Oh!" Rattled, she filled a glass of water and splashed it on the small flame, which hissed and scattered, dividing into bright rivulets that streamed across the stove and countertop then down onto the floor. It was not a large fire, but a fire nonetheless, and one of the thin streams advanced toward the curtains at the kitchen window. Jamie and I jumped to our feet, and his chair toppled over, rattling hard against the linoleum. Startled, his mother dropped her glass, which shattered in bright, sharp slivers that skittered across the floor. Jamie's father apparently heard all the commotion, because he ran into the room, shouting, "Baking soda! Get some baking soda!" while Jamie's mother backed away from him, her mouth open, hands raised. The reverend yanked open the refrigerator so violently a jar of pickles clattered down from the door and broke at his feet. He snatched a box, ripped the lid away, and poured baking soda over the thin flames, following the line of fire across the counter and down to the floor, swiftly efficient. I thought there could not possibly be enough or that it would not work, but it proved a miracle, the minister's own moment of loaves and fishes, a sufficient enough supply from so small a box that the flames surrendered with barely a hiss, meek as smothered kittens.

Jamie's father turned off the burner and switched on the vent hood, which erupted into an industrial roar. "Everything is fine," he called out above the fan, trying to sound reassuring, even trying to laugh. "Just a little grease fire!" But Jamie's mother retreated to the sink, fumbled at the valves, then put her hands beneath the scalding water. McAllister shut it off, gently pushing her back. She kept clearing her throat. "I can't," she said, "I can't," clearing her throat as if she were gagging on the smoke. The roaring stove fan vacuumed the room of its air. "It's fine, Carol," the reverend announced, his voice loud above the fan. "Everything's all right now. Just a little grease fire."

"But I can't," she said and moved back toward the sink. He blocked her. She waved her hands at him, palms out, as if shielding her face from a strong light. "I have to go." She hurried from the kitchen, and we heard the bedroom door slam shut. "Carol!" he called after her, "we have a guest!" But he didn't follow. The three of us stood in the kitchen, drowning in the noise, the floor splattered with pickle juice, broken glass and baking soda, the bubbling broccoli getting low on water, announcing itself in a tart odor beneath the smell of burnt bacon. The fan roared on, manic and unceasing, until Jamie's father switched it off. I felt grateful for the silence. "Damn fan," the reverend muttered, opening the window wider. "We've got to get it replaced." Then he turned and looked at us, artificially cheerful, and brought his hands together in a single, resolute clap. "Well, that was dramatic!" he said. "Everyone okay? Little, you all right?"

"Yes sir," I said, though the smell made me feel like I might throw up. The reverend gave Jamie a roll of paper towel, handed me a dustpan, and grabbed the broom for himself. It took the three of us the better part of twenty minutes to clean up the mess. The counter was scorched.

Afterwards, we ate a morose dinner, and I forced down a piece of the limp broccoli smeared with mayonnaise. No one made me eat vegetables at home, but as a guest, I knew what was required of me. Neither Jamie nor his father mentioned his mother, though we felt her presence down the hall.

Since Jamie's bedroom was too small for the two of us, Reverend McAllister opened the folding couch in the living room. After he turned out the light, Jamie and I lay side-by-side on the thin mattress. I could feel the bar of the couch frame beneath my hip. When a car passed, its lights swept the ceiling. The tall vases on the end tables towered above us, the climbing dragons yellow-eyed, listening in the dark.

"Poor Mama," Jamie said.

"You think she's all right?"

"She's fine. At least she will be fine. She just gets too wound up about things. I told her how Bit fixes your dinner every night, and she got this idea that she wanted us to have a nice supper like that, so you would feel at home, but she almost never cooks. She just heats up Chef Boyardee or gives us hot dogs or Daddy grills something. I told her you'd be fine, but once she gets an idea in her head, you can't change her. She was trying so hard to have this perfect family supper all laid out for you, and well, you saw what happened."

"Why not get a maid? She could cook for y'all."

"Mama doesn't like them."

After Jamie fell asleep, I lay awake listening to the sounds of an unfamiliar house. The couch frame poked my back through the pitiful mattress. At home, our dog, Smoke, sometimes came into my bedroom and curled on the foot of my bed. I wished I was home with him. They had a cat somewhere, a creepy Persian named Jezebel. I hoped she wouldn't come and lick my hair. As I lay there, I could hear the ticking of the rafters and the crickets outside. I could smell the scorched counter, the pickle juice and over-cooked broccoli. The sound of Jamie's breathing felt very close. He could sleep, but I could not. I imagined the reverend and Carol McAllister in their dark bedroom. He would be sleeping too, but not her. I knew she was watching the ceiling, just like me. I closed my eyes and saw the image of the bone-colored flame spreading across the counter. I turned and pulled the sheet high. Jamie's breathing was even and slow, the sawing crickets musical and strange, the night air damp. I fell asleep.

"What the hell?" I woke abruptly to the sound of Julia's voice, so close she could have been standing next to the foldout couch.

Then another voice, the reverend's, and I rolled over and saw a harsh fluorescence framed by the kitchen door, the two of them facing one another, Jamie's father with his back to me, in his pajamas, and Julia in makeup and a skirt, still standing at the open door to the garage, looking around the room. "You're late," he said.

"What the hell?" she said again. "Look at the counter! What happened?"

"Have you been drinking, Julia?" he demanded, his voice stern.

"Really, Daddy? You want to talk about me drinking? While you've been doing what? Burning up the kitchen?" Julia laughed. "It stinks in here!"

She moved to open another window, but he stopped her. "I want you in bed this minute. I won't have this. Not in this house."

"You mean in this house that smells like a burnt pickle factory?" she said. She couldn't keep herself from laughing.

"In bed! This minute!" he said, struggling to keep his voice down. He closed the kitchen door, and the room went dark.

I never told my mother about the grease fire or about Julia, either. I had seen plenty the McAllisters would want to keep private, and I had reached that age when I no longer told my mother everything. My life was not her life, and just as she did not tell me some things, I kept things to myself, too.

But Bit wasn't my mother, and I knew Carol's cooking episode was the kind of story she would enjoy. She had an irresistible laugh, eyes closed, her hand across her mouth, and it was so pleasing to watch, so infectious to hear her giggle, that I could not resist regaling her. By the time I got to the part of my story where the flames were spreading and Jamie's mother filled a glass, Bit was shaking steadily, and she said, "Now, don't you tell me that! Don't you be telling me she threw that water on that grease! I know you teasing me now!" And when I proceeded to tell her about the burning grease floating on the water across the counter and down to the floor and about the reverend running into the kitchen, Bit had me laughing so hard I could barely go on.

I spent a good part of my childhood in the kitchen with Bit, talking to her about everything and nothing at all, watching her cook. Her hands were constantly moving, slicing carrots, shelling peas, dredging pork chops in flour. She kept a glass of ice water by the sink, and when she drank, she closed her eyes and lifted her little finger from the glass. When she chopped onions, it amused me to see her wipe tears from the corners of her eyes with the back of her wrist. "You got a trampoline out there," she'd say. "Why don't you go jump on it?" Or, "Why don't you put on your swimsuit and go out to the pool?" But I did not want to do those things. I wanted to be in the kitchen with her, watching the rhythm of her work. I was chronically underfoot.

Most of all, though, I loved Bit's laugh, and would frequently tease her just to hear it. I'd sneak up behind her and tie her apron in knots, knot upon knot upon knot, then laugh as I watched her struggle to free herself. She always laughed along, too, until one afternoon when she didn't. I remember it as the day after Christmas. I was in a glorious mood, happy with my haul. The house was a wreck, with presents, evergreen needles, and ribbons scattered everywhere, dishes piled in towers in the sink. I sneaked up and began tying knots, and she whirled and swatted me away. "I ain't got time for your silliness now!" she snapped.

I'm mixing memories here. Bit scolded me at Christmas, and I slept at Jamie's house the following summer. But we remember the jarring moments, not the routine in-between. That little grease fire stays with me, the smoke, the smell, the reverend running into the room. When I saw Jamie's mother hold out her hands as if to ward away a swarm, my orderly world began to crack. By summer's end, it lay in shards.

CHAPTER 4

BOTH my parents were born in a town called Cemochechobee. The local joke about Cemochechobee was that you could drive through it faster than you could pronounce the name. My father's family lived on a farm outside of town, but my mother grew up close to the small commercial center with its grocery store, churches, and icehouse. Whenever we went down to Cemochechobee, we stayed with my maternal grandmother, and Allyn and I had free run of the town. We felt like minor royalty when we walked into the hardware store and heard the proprietor say, "You're Mo Nickerson's children, aren't you?"

On summer visits, my father drove us out to the farm, where my uncle lived in the old family house. We ate lunch with my cousins, a country spread of ham, corn, sliced tomatoes, field peas, and iced tea, then my father would announce, "Well, maybe we'll go say hello to Brother before we leave." Brother was an African American of my father's age with a lean frame and a quiet smile, a man who rarely made eye contact. It amused Allyn and me that my father called his older sibling "Bob" and the farmhand "Brother." "We grew up together," was how my father explained a kind of relationship now rare or nonexistent.

It did not require an advanced degree in psychology to see that my father and his true brother were different types. Bob was chronically taciturn and my father naturally social. Our visits to Bob's house felt like an obligation; going to see Brother was fun. The two men had a laconic, perpetually ironic way of addressing one another that I liked to hear. Standing in a swarm of flying mites, my father might remark, "Seems like you got a good crop of gnats this year," and Brother, sweeping his hand before his face in a futile gesture, inevitably replied, "One of the best I can recall."

On one of our visits to the farm, my father said, "I need to go talk to Bob, but maybe you can help Brother feed the ducks." I had never been alone with Brother, but when I climbed into his pickup, he ignored me in a friendly way, as if we had made this ride lots of times. There were no seat belts, and as we bumped along the rutted clay road, I had to brace myself to keep from sliding around on the bench seat. I watched Brother work the clutch and gearshift. We rode in silence, and he studied the fields as we passed, pausing at one, putting the truck in neutral. Then he grunted and shook his head, making note of some mystery there, and we drove on.

Brother parked at an aluminum gate between fences of rusted barbed wire. He handed me a ring of keys, one with a spot of red paint, another with a spot of blue, and a third with the green mostly worn off. The padlock was heavy, gritty with rust, and I struggled with it, convinced Brother had picked the wrong key, until it opened with a clunk. I had to lift the gate to keep it from bumping on the road as I swung it open so Brother could drive through.

The barn was an elevated structure of weathered gray boards, its floor almost waist high on me. I thought it odd that the barn had no steps, considering that it stored sacks of grain, a feed tub, rakes, shovels, and even an old wheelbarrow heavy as a truck, but Brother didn't seem to notice. He jumped up and hauled sacks from the dark interior while I examined an abandoned snakeskin, wondering whether the snake that had grown too large for it might be lurking close by. I staggered beneath the weight of one of the bags, hauling it out to my uncle's boat. Brother followed, a bag under each arm. We loaded the bags, paddles, and a tin bucket into the boat. Brother climbed in front and waited for me to unlock the chain, but this one I could not manage, so he climbed out to do it.

It did not look it, but the lake was artificial, one of my uncle's improvements to the property he had inherited from my grandfather. My uncle stocked it with bass and bream. Pines and oak trees surrounded it, with a few dogwoods sprinkled in. If the boat had tipped twenty yards offshore, we probably could have walked out, but the muddy water hid the bottom only a foot or two from the bank. At different times of the year, water moccasins, bullfrogs, mallards, dragonflies, whip-poor-wills, and mosquitoes made this patch of water home.

Brother paddled out, the lake smooth and faintly fragrant. It was late autumn, but not cold. Brother wore rubber boots, a light jacket, and his perpetual cap. He examined the water, and I pretended to do so as well.

"Looks like we've had a few," he said.

"It sure does," I said, looking down into the blank water, seeing nothing.

"Look here," he said, pointing across the flat water, "you see these feathers?" I noticed them now, curled bits of fluff floating on the surface. "That's how I know."

We went around a small bend and anchored. There was no wind, the water still, the inverted limbs of the bare trees painted along its edges. Brother shook out some corn, stood, and swung the half-filled bucket, sending an arc of grain over the quiet water, each kernel lifting a blip as it hit the surface. He fell into the rhythm of his work as I sat in the front of the boat with a paddle, trying to hold us steady. He shook out corn and swung the bucket up and out, each toss sweeping a dark arc across the sky. The lake answered his labor in faint echoes, mild reverberations that deepened all he did, the thump of the bucket in the bottom of the boat, the clatter of corn in tin, the sputter of grains as they hit the surface. We moved the boat to make sure of an even spread.

"Why are we doing this?" I asked.

"Mister Bob likes to hunt ducks. They enjoy this corn."

"Isn't that called 'baiting a lake'? I thought that was illegal."

"I expect it is," Brother said. "You want to try it?"

"I guess so."

"They ain't but one thing you has to remember."

"What?"

"Don't fall out the boat."

When I stood holding the bucket, I saw that Brother was not entirely joking. Though the water was calm, I could feel the boat tilting beneath me. Trying both to balance myself and to swing the bucket, I sent out a feeble arc, much of the corn clattering down into the bottom of the boat. "That's right," he said, "Try again."

We emptied the sacks, then I scooped up as much of the corn from the boat bottom as I could and threw that out into the water. Brother let the boat drift. Some light remained, but the sun had sunk below the trees, their reflections larger now. Out toward the center of the lake, the muddy color of the surface gave way to silver. "You like it out here?" Brother said, looking out over the water.

"I guess so."

"Me too."

If it had been summer, we might have listened to the croak of a bullfrog or the call of a whip-poor-will and enjoyed more time to drift, but it was November, and nothing moved, the quiet lake gathering the sky's last light. It was altogether dark when Brother dropped me off at my grandmother's house in town. I thanked him.

"You're welcome," he said. "I enjoyed the company." His eyes met mine for the briefest of moments, light as a dragonfly.

My father was five years older than my mother. Their families were acquainted, as most families in Cemochechobee were, but my parents were not childhood sweethearts. They began dating after both had left town, when my father was a Marine home from the Pacific, and my mother, fresh out of college, was working as a secretary in Atlanta, the big city. He was confident and easygoing, a man in uniform, while she tended to be cautious in everything she did, anxious to avoid another headache. My father could not cure the headaches, but he did, in a way, free her from herself, bringing her along to ride in the slipstream of his cheerful, capable pragmatism. She lived a better life because of him, and I think she appreciated that. When I came along, exhibiting the same hesitancies she had learned to overcome, she may not have been altogether delighted. I was a child "just like her," and she did not love every aspect of herself. Our similarities created an oblique tension between us, which I, as a child, did not understand.

When I was eight or so, I was invited to a costume birthday party. My mother decided that I should go as a sailor, and she used a ballpoint pen to draw the tattoo of a ship on my chest. I resisted the idea. I did not want to attend anyone's party without a shirt. "Don't be so fussy," my mother said. "Lots of boys go all summer long without a shirt." She wanted me to be a carefree kid, barefoot and happy. The exposure horrified me, and we argued, though I worried that any kind of resistance would trigger one of her headaches. As a compromise, she allowed me to go with an open shirt. As soon as she dropped me off, I buttoned it to the neck.

My mother's father, a man I never met, came to Cemochechobee sometime around 1915, when the Columbia Peanut Company sent him south from Norfolk to manage one of their mills. Lang Hayes was only in his forties and his eldest daughter only in her teens when he died of a stroke. His funeral was a town-wide affair. At the conclusion of the graveside service, my mother stood with her younger sisters next to her mother as the mourners approached them, first people they knew, then others they did not. They told stories of what Mr. Hayes had done for them, lending one a few dollars, sending a doctor to another, helping a recent widow find a place to live, acts of charity he had never mentioned to his family. As my mother told it, the line was nearly endless, the stories heartrending and warm. Growing up, I accepted her story at face value, and I regretted never having known this paragon of a grandparent. Looking back on it now, I can see how a teenage girl, upon suddenly losing her father, would turn him into a hero, and, with the passage of years, multiply the stories she had heard from one or two grateful strangers. This perfect father, tactfully charitable, widely respected, irretrievably lost, became the standard against whom she measured all others.

My father's family were country people. My parents maintained that Uncle Bob, the oldest child, was just like Robert Sr. A humorless soul, he felt none of my father's sentimentality toward Brother. Bob paid Brother to work the farm, just as Robert Sr. had employed Brother's father. It was a business relationship. When Brother came to Bob's door, he was not welcomed into the house.

Bob farmed the miscellaneous. He had a field of peanuts, a field of soybeans, another of melons, and another of corn. He had a pigsty, chickens, a couple of goats, a donkey, and a mule. Through our visits to the farm, I formed my opinion that pigs were mean, chickens stupid, and a donkey easier to ride than a goat. One day, my mother, Allyn, and I were riding in the car with my father when we spotted Brother out in a field of cantaloupes. My father rolled down the window and called out to him. He told Brother we were headed to the spring for a swim. He said it was too hot to work and that Brother should cut a few cantaloupes and meet us at the spring.

Brother called back, "I'm going to need help choosing some."

"Y'all hop out and help Brother," my father said. "He can bring you over in the truck."

Allyn and I hurried out through the tangle of vines to where Brother stood among the melons. The field was roasting in the sun, the air rich with gnats. "Y'all squeeze a few of these and see can you find us a good one," he said.

Allyn busied herself squeezing melons, and I began squeezing them myself, though they all felt the same to me.

"Here's one!" Allyn called. Brother and I walked over.

"Squeeze it again, Allyn, just to be sure," Brother said. Allyn dutifully squeezed. "Perfect," he said. He pulled a pocketknife out, unfolded it, and handed it to me. "Cut that vine for me, if you would please, Little." I cut, then Brother cut several more, handing two to Allyn, two to me, and keeping two for himself. He set the melons on the bed of his pickup and said, "Allyn, you ride back here and hold them steady."

I climbed on the front seat with Brother. As the truck lurched slowly toward the spring, I heard the cantaloupes rolling around, and I turned to see Allyn stretched out on the truck bed, struggling to keep them under control. Brother glanced in the rearview mirror, smiled, and said nothing.

He parked at the edge of a field, and we tramped through the thick brush behind him, toting the cantaloupes. My parents were already there, my mother with her slacks rolled up, cooling her feet in the clear, sun-dappled water. Her feet beneath the surface looked slim and white. She was laughing at something my father had said before we walked up. She handed us rolled towels, and Allyn and I went back into the woods to put on our bathing suits. I went a long way because I didn't want anyone looking at me. When I got back to the spring, my mother said, "There you are. I thought I was going to have to come look for you."

The cantaloupes floated in the spring water like buoyant cannon balls, and Allyn was walking the sandy bottom on tiptoes, trying to keep her waist above the surface. I saw why when I followed her into the water. It was remarkably cold. We ventured out toward the spring, a submerged volcano of roiling sand. "Brother," my father said, "did y'all ever find that cow that stepped down in that spring?"

"No sir," Brother said, "She went under, and that was the last we seen her."

Allyn laughed, and I laughed because she did, though I was wary of the bubbling hole. I heard my mother say, "Are you sure this is safe?"

"Nope," my father said. I looked back at him. "Y'all go one at a time," he called. "That way, if one of you goes under, I'll have one left over to care for me in my declining years."

"Be careful, Little!" my mother called.

We steered the floating melons out to the mouth of the spring and tried to push them down. They popped out, each bursting from the surface in a silvery splash, their veined rinds rough in our hands. I dared Allyn to jump in the hole, but she said I should go first because the gods were demanding a virgin sacrifice. I wasn't sure what a virgin was, but I said I would if she would, and we held hands and plunged feet-first into its sandy, churning center. The water rushed up under my bathing suit, gritty and cold. We laughed and hooted, struggled out, and jumped in again. After we were done swimming, we pushed the melons to the edge, and Brother cut them open, digging out the now cold, orange meat for us to eat.

We sat beside the spring and ate our melon, as my mother asked Brother about his wife and children and the people in Cemochoechobee they knew in common: Miss Pearl Hallett, who must be, what, at least ninety now, and Myrtiss Rae, who had a granddaughter working for Mrs. Mobley and another working for Mrs. Cane. Myrtiss Rae was even older than Miss Pearl Hallett, maybe even close to a hundred, and she had, according to Brother, her same sweet disposition. My mother asked about Walter Wetherbee's sorry boy, Chris, who had been sent to the state penitentiary, and Brother said he was still there. My father said that whole family had always been sorry. Brother reported that Flo Michaels "fell out" a few months ago and no longer knew who she was, and that Ernie Rogers had died, which my mother was sad to hear. Then my father said it was time for us to go, so Allyn and I went back into the woods to change out of our wet bathing suits. My father slipped Brother a roll of bills, and we left him by the spring to pick up the rinds.

Every trip to Cemochoechobee featured a transfer of cash. Big M reached into his pocket for a roll—he never counted out the bills—and, keeping his hand below his waist, slipped the wad to Brother, who slid it into his own pocket, also never counting, and said, simply, "I thank you for that." Nothing more, neither man looking at the other. The protocol preserved Brother's self-esteem and spared my father the embarrassment of accepting thanks, one man taking the time to count out the bills and roll them before each trip, and the other, hours later, closing a door in his dilapidated farmhouse and counting them again, their reckoning mysterious to me.

CHAPTER 5

I may be guilty of some nostalgia for my lost childhood, but I know I can't depict that time and place as innocent. Not so many years before our idyll in the farm spring, my father witnessed a lynching only a few miles away from where we swam. He told me the story more than once, each time in that matter-of-fact way of his. He remembered standing on the church steps, holding his mother's hand. They heard the toot of a horn. A small truck came down the street toward them, moving no faster than parade speed, the two men in front of the truck smiling and waving, sole dignitaries in a parade of their own making. He recognized the man driving the truck, Buford King, and the man riding next to him, Buford's sister's husband, Lonnie Rice. The truck, an old Model A pickup, belonged to Lonnie, but Buford was driving it, which was just like Buford. He was always one to have his way.

The truck was dragging something, though at first, my father didn't recognize what it was. He remembered his mother squeezing his hand when she saw it, her grip going tight. When the pickup came past the church, he saw the chain from the bumper wrapped around the ankles of a man's body. The truck dragged the corpse past them, the body's arms extended, its hands open and limp, the upturned face bouncing and turning on the uneven road, as if, even in death, to acknowledge the parade watchers on either side. Lonnie and Buford sat up front, tooting the horn.

My father broke free from his mother and chased the other children as they ran into the road behind the truck, the road, in those days, still dirt. Years later, when he was in the Marines, he traveled on leave to a friend's house in Pennsylvania, where he saw snow for the first time. His friend, a fellow Marine, lay in the snow and waved his arms, making a snow angel. The imprint in the snow reminded my father of the track the body left in the road, though he did not tell his friend that. He remembered a damp line in the middle of the track where blood was seeping into the road.

On the way home to the farm, my father rode in back with his brother. He remembered that his father, my grandfather, was angry at Buford and Lonnie, not so much for lynching a man, but for dragging the body through town. Though he didn't confess to feeling any trauma, my father told the story in surprising detail, describing how the back of my grandfather's neck looked razored and raw, his hair cut for church with kitchen scissors. As my father remembered it, his own father never turned to his mother but kept his eyes down the road, his hands at ten and two on the wheel, his words bitter and low. He was outraged that children should be exposed to something like that, after Sunday school, no less.

When they pulled up at the house, my father leapt out the door to find Brother. He thought he had news for Brother, an exciting story to tell, but Brother already knew, because he had seen the body as well. After passing the white churches, Buford and Lonnie pulled what was left of the corpse to the colored section of town, came to a stop in front of the Baptist church, unchained the bloody mess, and spat on it for good measure. Brother saw Buford tip his hat to one of the younger Black women as he drove away, leaving her, horrified and enraged, in his dust.

Brother had known the victim. My father realized he had, too, once Brother told him the name. Everyone knew Sonny Coleman. He loaded sacks at the seed warehouse, a man with a melodious whistle and handsome smile. The shape my father saw pulled behind the pickup truck was broken and limp, nothing like the Sonny he knew. Brother told him that Sonny had been accused of looking at a white woman, though my father would later hear that Sonny had tried to rape her.

When I expressed sympathy for Sonny, my father shook his head. Not every man who got lynched was innocent, he said. He sometimes described my grandfather, who died of lung cancer before Allyn was born, as a hard man, and my father, though he had a sense of humor and a sociable disposition, could be hard himself. He was skeptical of Black people, suspicious of all they said and did. That country attitude came with him to LaSalle.

As for Brother, he never lived anywhere but on my grandfather's farm. He attended, as my father did, the trial of Sonny's murderers, when an all-white jury concluded that Sonny broke his own neck. My father left Cemochechobee, but Brother remained, living out his life in the presence of killers. I never heard Brother speak of the lynching of course, but I can remember riding in the back of Brother's truck with Allyn, my cousin Bobby, and Bobby's friend, Bo King, Buford King's grandson.

As a child, I thought of my father's story as ancient history, a colorful fable from long ago. I don't see it that way now. I recognize that not so many years passed between my father's youth and my own. I struggle to reconcile my memories of a benign childhood with a collection of facts, some of which I know to be horrific. My sister helps me in this process. With my parents gone, only Allyn and I can remember the details of our family's life in LaSalle and our visits to Cemochechobee. She recalls what I may have forgotten or ignored, and when I compare her interpretations to my own, it helps me find a balance. All our phone conversations start the same way.

"Hey, Allyn," I say.

"Hey yourself," she answers.

I ask about her aching joints, her husband's heart condition, then guide her back to Cemochechobee, her memories of Brother. This time, I find myself talking about Carol McAllister and the time she nearly burned the house down. Allyn laughs. "She was a weird bird," she says. "I never really knew what the reverend saw in her." She pauses, then says,

"I had a crush on him, you know."

"You must be kidding me," I say, laughing. "He had white hair, for crying out loud."

"And blue eyes."

"I do remember those eyes, pale blue. And dark eyebrows. He could have been a Husky. But really, Allyn. Our minister?"

"I might have been sixteen, but I had the brain of a fourteen-year-old. Boys terrified me. I think I latched on to Reverend McAllister because I knew it was safe. Believe me, I wasn't the only one to notice."

"Who else?"

"Mama."

"No!"

"It's not like they had an affair. Nice people don't have affairs, but she did notice. Think about it. Big M was Mister Gruff, the old leatherneck, and he never read anything but the newspaper. Rob McAllister was a head taller than everyone else, full of ideas, well-read, inspirational. He was romantic. I think part of his problem was that all the men in the church knew that all the women in the church were infatuated with him. Have I mentioned those eyes? I want to make sure I mentioned his eyes."

"The person I remember being interested in Rob McAllister was Bit, not in terms of any kind of physical attraction, of course. Just interested."

"You're such a prude! Why couldn't Bit be attracted to him? She was female, wasn't she? If you were female, you noticed those eyes."

CHAPTER 6

A twelve-year-old boy doesn't pay attention to that kind of detail, but a sixteen-year-old girl does, and she remembers. I've condensed my youth to a few sentimental memories, like the day at the spring. Allyn does not think of LaSalle as I do, as a world left behind. She still has friends from high school down there, and she keeps up with the graduations and marriages of their children. Looking back on our parents or Rob McAllister or Brother, she sees them as an adult would, whereas I am trapped in the perspective of my tender years.

Rob McAllister dazzled me. He commanded the pulpit at First Presbyterian, one of LaSalle's largest churches, a man whose image was broadcast to thousands every Sunday morning. Whenever he came to pick up Jamie, he did not wait in the car, as Jamie's mother did. She would sit out there sometimes for five minutes, sometimes ten, because she preferred to wait alone than talk to someone, even my mother. If my mother walked out to talk with her, Carol smiled politely and made some excuse that she was catching up on her reading, though it had to be hot reading in the car. My mother didn't challenge her, but stood beside the car window and made conversation, asking about Carol's book or telling Carol about the book she was reading. She might even invite Carol inside, though she knew that Carol preferred to roast in privacy. I'm sure my mother sympathized with Carol, but I suspect she had another motive. I never told my mother about the kitchen fire, but she knew Carol McAllister was quirky. She may have gone out for a quick diagnosis, to assess the risk of sending her child into Carol's house, and Carol, understanding that, tried to smile and present herself as normal.

Once I stood at the kitchen window after Jamie had left. My mother leaned at the car door, talking with Carol, and I saw Jamie climb in the far side. As my mother came up the walk, her back to the car, I saw Carol get out with a tissue and wipe the door where my mother had touched it. That convinced me that Carol McAllister was not well. The kitchen fire I could forgive, but I could not imagine that any sane person would regard my mother as unclean.

Reverend McAllister would come to the door in his minister's collar and dark suit, with his smiling, brilliant eyes, and he stooped slightly to say hello, making conversation with whoever answered. He kept up to date on Allyn's horseback riding lessons, asked Big M if the shop was busy, and seemed genuinely interested in learning about our lives, even Bit's life. It galled my father. One day, we heard McAllister in the front hall talking to Bit, and Bit was going on about her church, telling the reverend he should come visit sometime. Jamie and I sat in the living room with my father, who read aloud an article about two Negroes arrested for blocking the entrance to a restroom at Patterson's, the local department store. That article irritated Big M, as did Bit's conversation in the hall. I knew what he was thinking. Only a lunatic could imagine that our minister would visit a colored church, and it was silly of Bit to suggest it. What a heap of foolishness for Rob McAllister to pay so much attention to the maid when we were seated just one room away. Exasperated, Big M went into the front hall and interrupted them, saying, "Robert, how are you?" He brushed past Bit, interrupting her mid-sentence. Bit, who knew the role she was expected to play, stepped back. McAllister, always gracious, took my father's hand, shook it, and delivered up his incomparable smile. Seeing Bit retreat, he said to her, "Bit, I'll catch up with you later, all right?"

Bit, pleased with this opportunity to twist a small blade between my father's ribs, said, "Yessir, Reverend. I'll see you soon, I know."

CHAPTER 7

WHEN we visited my father's cabinet shop, Jamie was enthralled. I guess most boys are interested in how men make things. If the process is exotic, as the shop was to Jamie, all the better. I cannot imagine a place farther removed from McAllister's quiet study than the shop floor at Nickerson Millwork, a war zone of wood shavings and chips, sawn boards, and rolls of stacked and torn house plans. Pencil-marked boards of varying lengths leaned against every wall, table, and chair. Shelving lay strewn across the floor, and boxes of finishing nails spilled across the counters. A film of sawdust coated every surface, the floor so thick with it, you might as well be walking on a beach. Someone was always hammering something, prying a nail free, dropping a board, crooning along to the non-stop AM radio where Porter Wagoner sang: *I've enjoyed as much of this as I can stand.* The stain-and-paint shed out back reeked of toxic fumes. Everyone smoked, from the foreman, a scrawny white man named Homer Fountain who sported a mouth of unnaturally even dentures, to Miss Bannister, the bookkeeper, a dyspeptic widow with the face of a fallen pie, to Willie Ed, the "clean-up" man, a forlorn Black man with a withered arm and crooked, filmy glasses. Willie Ed shoved sawdust dunes across the floor with a broom that kept dropping its head, the brush falling from the pole with a clunk. Table saws shrieked. Shafts of sunlight seethed and writhed in shades of gray and brown.

I once got a migraine at the shop and had to rush to the workers' slimy toilet to throw up. I hated the place, but I was my father's only son, Morris Nickerson Jr., and he saw me as heir to the family empire. He wanted me to spend time around the shop, to watch him work so I could learn the trade. Someday, it could all be mine, the paint shed leaking cherry stain, the shavings and shelving and twisted nails, a legacy of lucrative dust. The thought left me cold. I preferred Reverend McAllister's quiet study, the solitude of his books, the mysterious art of his sermon-making. I did not like the shop's commotion, Homer Fountain digging at his privates as he leaned over a set of drawings, a bead of tobacco juice draining down his chin, the country music blaring on the radio, a truck honking at the loading dock, the insurance company calendar hanging crooked on the wall, a month out-of-date. I watched a worker named Rudean rip plywood with his table saw, squinting through his cigarette smoke, chips of wood bouncing from the blade, the nub of his missing thumb held high and clear. Every inch of that place sickened me.

Not Jamie. He loved it. We stood in the stinking, fibrous haze, and Jamie had so many questions my father held up his hands to slow him down. "Hold on, now," Big M said, laughing. "Hold on. Let me walk you through the flow." The flow began at the loading dock, a slab of truck-bashed concrete where a clipboard hung from a nail on the wall. From there, it proceeded to "inventory," the deep shelves a haven for spiders, then to the shop floor itself. "Homer, let me borrow those plans for a minute," my father said, and Homer stood aside. Big M explained a kitchen plan, running his finger along the lines of the drawing, and Jamie gave it a level of attention worthy of the Old Testament. We walked around the shop floor, my father showing Jamie the coarser wood used for backboards and the finer wood for shelving. "Look at this piece here," he said. "See how straight that grain is? That's walnut. Walnut is a fine wood, too fine for a lot of the work we do."

Jamie ran a reverential hand along the board. "How do you know it's walnut?" he asked. "Because of the grain?"

"That's part of it," my father said, "but also the color and the hardness. Knock on that, feel how hard it is? The grain depends on which part of the tree you're using. This piece here was cut from the crotch of the tree, and that's what gives it this flaring pattern in the grain. And it also depends on how it's sawn. Look at this piece here, see how the grain moves in parallel lines? That's quarter sawn. Now look at this piece over here, see those rings? That's flat sawn. Could be the very same tree, but depending on how you cut it, lengthwise or horizontal, you'll get your different grains. Now, let me show you something really interesting. Homer, where's that piece of burl we were looking at the other day?" Homer gave his testicles a quick hoist, as if they too had been on break and were now summoned into action, and he peered around with his bifocals, his long neck craning, his Adam's apple enormous. He searched the counters then leaned to look under one, finally pulling a piece from a pile I would have sworn was scrap.

"See that?" my father said, alight with pride, "That's a piece of burl wood. You know those bumps that grow on trees, like warts? You've seen those, right? That's where you get your burl. You see all those whorls and patterns here? You put a nice stain on that, something that will bring out your grain, and you've got one very nice veneer."

By the time we arrived back at the house, Jamie had decided we should start a business of our own. Jamie's interests inevitably turned into obsessions, and once in the grip of an idea, he became relentless. Track, train, and engineer, he pulled me, the little red caboose, behind him. We spent the better part of the next day discussing entrepreneurial schemes. Drunk on the fumes of my father's cabinet-making shop, Jamie at first decided we should open a small factory, but neither of us could imagine a way to make this plan remotely possible. We knew we needed to sell something, but what? And who would buy it?

At the shop, Jamie was intrigued when my father broke down the price of a finished set of cabinets into a series of markups, one percentage on the labor, another on the hardware, and a series of markups on shelving, cabinet doors, and backboards. "What we need to find," Jamie said to me with the authority of one with years of experience, "is a product with a nice markup." He hit upon the idea of selling Cokes to the workers from the textile mills. We could set up a table at the mill parking lot, and when the workers came off their shift, hot and thirsty, there we would be, selling cold, refreshing Cokes at a very sweet markup. When Jamie stayed with us for dinner, he mentioned this scheme to my father. "It'll never work," my father said. "Every one of those workers knows that a Coke costs a dime. If you're there trying to sell drinks for a quarter, they'll know you're trying to gouge them. The secret to a nice markup is a product the customer can't get too easy someplace else. If you're selling Cokes, you're in competition with every gas station and grocery store in town. When I sell kitchen cabinets, there are only a few other places folks can go to buy cabinets, and if what I'm selling is something unique, like that piece of burl wood I showed you, then there's virtually no competition. That's where you get your nice markup."

For the next couple of days, we saw the world through a new lens, not as a familiar collection of houses, cars, and groceries, but as a series of markups. What was the markup on a shirt, a Cadillac, a baseball, an onion? We came to appreciate the difference between the amount of the markup (thousands on a Cadillac, pennies on an onion) and the percentage markup. We wanted to make thousands, but that meant scrounging up thousands to spend on raw goods. We needed to find something cheap we could resell at a high percentage markup. But what? Cokes wouldn't work, and neither would Baby Ruth bars, chewing gum, or newspapers. We gave serious consideration to boiled peanuts, but neither of us knew how to boil a peanut. Mentally, I walked down the aisles of the grocery store, considering the markup we could ask on every item. "What about watermelons?" I said.

"Everyone knows what watermelons cost," Jamie replied wearily.

"Not if we cut it up. No one knows what a slice of watermelon costs."

Jamie's back stiffened. He studied me hard. "Little," he said, "You're a genius!" I didn't disagree. Thanks to my meager spark of inspiration, we now had a plan. We had a product (watermelon), a manufacturing process (slicing it), and customers (workers at the mill).

Transporting a watermelon on a bicycle is no minor feat. Between the grocery store and the mill parking lot, we came close to losing our inventory more than once. Did I mention that Jamie was also carrying a butcher knife? We arrived at the mill before the shift change. We split one of the watermelons in half, and carved a few cold, sweet, delicious, nutritious, ruby-red wedges. Jamie set up our sign:

Watermelon

10¢ a Slice!

We discussed the exclamation point. I wasn't sure we needed it, but Jamie insisted. "It's sales," he said. Our two watermelons cost us thirty cents each. If we sold three pieces, we would break even on the first watermelon. Three more, and both melons were paid for. Every piece beyond that counted as pure profit.

Our first prospect approached the table, an arthritic white man, ancient, almost sixty, with a glaucous eye and scraggly beard, frightening to look at, not my idea of a customer, but Jamie smiled and said, "Hello, sir. Can we offer you a delicious slice of watermelon?"

Our prospect wheezed out a laugh, and the color of his eye unsettled my stomach. "How much?" he asked.

"Ten cents a slice, sir," Jamie said. I pointed to our sign.

"How do I know it's any good?"

"Because," Jamie answered, "my partner and I planted and raised this watermelon ourselves. We put the seed in the ground, and we nurtured this melon from the day it was a flower on the vine."

"Is that right? You and your partner?" He nodded toward me, but kept his good eye on Jamie. "Is it mealy? I don't like my melon mealy."

"Me neither," Jamie said. "Mealy means old. We sell them young and firm. This melon was sleeping on the vine just last night."

"Young and firm, huh? Sounds like the farmer's daughter." A phlegmy laugh.

"Yessir," Jamie said, his face solemn, a shade beyond sincere.

"How about sweet? I can't eat it if it ain't sweet."

"Sweet as the farmer's daughter," Jamie said, and I was thinking, *Who? What farmer? What daughter?* "My partner and I are just like you," Jamie said. "We like them firm and sweet. You know the secret to a really sweet watermelon?" Now Jamie leaned forward.

"What?"

"The soil."

They studied one another. "If this isn't the sweetest slice of watermelon you've ever tasted," Jamie said carefully, "we'll double your money back." And I was thinking, *What? We'll do what? With what money?*

"Deal!" our prospect said. "Give me one." We completed the transaction, and he stood before us, eating the slice, his functioning eye keeping watch on Jamie. Then he dug into his pocket again. "One more," he said.

We were in business. Workers from the mill gathered around us. I sliced and Jamie sold. In no time, our inventory was gone, and we were heavy with dimes. We mounted our bikes. "We will see you gentlemen tomorrow!" Jamie called with a triumphant wave of our dripping blade, and off we went, a pair of entrepreneurs giddy with our riches.

We talked my mother into lending us her folding card table, and over the next few days, we stored it among some bushes near the mill. We displayed our product on the table along with Jamie's new sign, which announced the name he had given our enterprise:

Universal Gourmet

Presents

Hand Grown Watermelons

10¢ a Slice!!!

We converted melons to coin, establishing a stream of income so steady it would have put the electric company to shame. It pleased us. No longer the little boys of last week, those innocents who swam in the pool and played their childish games, we sold slices, bought product, and wrapped dimes. We had arrived in the world's bazaar to claim our lucrative share.

CHAPTER 8

IN 1984, I was practicing corporate law in Boston, one miserable attorney among many. Returning to a dark house after my wife and children had gone to bed, I would drink a couple of glasses of wine, convinced I could not sleep without it. When the alcohol wore off at some ungodly hour, I lay in bed and agonized over deadlines.

I became an attorney because I liked working with words, and I wanted to be a professional. Some aspects of law I enjoyed, the craftsmanship of definitions, the nesting of paragraphs, but I did not grow up in a family that argued a lot, and the competitive aspect of law felt unnatural to me. My more rapacious clients pushed me to make demands and contest every point. I didn't like arguing over nits. I wasn't a bad lawyer, but younger attorneys were charging higher rates and bringing more business to the firm.

One client, Integrated Labs, I particularly loathed because of the CEO, Jeff Saliba. IL acquired regional testing labs, eliminated excess staff, and consolidated work to keep the instruments busy. My firm made a lot of money negotiating IL's acquisition contracts, and we understood that Mr. Saliba believed in buying low. Saliba and I visited prospects together, each lab like the one before. The owner would meet us in the lobby, confess he was more of a chemistry guy or engineer than businessman, then offer to walk us around the place while Saliba smiled and asked questions, praising the clean labs for their polished floors and the disorganized labs for their devotion to science. He'd examine a spectrometer, bending close, then stand erect to ask an esoteric question that never failed to surprise and please the lab owner. This from a finance man? Where did he learn about spectrometry? It was always a spectrometer, and the question never varied. We'd join the owner for lunch around the corner, where he teased the waitress and Saliba picked up the tab. After lunch, while I browsed the corporate records, Saliba would join the self-confessed mediocre business guy in his office for a private one-on-one. Following goodbyes, as we turned out of the parking lot, Saliba would say, "So, what did you find?" My role was to discover irregularities, excuses to lower whatever offer Saliba had floated. When we returned for the follow-up, I searched for more legal anomalies while an accountant named Larry Shine took apart the financials.

What my senior partner referred to as "performing due diligence for IL," Larry Shine called, "finding the shit in the soup." One day, I was reviewing the contracts of Erie Labco, parsing the shit, when I realized I had worked through lunch. I stepped out of the office to find a bite. I'd always avoided the food truck closest to our door because it attracted a crowd, and attorneys can't afford to wait. At this late hour—past two —the line had dispersed, and the man in the truck was packing up. He was altogether Irish, with pink skin, broken capillaries, thick black hair, a magnificent brush of eyebrows, and glittering eyes. I called up to him, "Am I too late to get lunch?"

"For you, counselor? Never."

"How do you know I'm an attorney?"

"You're eating lunch after two o'clock, and most pipefitters don't wear ties. What'll it be?"

I studied the menu on the board above his window. "There's always a line here at lunchtime," I said. "What's the most popular thing you've got?"

"Picanha."

"Never heard of it."

"Brazilian barbecue."

"Funny," I said, "you don't look Brazilian."

Dermot Bogue laughed at that. "I don't serve what I eat. I serve what they eat. That's called marketing, counselor. Most of my clientele aren't like you. They don't work inside these buildings. They build these buildings. Lots of them are Brazilian, and I serve them what they want."

The picanha was delicious, as was the Bolinho de Bacalhau he served me the next day. Both tasted better than my typical slice of pizza. I made it a new routine to visit Dermot's truck just before he packed up for the day. He wasn't busy then, and he loved to talk, so we chatted as I enjoyed my late lunch. Before long, Dermot was staying late just for me, a gesture that won my loyalty.

I soon learned the names of his children (he had four, with a fifth on the way), where he lived (Braintree), and his goal for 1985 (to buy and operate a second food truck). He had a nephew who would man the truck, and Dermot knew just where to park it on the edge of Chinatown, at the construction site for a new office tower. The neighborhood teemed with hungry steelworkers, pipefitters, carpenters, and electricians. Why 1985, I asked, why not now? "Trucks cost money, counselor." Couldn't he get a bank loan? No, he didn't feel comfortable doing that.

I sat on a park bench near his truck, and Dermot lowered the truck window and sat with me. He tutored me in Food Truck Economics 101, the cost of beef, fuel, and permits, how to price soft drinks and how to price Pé-de-moleque. Returning from a lesson with Dermot, I found it hard to concentrate on my work. Although he didn't have a college education, Dermot had a head for numbers, and for him, running a business required nothing more than common sense. I made more money in my office than Dermot made with his truck, but he enjoyed his work, and I resented mine.

"Say, Dermot," I said one day, folding a paper napkin soiled with barbecue sauce, "why don't we buy the new truck now? Why wait a year? I'll work out the financing—I do that stuff all day—and you operate it. We'll be partners, fifty-fifty. If it doesn't work out, I'll own a food truck and you will have wasted some time. If it does work, we'll both enjoy a little incremental cash flow."

"Incremental cash flow," Dermot said slowly. "I don't remember the sisters ever teaching me the term, but it has quite the pleasing ring to it, doesn't it?" I saw the gleam of turning wheels. "I've never had a partner though, and I'm used to making all my business decisions myself. I don't know anything about finance, and you don't know beans about operating a food truck other than what I've taught you, and that's not half of what I know. Going into business together means we would have to trust one another."

"Yes, it does," I said, holding out my hand. Dermot took it, and with that, Never Dull, LLC (Dermot's choice of names, my choice of corporate structures) was born. I handled the paperwork and showed Dermot where to sign. He found a cousin to track our receipts and expenses, and Larry Shine introduced me to a young associate who prepared our books for the bankers. In a couple of years, we had five trucks, each with its own cuisine. Our chief marketing officer, Mr. Dermot Bogue, waded into groups of workers, introduced himself, and began to talk, unembarrassed by his few phrases of abominable Spanish or Portuguese. He came away knowing what they carried in their lunch boxes. He even got to know two of their wives, and they joined Never Dull, teaching Dermot's relatives how to fry a taco shell and fold a burrito. When one of the cousins balked at taking instructions from a Latina, Dermot did what his mother had warned him never to do. He fired the cousin and gave the mujer her own truck.

My equity interest in Never Dull did not mean that I was making more than the young hotshots in our firm, but I pitied them for the hours they worked. (Well, I almost pitied them. A better person would have pitied them.) My incremental cash flow grew as steady as a March melt. It trickled in brave little rivulets that conjoined, forming a stream of gathering strength.

Dermot parked our fifth truck way out in Framingham, nowhere near an office project. He had found a Home Depot under construction, the first either of us had seen. Dermot watched the big box go up, amazed that a hardware store could be so large, and he reported back to me. After the workers go, he told me, shoppers will appear, lots of them. "That first little restaurant," he said, "will do quite well. Nothing grand, you know.

Just a little place that serves mud in the morning and subs for lunch." He had heard of a local developer with plans for a retail strip near the new store. I called the man and told him Never Dull might consider signing a five-year lease on a little restaurant space. We came to terms, and the first Never Dull Deli opened its door. We followed Home Depot and the other big box stores around the country. Let them research the site, build the box, and bring the traffic. We planned to duplicate our experience in Framingham nationwide. We imagined offering pulled pork in one town, fried chicken in another, and pierogies in a third. Our patrons would believe they had discovered a great little local eatery that just happened to be near the new Walmart or Lowe's. We expected to hire locals to cook and manage the shop, and if they proved to be energetic and honest, to award them equity interests.

We worked hard enough—Dermot spent his life on airplanes, and I had to quit the law firm to focus on loans, leases, and LLCs—but we worked for ourselves and kept the profits. The big box stores, with their teams of market researchers, took all the risk of entering a new market. We just followed along, industrious ants, happy to haul away the crumbs.

I often think I owe my good fortune as much to Jamie as Dermot Bogue. They share an entrepreneurial elan, a quality I recognized in Dermot because of my early years with Universal Gourmet. Like Jamie, Dermot combined a sharp mind with a bold and persuasive patter. Working with Dermot, I played second fiddle, but I knew the part from my time with Jamie. It suited me.

CHAPTER 9

I have a copy of the book Reverend Rob McAllister wrote about his time in LaSalle, a bit of autobiography, excerpts from his sermons, a testimonial of one man's experience at the front lines of the civil rights movement. Most of his story takes place, as this one does, in 1962. In his book, McAllister describes his work with The Joint Mission for a Better LaSalle, a group of white ministers devoted to charitable causes. The Council for Improvements in the Colored Community served a similar role in Baker Bottom. The Council focused on the needs of less fortunate Black people, while the Mission concentrated on the whites. But these needs overlapped. If a white Lutheran found herself with an old refrigerator or stove, her minister called a member of the Council, who might know a Black family in need of an appliance. If a Black family had a boy old enough for yard work, their minister reached out to a member of the Mission, who found a white household that wanted him.

Through that work, McAllister came to know Timothy Butters, pastor of Mount Calvary Baptist, the largest church in Baker Bottom. Butters was of average height, slightly pear-shaped, thoroughly bald. He could not shake hands without using both of his own. He exploded with laughter at the mildest of witticisms and listened with an almost preternatural stillness. Like Dr. King, he'd graduated from Morehouse College. He did not, as King did, travel to Boston for his graduate studies, and, as McAllister would discover, he preached in a less florid style than King, his delivery more down home. When Bit told McAllister she attended services at Mount Calvary, it occurred to him that Tim Butters led her congregation. When she surprised him by inviting him to a service, McAllister was inclined to brush her off, but Butters intrigued him.

Representatives of the Black and white councils tended to interact with an almost comic politesse. Just as members of Congress will refer to one another as "my good friends across the aisle" and "my distinguished colleagues," these ministers would say, "I wonder whether I may solicit the generosity of the good members of your congregation," and when granted the favor, they indulged in the most extravagant expressions of gratitude. They quoted the Bible to one another, gently sparring, dipping more often into the New Testament than the Old. McAllister noted that Butters knew his Amos, Esther, and Ezra, as well as his Matthew and Mark. After Bit planted the seed, the men began to engage in a more honest dialogue.

They traded sermons, affording each man an opportunity to read how the other thought and to discover how he spoke to his own congregation. McAllister could not, of course, invite Butters to visit our church, but when he casually mentioned that one of Butters' congregants had invited him to visit Mount Calvary, Butters enthusiastically agreed. The occasional rabbi from New York or Philadelphia had visited Mount Calvary, but never a minister from one of LaSalle's white churches. Ultimately, McAllister attended at least half a dozen services. He heard the standard exhortations to follow Christ and do good, but he heard another message as well, as seditious and liberating as the Gospel itself, and he saw how Butters' congregation responded. Long before most of white LaSalle, Rob McAllister foresaw what was coming.

On the night he took Jamie and me to Mount Calvary, we were riding in the car before I realized where we were going, and we stepped out on the sidewalk in Baker Bottom before I could express my apprehension. I knew we should not be there. This was their world, not ours. McAllister rested a reassuring hand on my shoulder as we approached the door.

"Little" he said, "This is Reverend Butters," and the minister welcomed me with a jolting handshake.

"Thank you," I said and then, "thank you, sir," because I did not know what else to say. We headed upstairs to the balcony, which curved above the pews below. We were the only whites in the rapidly filling church. I kept asking myself, *What would Daddy say?* He had told Allyn and me that, as a young man, he used to sit on the steps of the colored Baptist church and listen to the singing. When one of the old ushers stepped outside, my father and his friends dropped nickels into the collection plate. I knew Big Mo had never set foot inside a Black church, as I was doing now, and the thought of going where my father dared not go, of seeing what he had never seen, felt thrilling and transgressive. This visit counted as another of Rob McAllister's small rebellions, as when he took time to speak with the maid.

A tall man in horn-rimmed glasses and a three-piece suit took the seat next to me in our pew. I could smell his after-shave. He nodded solemnly to Jamie's father, muttered *Reverend* in a rich baritone, then crossed his long legs and tilted his head to examine the scene below. People filed in, the women in brilliant dresses of red and plum, the men in dark suits with a white stripe of handkerchief at the breast pocket. The women smiled and greeted one another, raising their hands and popping their fingers to their palms in little waves. The men nodded and leaned close to exchange a word then broke apart in low laughter. My mother had dragged me into the First Presbyterian church countless times, but I never studied it as I did Mount Calvary. Finding myself in the minority, I felt like a pilgrim away from home.

I was surprised to see Bit and Emma G take their seats below us. I felt exposed, then fascinated, like a spy hiding in plain sight. Bit never turned, but surely, she saw us. One does not hide a white face simply by sitting in the balcony. She understood, as did everyone else there, that McAllister had crossed a line when he entered her church. Best not to acknowledge him.

Emma G smiled and looked around, enjoying the flow of traffic. In those days, I saw her rarely, only when she came to help her mother turn rugs, or when we dropped Bit off, and she came out to talk to my mother. Seeing Emma G now, I felt I had somehow lost touch with how she looked. From this new vantage, I noticed her slender neck and jaw, an earring that dangled and shined, how her dress, which looked familiar, shifted on her shoulder as she turned.

A woman in white robes took a seat at the piano, and the congregation joined the choir in singing *Surely God is Able*. When we rose for the hymn, the man next to me stood, unfolding his long limbs. He lowered his head and clasped his hands, not bothering with the hymnal. Others sang and swayed, the women more than the men, and he murmured along in resonant harmony, rocking left to right and back again, graceful as an old pine. Tim Butters took the pulpit, his bald head burnished, the pulpit reading light reflecting in his glasses. He began to speak in an almost conversational tone, telling a story from the book of Matthew.

"Jesus has finished preaching for the day, so he says to the disciples, 'You go ahead on. I want to be by myself and pray for a while.' So, the disciples, they get in the boat and head off back towards home. They are out in that boat—it's good and dark—and what does Matthew say? He says the wind was boisterous."

Here, one or two members of the congregation laughed softly. I saw Bit shift, smiling and satisfied, anticipating what was to come. Emma G recoiled, a barely perceptible retreat from her animated mother, but they were crowded close on the pew with no place for Emma G to go.

"Their little boat is getting tossed around, rocking up and down, waves rising and falling, and foam blowing off the whitecaps. The moon is nearly full, but it's starting to cloud over. Sometimes the sea is lit up, then it suddenly goes dark, big sheets of shadow passing over. Peter looks out, and he sees something, a shape, coming over the water towards them. He tells himself it must be another boat, but it's not big enough for a boat, then he thinks it may be a waterspout, but a waterspout doesn't move that way. He's sitting there in that boat and watching, and this form, this shape, this moonlit presence is coming closer and closer and closer."

Almost a ghost story, the way Butters told it. Emma G looked left and right across the hushed congregation, monitoring the crowd's reaction.

"Well, Peter is sitting there in that boat, and he doesn't say a word, because he's waiting for his mind to make sense of what his eyes are telling him. He knows what it is. The light is not good, but it's good enough for him to make out that this is a man walking across the water toward them. He sees it, all right, but his mind knows that can't be right, so he just sits in that boat and watches, waiting for his mind to catch up to what his eyes already know."

"Watch now!" the man next to me said aloud, and I started. I had never heard anyone interrupt a sermon. I shot a glance at Reverend McAllister. He was looking down at the pulpit, his thin lips creased in a faint smile. His elbow pressed once into my ribs.

"One by one, they all see it, falling silent in the boat, just staring out at it. They watch it come on, trudging up the side of one wave and down the next, stepping over the crests. When the boat sinks down or a wave rises, it may disappear, but then there it is again, still moving toward them. One of the disciples begins to moan a little bit, the way a man will do when he is deathly afraid, kind of whimpering, and that releases something in all of them, so before you know it, they are all crying and carrying on, convinced that this ghost or devil or whatever it is has come to drown their little boat."

"Make it plain!" the man next to me called out, and below us, other voices fell into the rhythm of Reverend Butters' story, spurring him along.

"The apostles are carrying on this way, fearing for their very lives, weeping and crying and such, when suddenly the figure stops, stands tall right out there in the water, and raises his hand. And what does he say? I think you know. He says, 'Be of good cheer. It is I. Be not afraid.'"

"Yes, Lord," members of the congregation called. "Let's hear it plain, now," the man next to me called. He rocked his head softly, as if astride a softly cantering mare. I looked down, and I could see that Bit was swaying too, not back and forth like the man next to me, but side to side, with each sway pressing Emma G into the shoulder of the woman next to her. Bit had her hand raised, palm out above her head, and when

Butters described the tremulous Peter climbing over the side of the boat, stepping down into the dark, boiling water, then crying out as he begins to sink, and Christ reaching out and catching him, Bit's hand snapped shut, and I realized she knew this sermon well.

The rapt congregation waited for the story to continue. I glanced at Jamie's father. He sat erect, legs crossed, hands folded, eyes bright in the dark balcony. Butters paused, folded his glasses, set them down on the lectern, leaned forward on his elbows. "I reckon by now one or two of you may have guessed what it is I'm getting at," he said.

Scattered, knowing laughs rippled through the pews. People smiled and looked side to side, as if to acknowledge that the reverend had done it again, telling some old story that pulled them in. Emma G leaned forward and grasped the back of the pew in front of her.

"Well, there is no need to guess. The time for guessing is long gone. Guessing is but a child's game, and what we're talking about now is a serious business, a matter for us as adults to consider. I haven't told you this familiar story just to entertain you. No, I've been telling you this because of a message I need to deliver here tonight: it's time. It's time to leave the boat. Now, I know it may not feel that way to some of you. The water looks cold, and the wind boisterous. Nevertheless, it is time we acknowledge a perverse, but irrefutable truth. We have arrived at one of those odd moments of civic progression neither anticipated nor planned but now undeniably real, and therefore, unmistakably urgent. We have come to a junction in the history of our race where safety and danger have reversed themselves, making the most dangerous way our safest course. It is time to leave the boat!

"I know you all have been reading the news and hearing the news. Maybe you remember what happened in Montgomery. Or maybe you've read about what happened at the lunch counters in Nashville. And you know what troubles me? You know what grieves me when I hear this news on my radio and watch it on my TV? What grieves and troubles me is what is not happening right here in LaSalle!"

Emma G lifted her face, jaw forward, back arched. Bit was no longer watching Butters. She was watching Emma G.

"How can it be that in all those places, in Tennessee, in North Carolina, and even right over there in Alabama—Alabama, for heaven's sakes!—folks have begun to stand up for themselves, but here, right here where we live, right here in LaSalle, Georgia, we are all just as meek and quiet as the youngest mouse in church." Emma G shook her head, disgusted. "Let's talk for one minute about the intolerable situation in this community. If a member of this congregation—you or you or you or you—gets on a bus after a long day of work, after hours and hours and hours of sweeping and washing and vacuuming and folding and cooking and picking up and putting away, carrying out the garbage, bringing in the groceries, hanging out the wash, taking clothes off the line, even if you're so tired you can barely walk and your knees hurt and your ankles hurt and your hips hurt, if the driver of that bus tells you that a white woman needs your seat, you are expected—no, not expected, you are required—to give up your seat!"

He shouted the words, and the congregation answered in kind, jolted by the minister's transition. "That's right!" people called out. "Tell it now!" They drummed the floor with their feet, thundering the pews.

"Any of you ever tried to use the restrooms down at Patterson's department store? What did they tell you? 'Whites only,' that's what they say. But they don't say that when they're taking our money, do they? If I hand the man a five-dollar bill or a ten-dollar bill or a twenty-dollar bill, he never says to me, 'No, I'm sorry. It's whites only.'"

Bitter laughter coursed through the church. Women fanned themselves with palm fans and said, "Ain't that the truth!" Bit placed her hand on Emma G's back, and Emma G flinched, flashing her mother an irritated look.

Butters shook his head, incensed, the congregation clapping and calling out. "Shameful," he said, "Shameful, shameful, shameful!"

When Butters concluded his sermon, we rose for the final hymn. The old pews creaked and groaned in a chorus of sighs. *Go, tell it on the mountain*, the congregation sang, *over the hills and everywhere.* Emma G looked transported, smiling, singing, and clapping her hands. Bit sang too, and Reverend McAllister as well, everyone but me. Singing embarrassed me.

We stood in the balcony to watch the congregation file out. They lingered and talked and hugged and laughed, as if reluctant to leave. Every church-going Presbyterian I knew had to get home to put a roast in the oven. Not these people. The sermon, it seemed, was the warmup act, teeing up a social hour. Bit commanded a position at the end of her pew, a knot of people around her, one holding her hand, another placing a palm on the small of her back. Bit was animated and talkative, trading handshakes and hugs, holding and squeezing, continuously touching, and I could see how the group responded to her, throwing their heads back to laugh at something she said.

And not just women. Men joined in that circle around her, apparently single men. One of them took her hand in both of his, and smiling, watched her speak, then broke into a hearty laugh, pumping her hand as he laughed. Bit laughed as well, and they hugged one another. It took me a minute to recognize what made Bit's face different. She was wearing lipstick, a strong crimson that lit up her smile. If Bit knew we were watching her, she performed her role well. Every look and gesture seemed to say, *This is my church. These are my friends. I am* someone *here.*

Even Emma G seemed to enjoy watching her mother perform. A woman came up behind Bit, placed a hand on her shoulder, and whispered in her ear. Bit listened, head cocked to one side, her chin tucked close to her clavicle. Her answer sent the woman into a laughing paroxysm of pats and squeezes. When a woman in front of her spoke, Bit rested her fingers on the woman's forearm, a gesture of undiluted attention, that, of course, she could never use in any conversation with us.

Rob McAllister would name his book *Leaving the Boat, A Southern Minister's Ordeal.* He didn't explain the title, and I have not decided whether he was stealing from Butters or paying homage to him. I suppose theft is a form of homage. McAllister didn't explain when or how he decided to attend a Black church, but I remember who gave him the idea. She set in motion his ordeal.

CHAPTER 10

IF not for the McAllisters, I never would have ventured inside Mount
Calvary or sold watermelons at the mill. I was content to stay home,
close to my trampoline and swimming pool. I attended school with children of my own race and played ball on a team with boys like me. The
white adults I knew best were polite people with college degrees. The
men at the mill, known as "lintheads," punched timecards and carried
lunch boxes. They drank in neon-lit bars to the twang of Tennessee
Ernie Ford and Grandpa Jones. Tattoos littered their arms. Tobacco
crammed their cheeks. Some of them stank to high heaven.

When one called out across the parking lot, "My Lord, if it isn't Universal Gourmet!" I knew he was laughing at us, and the other workers
were laughing with him, but Jamie didn't care. He waved and laughed
along, pouring out his shameless sales pitch. *Sweetest melons south of the
Fall Line. Rinsed in pure spring water.* A head taller than me, Jamie
looked our customers straight in the eye. He liked these men, they liked
him, and we raked in the dimes Monday through Friday. We came to
know some of them by name – George, Bobby, Vernon, and Cal. They
teased Jamie just to hear how he would answer. "I don't know about this
piece here," Vernon said. "I believe your quality might be slipping. I just
might have to ask for my money back."

"We're not selling melon," Jamie answered. "We sell satisfaction.
Anytime you want your money back, just say so."

They looked worn out, these men, addicted to their cigarettes, weary
with mill life and low wages, beaten down by a long day's work, and yet,
someone was always teasing someone else, their banter predictable and

continuous. White and Black, they worked together at the looms, and while they did not eat lunch together, or go to the same bars, or socialize after work, harmony prevailed at our table in the parking lot. Our pursuit of cash was color blind, just as Reverend Butters had said. Their coins carried equal weight.

Universal Gourmet shut down for a week when my mother announced that we were going to the beach and that Jamie was coming with us. We never took spontaneous trips, but suddenly Bit was packing beach towels, and my mother was shopping for suntan lotion.

"But why do we have to go?" Allyn said. "Can't I just stay here? Bit will be around."

"No," my mother said. "We're all going. It'll be fun."

"I thought you decided you didn't like the beach. I thought the sun gave you headaches."

"Sometimes the sunlight on the water does bother me," my mother conceded, "but I'll be more careful this time. We'll enjoy it, I promise. Besides, we have to go. There's been a little dust-up at the church. Nothing major, but it's put quite a bit of strain on Carol McAllister. She'll be going away for a while, and Rob needs to get her settled. I told him we would look after Jamie while they're gone. Your father and I talked it over, and we decided, why not make it a vacation?"

"Why can't Julia take care of Jamie?"

"Allyn! You act like I'm torturing you by taking you to the beach! When you grow up, you can tell your psychiatrist all about it. Get packed."

Allyn stormed out, blowing past Bit, who stood aside to let her pass. My mother closed her eyes and shook her head. "I hope you're praying for me, Bit," she said.

Bit giggled. "Yes, ma'am, I sure am. I pray for you and her both, every night. I got one of my own, you know."

On our previous trip to the beach, the day after we arrived, my mother retreated to her bed with a headache. My father had rented two rooms, one for Allyn, the Princess of Sheba, and the other for my parents and me. I was supposed to sleep on a cot in my parents' room, but when my mother got sick, my father moved the cot into Allyn's room. I knew Allyn didn't want me there. She wanted to stay up late making long-distance calls Big M would not know about until he paid the bill. Allyn made me sit in the bathroom while she changed clothes, which seemed to take forever. I didn't like being stuck in there with the toilet and tub, streaked mirror, and dripping shower, but when I threatened to come out, Allyn yelled for me to stay inside. Then she sneaked out of the room, closing the door so softly I couldn't hear it—just for the pleasure of leaving me behind.

With my mother sick in her motel room, I moped outside her door. I had miles of sand and the entire Gulf of Mexico to entertain me, but I pined for my mother's company. My father, frustrated with his wife for being sick and with his son for being such a mama's boy, decided to entertain me by taking me to fly a kite. He had a catalog of things like that boys were supposed to enjoy. So, we marched down to the beach with a paper kite and a ball of twine. He held the kite and told me to run while spooling out the string. I staggered over the soft sand with the kite flapping and bumping behind me but could not get it to climb. Big M began ripping a towel into strips to make a tail for the kite. The motel towel was cheap but tough, and he tugged and wrenched at it, the threads resisting, then snapping with a shriek. The sound of that ripping towel went right through my skull, but if my father noticed, he didn't care. He was determined to get the damn thing in the air. I told him I might be getting a headache (not true) and wanted to go back to the motel. He didn't believe me, but we trudged back to the room, my father in front and me in back. "Find something to do," he said and closed me out of their room.

Before we'd left on the trip, Bit had promised me my father wouldn't make me eat shrimp. He did though. He ripped out the shrimp's eyes and tore off its legs, then passed the plate to me. I lifted the shrimp, trying not to smell it, and picked at the vein that ran down its back. I forced the rubbery flesh into my mouth, wishing I were home with Bit.

Bit had learned to cook before doctors invented cholesterol. We ate fried chicken, fried cornbread, and fried pork chops. She cooked grits in whole milk instead of water and served biscuits dripping butter. She mashed our potatoes into valleys of decadent yellow and gave us sliced peaches sprinkled with sugar. After lunch, we ate cantaloupe and orange sherbet for dessert. She baked caramel cakes and pecan pies sweet enough to make my head swim.

The beach skirted the Gulf of Mexico four hours south of LaSalle. We stayed at the air-conditioned White Sails motel off the Miracle Strip. I liked the green water, the brilliant, squeaking sand, the whump of falling waves, the hiss of their retreat, playing Skee Ball and Goofy Golf with Jamie, and going to Ross Allen's Snaketorium, where a man in a T-shirt and wading boots swaggered into a pit of rattlers with a balloon on a stick. The snakes struck faster than the eye could see. Jamie said he'd like to work at the Snaketorium someday. Big M said he'd stick to shop work. At night, we prowled the beach with a bucket and flashlights. Sand crabs skittered sideways as our lights hit their eyes. When we caught them, they fought in the bottom of the bucket, ripping off claws and legs in a delightfully gruesome spectacle. I poured a frantic crab down Allyn's back, and she ran shrieking down the beach. The sand scorched our feet at noontime, and we stayed in the water for hours, diving for sand dollars and chasing small fish, our shoulders getting sunburned. When the afternoon cooled off, we climbed back among the dunes.

Plumes of sea grass topped the sandy peaks, which cut us off from the shoreline and the real world. Sliding down the pristine sand, setting off avalanches, we could have been shipwrecked pirates, escapees from a caravan of Bedouin slaves, or Tigercat pilots shot down in the Pacific. Jamie's mind worked in overdrive, investing our treks with baroque detail. Always in danger, always hiding, desperate with thirst, draining our last ounces of adrenalin, we trudged up the merciless, sandy hills, only to fall back down, gunshot or skewered. Long after I was ready to return to the waves or go inside, Jamie insisted that we stay to act out another elaborate drama.

I did not ask about his mother, and he did not offer much, though he did mention that she was "drying out." Drying out did not sound so bad to me. All the adults I knew drank, and some drank a lot. Drying out sounded like something that could be accomplished in a weekend. I expected to find Jamie's mother waiting for him when we returned. If not, Julia would be there to cook and do the dishes. She was a rising senior in high school, practically an adult.

On our third day, Allyn suffered an uncharacteristic spasm of niceness and offered to take us for ice cream cones. I told her I didn't want to go because I didn't like ice cream. She gave me her exasperated sigh. "Oh, good Lord. Since when? Who doesn't like ice cream?"

"I just don't want any right now," I said. Jamie asked, "Little, are you sure?" and Allyn said, "Come on. It'll be fun," but I was adamant. We agreed that Jamie would go with Allyn while I stayed in the motel with my parents. I didn't tell them why I wasn't going, because I knew Allyn would laugh at me. Eating ice cream is stressful. The cones melt too fast, especially at the beach. I dreaded waiting in line on the hot pavement and rushing to lick the dripping mess. I couldn't bear the steaming asphalt and sticky napkin, how the scoop tumbled off when the cone collapsed.

In the cool motel room, my parents had pulled the curtains across the picture window. Stretched out on the bed in his boxer shorts, my father read a folded newspaper, his thick fingers resting in the coarse hair of his chest. My mother and I shared the narrow couch. She flipped through a copy of *Look* magazine, while I read *Riders of the Purple Sage*.

"Here it is," she said. "*The Case for Creative Contact* by Reverend Robert O. McAllister. Unbelievable. How on earth did he ever get in touch with *Look* magazine?"

"Oh, God," my father moaned. "Is it as bad as they say?"

"Hold on, I'm reading it," my mother said, scanning the page. "Here's something. 'For too long we've relied on leaders with a one-dimensional view of the race problem,' blah-blah-blah, blah-blah-blah, shouldn't do that and oh, here we go, 'We need a new approach, active engagement with the Negro leaders in their churches, schools, and other social institutions, a policy I call Creative Contact. We cannot expect to understand the Negro's concerns if we limit our interactions to those of the housewife with her maid or the foreman with his laborer.'"

"What does he want us to do, invite them for dinner?" my father asked, lifting his head.

"This is not a joke, Morris," my mother said, still studying the article. "I think he's trying to strike a balance here. It seems like he's just arguing that we should have more of a dialogue."

My father sighed and let his head plop onto the pillow.

"No wonder poor Carol went off the deep end," my mother said. "Once people read this, there'll be pandemonium at the church. We have to get back before the next session of elders meeting. Carol is delicate enough as it is, and I know she has her hands full with Julia, and now, on top of that, with Rob going public this way, people will blow their tops! Rob can handle it. He's remarkable that way, but Carol can't. Just the rumors pushed her over the edge. How can she come back now that this thing has actually been published?"

"He should have thought about that before he wrote it," my father said. "His first responsibility is to Carol and his children, and he has let them down."

"How does Jamie seem to you?" my mother asked, looking at me.

The question startled me. "Fine," I said weakly. To be honest, I felt relieved to be away from him for an hour. Better to rest in this quiet room than to march up more dunes and crash through the waves in another round of desperate play.

When Jamie and Allyn returned, my mother closed the magazine and slipped it into her beach bag, but Jamie saw it. "Is that it?" he asked. "Did they publish Daddy's article?" My mother nodded and handed him the magazine, looking reluctant. Jamie sat and read. Someone who did not know Jamie might think he was too outgoing and social to have the patience of a reader, but Jamie brought to his reading the same intensity he brought to a conversation. He burned through books, and he was always talking about them. (Just the night before, he had read to me from Hersey's *Hiroshima* before we turned out the light, "He saw there were about twenty men, and they were all in exactly the same nightmarish state: their faces were wholly burned, their eye sockets were hollow, the fluid from their melted eyes had run down their cheeks." Jamie enjoyed selecting details sure to horrify me.)

He studied the article, holding it close as his eyes raced down the columns of words. We watched him read.

He closed the magazine and said, "Pretty good, don't you think?"

My father went to the window and parted the curtain just enough to look outside.

"I think it is very interesting," my mother said.

"I feel like I know half of it by heart," Jamie said. "Daddy's been working on it for a long time, and he's read all the different versions to us at dinner."

"And how did your mother react when she heard what he was writing?" my mother asked.

Jamie lowered his eyes. "She tried to talk him out of it. It seemed like every night they'd argue about it, not shouting, just debating, going back and forth. He'd say we have to change things, and she'd say nothing is going to change until colored people change, and that is going to take hundreds of years."

"Your mother said that?" I could see my mother's shock, not at the idea—common enough in those days—but that Carol McAllister had expressed it. I'm sure my mother saw Carol as I did, as an intelligent but fragile person. For her to give voice to a bigoted thought was, well, common. Beneath her. My father listened closely but said nothing.

"Mama doesn't always mean what she says. She'll start drinking, and these words just come out of her. Daddy understands that. We all do. And he knows that what she really wants is for him not to make trouble. But Daddy says his job is to speak his conscience. If he doesn't do that, he isn't earning his salary."

"My God," my father said.

"Of course," my mother said. "Your father has an important role to play, a public responsibility, and certainly, he has to follow his conscience, but for the rest of us," she hesitated, finding her way, "for the ones who may feel a little differently, or who might not be as bold as he is, it's a little troubling to see him go so far. I just wonder if your father might not want to be a little more careful about what he puts in writing."

"He had to write it," Jamie said. "He had no choice."

"Of course," my mother said.

In his book, McAllister recounts the story of his article's publication. My mother veered off course in thinking that he found *Look* magazine. They found him. An editor called from Atlanta and told McAllister they were looking for a fresh perspective on the race issue. Hardcore segregationists, demagogic governors, and Klansmen were grabbing all the headlines. "We've seen the pictures of the white girls spitting on those poor colored girls," the editor said, "and the white boys squirting ketchup on those young men at the lunch counter, but we refuse to believe they represent the educated South. We need someone to speak up for the better part of the southern conscience, a voice of moderation."

McAllister put the editor off for twenty-four hours, telling him he needed to pray over the decision and discuss it with his wife. He doesn't say how she reacted, but I can guess. Carol McAllister did not feel comfortable ringing the doorbell at our house. She would have dreaded the scrutiny of greater LaSalle. When her husband decided to speak out on the most explosive issue of our day, she tried to stop him, but McAllister felt restless even before the editor's call. It tortured him to watch as Butters took his congregation to new heights, while our congregation held to its ways, stolid and self-satisfied, congealing in our own fat. Our minister understood that, politically, he was drifting away from us and to conceal the progression in his thinking felt wrong. He wanted to lead us, not brood or hide. He wanted to march in front. His book quotes a poem by Henry Hitt Crane:

Keep me from cowardice, compromise, quitting;
Force me to face every fact, God.
Fire me with courage and zeal unremitting,
Forever determined to act, God.

I imagine him reading those words to his son. The reverend seated in his wingback chair, a pool of light on the open book, Jamie on the sofa, just the two of them, father and son, in the quiet room. Those words, "zeal unremitting," shoot straight through Jamie's heart. Life should be principled, dramatic, inspired. The boy sees his father as the noblest of men.

As we sat in our motel room, I watched Big M. He stood at the window, the curtain parted but an inch, a slash of sunlight splitting his face. I felt his contempt for McAllister's words. Nonsense, this article, beyond naïve. Nothing will change, and no good can come from stirring up trouble.

I have read and reread McAllister's book, brooding over his decision. Maybe it's my advanced years or the fact that I am Morris Nickerson's son, but McAllister's explanation sounds, to my ear, a touch high-minded. A cynic could argue that this editor from Atlanta, whoever he was, played our minister like a fiddle, flattering his ego. *We don't need another racist Georgia redneck. We need to hear a finer voice, a call to conscience from some distinguished southerner. Our magazine sells coast-to-coast, Reverend. Your name in lights.*

McAllister knew he was taking a risk. Doing the right thing would be so much easier if not for family entanglements. He planned to protect his reclusive wife by discussing the article with the session of elders, my mother among them, prior to publication. With their advice and support, he would then introduce the topic to the broader congregation. Once the article came out, he felt confident that most members of our church would applaud his moderation. A few hotheads would grouse, of course, but now he could seize the opportunity to lead most of us to higher ground.

But *Look* moved publication of the article forward, because it happened to fit in an issue going to press. Before McAllister could speak to a single member of the session, rumors swept the church. People felt blindsided and outraged without having read a word. Carol fell over the edge before the magazine hit the stands. As the congregation howled and gnashed its teeth, my mother placed a quiet call to McAllister's office and asked whether Jamie might join us at the beach. That's the kind of person she was.

I'm sure my father believed that the publication of McAllister's article led to Carol's breakdown, but that leaves out Julia, Carol's natural rival. Julia did not inherit her mother's red hair and fair skin, but she had her father's eyes, intelligence, and height. She never shied from standing near her mother to look down on her. As Carol faded, Julia bloomed. She advanced through her late teens like Liberty Leading the People. A top contender for homecoming queen, good-looking, sarcastic, and popular, Julia did not want to hide, excuse, explain, or protect her mother. She was looking for bridges to burn.

Julia refused to forgive Carol's smallest eccentricity. She made rough what her mother tried to smooth, left out what her mother put away. Julia and Carol brought out the worst in each other. Julia was already abetting Carol's decline when the reverend engaged in his high-minded martyrdom. Carol wanted quiet nights at home, a little television, the whisper of turning pages. She liked to snuggle on the couch with Jamie as he read a book. Meanwhile, Julia was coming home late, ready for war, wobbling, smelling of cigarettes, the buttons on her blouse askew.

CHAPTER 11

WHILE we played in the waves, Bit emptied the kitchen pantry, wiped down shelves, cleaned out the refrigerator, and scraped away traces of mold. With Emma G's help, she moved furniture and turned rugs. Bit took pride in her work, and she held strong ideas about what it did and did not entail. Once, my mother decided to start a garden. She wanted to serve a salad of lettuce and tomatoes from our own backyard, but Bit scotched the idea. "I don't weed," she said.

Bit knew my father would suspect her of moonlighting during our vacation. She already engaged in a variety of side ventures that he knew about. For years, she had been finding clients in our neighborhood for a gifted seamstress in Baker Bottom. Bit picked up and delivered the needlework, extracting a commission she called "the cut." Likewise, she claimed a cut for arranging catering when our neighbors wanted to host a cocktail party. "I need to put you in touch with a friend of mine," Bit would say to the hostess. "She handles all the nicest parties." My father grumbled that Bit was so busy collecting her various cuts she barely had time for housework, but Bit knew how to manage him. She made sure our house looked spotless when we came home.

Carol McAllister still had not returned, so Jamie spent most days at our house then went home for dinner with his father, a meal Julia was supposed to cook (although in fact she struggled to boil water). Jamie grumbled to Bit, Bit confided in my mother, and together, Bit and my mother developed a new routine. In the afternoon, Mama drove us to the McAllister's house with Jamie and Bit in back, each holding a covered dish or a pan wrapped in aluminum foil.

Reverend McAllister met us at the door and held it open, saying to my mother, "You know you don't have to keep doing this, Elizabeth," and then, "Come on in, Bit. Oh, my goodness, what do I smell?" Bit came through the door sideways, cradling her tray, and said, "Just a few pork chops" or "Just a little casserole." She laid the tray on the counter and looked around for the empty bowl or pot from the previous meal. When Reverend McAllister told her she was going to make him fat, Bit cocked her head, sizing him up, and said, "We got a ways to go yet," and they both laughed. Bit and my mother worked in concert, my mother defending McAllister at the church and Bit fixing his dinners. My mother did the shopping and told Bit what to cook. Once, when she told Bit to prepare a beet salad because my father loved beets, Bit objected, "No ma'am. The reverend don't like beets," and that was that.

Late one morning when Jamie was visiting, Bit pulled a tray from the oven, and the warm smell of sausage and biscuits filled our kitchen. She served us pigs-in-a-blanket, two each. The sausage was juicy and salty, the crust flakey and warm. I walked over to the fridge to get mustard for my second pig, but Jamie finished his and asked Bit for two more. When he cleaned those off his plate and asked for more, Bit said, "I'm thinking you like these, Jamie."

"This is the best thing I've ever eaten in my entire life," Jamie said.

"Well, then, I guess you better have one more," she said.

Bit dropped the pig on his plate, and returned to her position beside the sink, studying Jamie. "Say, Jamie," she said, "What you think you could sell one of these for? Down at the mill, I mean."

Jamie studied his pig. "At least a dime, I guess."

"A dime? That's nothing. I'm thinking more like twenty cents. Three for fifty cents. Folks like to feel like they's getting a discount."

Jamie's entrepreneurial instincts began to stir. He peeled back the biscuit to examine the pork. "What does it cost to make one of these," he asked, "if we had to buy all the ingredients, the sausage, the flour, the salt and whatever else is in here?"

"Practically nothing. A few pennies, I reckon. Maybe a nickel."

Jamie took another bite, then held up his half-eaten pig, inviting me to consider it. "Make it for a nickel, sell it for twenty cents," he said.

"That's a nice margin," I said.

"A very nice margin."

Jamie asked Bit if she could make one more tray, and she told him it was already in the oven. Next day, I carried a watermelon (investment: thirty cents), and Jamie carried a bag of pigs-in-a-blanket (investment: zero). We unfolded our table and set up shop. I wielded the blade, and Jamie wielded his charm, promoting our new product, offered at our introductory price of only fifteen cents each. We sold four slices of watermelon and threw the rest away. The scales had fallen from our eyes. We disdained watermelon now that we had discovered how a real product, a manufactured product, sells. Watermelon was difficult to transport and sloppy to cut, the growing season limited, and disposal of the rinds a bother. The margin, which had felt so rich the day before, now seemed pathetic. On the grand scale of commerce, watermelon ranked very low, on par with lemonade. A mere commodity.

And a pig-in-a-blanket? A work of craftsmanship! The crumbling, flaky crust and juicy pork carried our loyal lintheads to new heights of gastronomic ecstasy. What was fifteen or twenty cents for such a reward after eight hours of slaving at the looms? What began as a sales effort became an exercise in crowd-control. The men swarmed our table, eager for their pigs, surprised and delighted by our innovative offering. We left in triumph, weighed down with coins.

We found Bit in the kitchen. Jamie dug into his pocket, pulled out a couple of dollar bills and some coins, and passed Bit her cut. She examined the take. "How many trays you think you can sell?" she asked.

"We can sell all you can make," Jamie told her. "You should have seen it, Bit. We practically had to fight them off!"

"Is that right?" she said with a self-satisfied smile. "They like them, huh?"

"They love them! Way better than watermelon!"

"Watermelon," Bit sniffed. "Watermelon ain't nothing but a fruit!"

Now she turned to me. "If we going to do this, we got to be smart about how we use this kitchen," she said.

"I'll talk to Mama," I said.

"Ain't your mama I'm worried about," she said.

"I'll talk to him, too."

Bit grunted, twisting a dish towel as she planned. "All right then," she said. She held out her hand, shaking first with Jamie, then with me. Universal Gourmet had a new partner, and Bit had scored a lucrative cut.

Every member of the Nickerson household practiced the art of managing Big M, an art my mother and Bit had nearly perfected. They shared a common boss, and they collaborated to manipulate his behavior. My mother called it "making a little cornbread." Bit understood Big M's weakness for cornbread, and "making cornbread" became code for controlling him. I could not make cornbread, but I was beginning to learn a few tricks of my own.

When I offered to ride with him to the shop, he was surprised but happy to have me come along. I told him about our new product line, mentioning the margin. "With the watermelons, it was like we were selling shelving," I said, shamelessly pandering, "but now we're selling burl wood." My father did not say anything, but I knew how his mind worked. My mother's mind sometimes moved in cryptic ways, but with my father, I could read every thought. He was mentally repainting the shop sign to read "Nickerson & Son." I did not mention that we would be taking over the kitchen and bringing Bit in as a partner. Better to get him on board and sort out the details later.

Getting our new product to market turned out to be even more challenging than balancing a watermelon on a bicycle. We had ingredients to buy, dough to mix, and baking sheets to wash. When selling watermelons, we were distributors. Now, we were manufacturers, and manufacturing is a process. As it turned out, our new partner knew a lot more about process than we did. She knew what to buy, how to wrap the pigs, and how long to bake them, and before we could catch up to her, she began to innovate, diversifying our product line with spiced pork and sweet pork as well as two types of mustard.

Jamie made us a new sign:

Universal Gourmet

Presents

BIT'S BEST!

Pigs-in-a-Blanket

Plain, Hot, or Sweet

20¢ Each!!!

Your Choice of Mustards

1¢

He kept track of our receipts, set aside the capital required for raw goods, and allocated profits. He also took the lead on sales, keeping up a steady patter with the workers crowded around our table. "In Paris, they would call these crescent rolls," he informed them, "but the French don't have access to the pork products we have around here, and of course, our whole wrapping process is a trade secret."

With Bit supervising production and Jamie responsible for sales and finances, the menial labor fell to me. I hauled groceries, washed trays, pedaled my bike, set up the table and put it away. While Bit experimented with new ingredients and Jamie polished his pitch, I did the same old thing day after day. True, I was getting rich, but I was living a life of hard labor for money I didn't really need.

Jamie told Bit how the pigs were getting damaged when we carried the product loose in paper bags. "Half the crust ends up in the bottom of the bag," he said, so Bit developed a way to wrap each in wax paper, a process she perfected then turned over to me. I wrapped one after another, ripping each monotonous paper square, placing the pig, and folding it in. Bit watched closely and let me know when I did it wrong. She told Jamie to get rid of the paper plates ("Paper plates is low class") and to use plastic plates instead, which I had to wash. They experimented with presentation, comparing a pyramid of stacked pigs to an arrangement of concentric circles. Jamie reported that spicy pigs sold faster than plain or sweet, and Bit adjusted her production accordingly.

Jamie and Bit reveled in their collaboration, thrilled by the success of their joint business venture. I kept trying to offer up ideas, but none seemed to have much merit. One day, Jamie burned his hand on a tray right out of the oven, and Bit rushed to help him. She ran cool tap water over the burn, applied a Band-Aid, and kissed the top of his head. In all the years she was in our house, even when I had a headache, she had never kissed me.

If I was indifferent to the money, our new partner was not. Universal Gourmet supplied a meaningful difference in her weekly income, flowing more reliably than her other cuts. My father was getting fed up, but for Bit, that was just a cost of doing business. With extra cash coming in, she was not about to return to her pre-pig days. Her housework suffered. How could it not? There were only so many hours to vacuum, make the beds, cook our dinner, cook the reverend's dinner, and make pigs for Jamie and me.

"Bit," my father said one day, eyeing the counters crowded with bowls and baking sheets, "we need to talk about this pigs-in-a-blanket business."

"Yes sir," she said.

"I was all right with it when I thought you were just helping these boys out, and I know they appreciate it, but I can't be paying you for one job while you're working on another. That's not right."

"No sir," she said.

"I mean, it would be one thing if you were doing it on your own time, but when you're here, I'm paying you to cook and clean."

"Yes sir," she said. My father was inches taller than Bit, but she straightened her back and tilted her strong jaw. She wiped her hands with a dish towel, rubbing them long after they were dry. "If you has something that needs doing," she said, "just you tell me, and I'll get it done."

"You and I have always understood each other."

"Like I say, Mister Morris, anything you see that ain't getting done, you tell me, and I'll do it quick."

"It's not just the work, Bit. It's the money."

Her hands stopped moving. "What money?" she said.

"The money these boys are paying you to make their pigs."

"No sir," she said. "They ain't paying me nothing. I ain't got but one job, and that's working for you and Miss Elizabeth."

My father looked like the former Marine he was, thickly built, his nose raw with a recent sunburn. He turned from Bit to me, looking down on me as he did on her. "But I thought this was a business," he said. "I thought you and Jamie were paying Bit as your partner."

I could feel Bit watching me. "No sir," I said. "It's a business, but we don't pay Bit. I figured that was just part of her job." It was a mendacious but plausible use of the code on my part. Why would we pay her? She was just the maid.

Big M looked from me to Bit then back at me. "We'll have to see about this," he said and left the room. We had at least confused him, but I felt awful lying to my father. When he was gone, I turned to Bit, my co-conspirator, but her face was impassive.

"You heard what your Daddy said. Why don't you leave me alone and let me get some of this work done?"

My father did not enjoy confrontation, though he had seen plenty. During World War II, he served as Lieutenant Mo Nickerson, smart as a whip and tough as a knot, sent to the South Pacific to clear the Japanese from pillboxes and caves. He and his men would crawl toward a pillbox, open fire with machine guns, hand grenades, and flamethrowers, then crawl into the still-smoking hole to take cover and look for their next target.

"But what about the people in the box," I asked, "the ones you were shooting at? Where were they?"

"They were still there. But they were dead."

"You hid in a hole with dead people?"

"They were just Japs."

My father made clear to my mother that, when he returned from a long day at the shop, he expected the house to be "pleasant." Pleasant meant tidy, quiet, and calm. It meant that Bit had left our dinner on the stove. His sheets were clean, his shirts washed, and the towel he had left on the bathroom floor would have been laundered, dried and folded. When we joined him at the table, he expected to have a nice conversation. When things were not "pleasant," when there were trays still stacked in the dish rack and my mother was just getting home from the McAllister house, and dinner was late because my mother needed to finish what Bit had only begun, Big M's mood grew dark, his demeanor sullen and quiet.

I could hear them in the kitchen as my mother finished the dishes. "I won't have it," he said, "I'm not paying her to bake pigs-in-a-blanket all day when what she should be doing is sweeping my floors and fixing my supper."

"You're still getting fed."

"She's not keeping up with her work, and you know it. I'm tempted to find us another maid."

"Another maid?" my mother said. "Have you lost your mind? That's like saying you're going to replace a member of the family. You can't get rid of Bit any more than you can get rid of me. The children love Bit. We all love Bit. Jamie loves Bit."

"That's another thing! What the hell does Jamie got to do with anything? Here I am paying a maid who has decided to work half-time for me and the rest of the time for Jamie! What am I, a welfare agency?"

"I think it's sort of touching, really, the way Jamie and Bit get along. I think it's very sweet."

"It's expensive, is what it is, and I'm not sure it's appropriate. He's here all the time, and she dotes on him! Something's not right, Elizabeth. She's the hired help, for crying out loud."

"Jamie needs that attention, Morris. Things are hard for him at home right now, and if Bit can provide a little support, I'm not going to stop her."

"Shouldn't his mother be doing that? Not our maid, for heaven's sakes!"

"Well, Carol's not around, is she?"

Carol was taking more time to dry out than any self-respecting alcoholic should require. She was, in fact, in treatment for her mental illness, as well as alcoholism. She was not locked up in Milledgeville, Georgia's notorious state mental hospital, but resting in a private institution in the foothills of the Appalachian Range. I envisioned her with her legs wrapped in a blanket, watching the slow progress of shadows on the far side of a valley. McAllister spoke with her doctors regularly, and the reports he gave my mother were vague but reassuring. I came to understand that Carol McAllister was crazy, which I knew to be shameful, but still I felt a connection with her. Her reclusiveness appealed to me. Her hesitancy around others manifested what I sometimes discovered in myself. I liked to imagine my own days with an attentive nurse and hot chocolate, adrift in my thoughts, a blanket wrapped around my knees.

Weeks passed, and when I went to Jamie's house, I no longer expected to find his mother there. Many afternoons, Julia was entertaining her boyfriend, Tucker Gran, linebacker for the LaSalle Blue Devils. Star of the defense, gigantic in build, mildly if coarsely humorous, Tucker was the prize catch for girls at LaSalle High, and Julia had nabbed him. With Carol gone and the Reverend off at church, Tucker came often to the McAllister house, where he visited Julia in her bedroom with the door closed. "What do they do in there?" I asked, but Jamie only shrugged.

Tucker heard Julia call me "little Little" and took it one better, calling me "little Little lightweight." Julia's teasing never bothered me. She was pretty and energetic, and when she drove us places or fixed us one of her warm-it-up meals, she entertained me with her irreverent take on her family. She said that all her father's sermons about sin were about her, but when he invoked the congregation to have sympathy for the mentally infirm, he was talking about Jamie. She called Jamie "James," and Reverend McAllister "The Brow." "Just you and me tonight, James. The Brow has another Bible study with the fossils."

Nothing in Tucker's teasing sounded funny to me. He laughed at me, not with me, and either he wasn't smart enough to know the difference or too callous to care. Tucker led a small group of high school boys that had appeared at a couple of the recent marches downtown. They jeered at the demonstrators. When he and Reverend McAllister were in the house at the same time, I could tell the reverend didn't like him. Tucker minded his unctuous manners and served up a warm glop of syrup and insincerity. The reverend acted polite, but only that, and soon found a reason to retreat into his study. Tucker preferred to come around when McAllister was away.

Tucker was lounging in the McAllister kitchen one day when we dropped off a meatloaf. Afterwards, on the drive to Baker Bottom, my mother said, "What do you make of that boy, Bit?"

"He's up to no good," Bit said.

"I'm afraid you're right," my mother answered.

CHAPTER 12

WHERE I live now, in a comfortable little town west of Boston, the local fundraisers know me to be a reliable touch. I rarely attend their auctions. Ostentatious giving does not sit well with me, but I am always good for the anonymous donation. I've done my part for the artificial turf at the high school, the renovations at the library, and the new entrance at the museum. The truth is, I can give a good amount away and never notice it. It's easier to be generous when you know you have plenty. Having plenty means I don't have to work. A man my age shouldn't work anyway. It means I can eat breakfast on the terrace and look down a sloping lawn to trees that, in summer, block my view of the river. I drive a practical car, knowing that I can afford any car I want.

When the names of donors are listed on a brass plaque in a prominent place, or better yet, carved in stone, my friend Dermot Bogue enjoys seeing his top the list. He once talked me into attending a fundraiser, and he picked me up in a stretch limo with the tinted windows rolled down. When his wife complained that it was blowing her hair, he said, "What's the point of riding in a limo if no one can see you?"

We lunch together regularly. He'll pull up in my drive in a new Porsche or BMW or an antique Corvette. When I climb in next to him and ask, "Have I seen this one yet?" he cackles with delight. I credit Dermot's shameless hustle for much of my success. We had our share of debates while building Never Dull, but we were good partners. He needed me to handle the details of finance and law, and I needed his boldness and energy.

When we were starting out, we tried opening restaurants in the shadows of new Walmarts and Home Depots, but staffing and managing restaurants is a hard way to make money. We got rolling when we turned our focus to real estate. In a small town, a big box store literally moves the market. All one had to do, we learned, was invest in land or a new retail strip near the box. Obvious, easy, and lucrative. We flipped a few properties early on, but we kept as many as we could, sweeping in the lease payments month after month, year after year. I borrowed and re-borrowed, consolidating loans, cross-collateralizing properties. "It's a balloon loan with five years of partial PIK interest and an equity kicker," I would tell Dermot, and he'd chuckle and sign, having no idea what that meant. We were cautious in our selection of properties, conservative in our bids. We kept our greed in check and never ventured beyond the benign shade of the big boxes.

Dermot grew up in South Boston on the top floor of a three-decker with heat that came and went as his father found and lost work. He shared a bedroom with two brothers, Sean and Paulie, and waited in the freezing hall to use the bathroom. Some nights they ate oatmeal for dinner. I have eaten oatmeal for dinner only once, while camping in the Tetons. As a boy, Dermot hauled the garbage down two flights of stairs and saw rats scatter as he approached the cans out back. When I tried to give Dermot a history lesson on race relations in LaSalle, he brushed me off. "Whatever you saw," he said, "I saw worse. Don't get me started on busing in Boston. That was a nightmare." With his Boston accent, it sounded like *nightmeer*.

Dermot possesses a hunter's instincts for new markets and properties. I have stood with him on a piece of raw land and listened as he mapped out its development, telling me how the traffic will flow, pointing out the good lots and bad ones, showing me where drainage will create environmental headaches and noting where the afternoon sun will blind commuters, causing them to miss our signage. No one taught him how to do that.

"How do you explain me, Morris?" he'll ask. "I've told you how I grew up. If we had butter for the potatoes, we said a half-dozen hail Marys. Look at me now! I drive any car I want. Look at my shoes. You know what these shoes cost? You can't even buy shoes like this in America anymore. There are rooms in my house I've never even seen. How do you explain that?"

"Well, you had a brilliant partner."

"I've been blessed, Morris, but you know what? I also hustled. We both did. You some, me more. Remember, you have brains, but I don't. I'm just some lump. It's easier when you have your kind of brains. You know what I do have though? I have an Irish spine. I'm not afraid to work."

After Dermot's father's first heart attack, his mother took a job as a nanny for a wealthy family in Prides Crossing, on the north shore of Boston. The work was not hard, and though she didn't enjoy commuting by train, she came to love the old shingle style house with its big bay windows overlooking the Atlantic. She even came to love her charge, a lonely boy with alcoholic parents worn thin by their cigarettes and social life. Often, she walked him to the shoreline, first holding his hand as they climbed down the rocks from the house, then, as they both grew older, depending on him to take her hand. She told Dermot she was the boy's only friend, though that could no longer have been true by the time he began attending debutante balls. Helping him with his cummerbund and bow tie, then slipping a flask into his breast pocket, she told him in a conspiratorial whisper, "Here's a little Irish for you." She didn't tell him she had watered down his whiskey to keep him from drinking too much. Dermot heard that story years later, when the now-grown boy came to visit her in the hospital, where she was dying of congestive heart failure.

"That was nice of him," I told Dermot, "to remember her and visit her that way."

"You think?" Dermot said. "Here we are. The whole family, Sean, Paulie, all my sisters and me, gathered round for my mum's final hours, and this guy shows up. We're like, 'Who's he?' This guy ain't family. He's just some dosser trying to elbow in at her bedside. It didn't sit so well with us."

I feel a pang of self-recognition in that story. How was the boy to know the nanny wasn't family? What occurs in the maturation of the heart that teaches a child to distinguish between one loving figure, who is his own flesh and blood, and the other, who is just the hired help? Maybe he hears his father make a disdainful remark, and he finds himself amused by it, or maybe he recognizes a difference in the nanny's accent and choice of words, a difference he will learn to ascribe to class and education. In any case, boys do come to understand that a maid is not a mother, and in doing so, they substitute for love a lesser form of sentimentality. The boy who misses this difference or elects to gloss over it, a boy whose heart does not mature as expected, risks embarrassing himself.

In Dermot's story, I can understand why the lonely boy became so attached to the maid, but my case puzzles me. When I was a child, if someone had asked whether I felt close to my mother, I would have laughed. Is the sky blue? I have never questioned my relationship with her, not once, until now. Why was I was so attached to our maid? What did I see in Bit that my mother did not provide? The very question feels heretical, as if I were doubting the most important bond in my life. I keep returning to the image of my mother's "sick room" and its closed door. She's inside, suffering from a headache, and I'm outside, worried and needing her. My mother required her privacy. I felt her holding back from me, and not just when she had a headache. Even when she felt fine, she protected some inner chamber, locking me out.

I write a check to the Timothy Butters Memorial Fund and enclose a note: *In Memory of Elizabeth Nickerson.* I know the donors' egos will require a plaque somewhere near the monument. I like the thought of my mother's name topping the list. The size of my contribution does not compare to, say, a new wing on a hospital or a permanent college endowment, but it's enough to ensure the success of their campaign. Their cause has given me license to remember, and Emma G's dedicatory address provides a reason to return.

CHAPTER 13

BIT decided to move pig production out of our kitchen. She grasped that her ally, my mother, had done all she was willing to do to appease my father. In fact, the noise and confusion of our manufacturing line probably bothered my mother more than it bothered Big M. He left for the day, but she was stuck in the house, unable to escape the clatter and bustle of our factory. When Bit floated the idea of moving to the McAllister kitchen, my mother didn't object.

Bit talked to Jamie, Jamie talked to his father, and we made the move. Bit asked my mother to let her leave an hour early each day. When my father grumbled that he was paying Bit the same money for less work, Bit offered Emma G as extra labor. My mother thought Emma G had better things to do than sweep our floors, but she agreed, just to mollify my father.

Allyn and I knew nothing about the arrangement until we discovered Emma G in Allyn's bedroom, changing her sheets. Allyn usually barred me from her room, but she was so surprised to see Emma G that I slipped in without her noticing. Emma G straightened as we came in, her eyes on Allyn. The girls said hello, and Allyn told Emma G she did not have to make her bed, that she could do it herself, though I had never seen her do it. Emma G said she didn't mind, which also did not sound true. Emma G stood on the far side of the bed, gripping the sheet. She wore her hair pulled back, which emphasized the strong bones of her face and her frank, appraising eyes. Though she smiled at us, I detected a challenge there. She looked older than Allyn, more worldly. Lifting her chin, nodding toward an aluminum baton resting on Allyn's bureau, she said, "You in the band?"

"I was thinking of trying out. I wanted to be a cheerleader, but I didn't make the squad." This had been the most recent tragedy in Allyn's fraught life, another excuse for her to act mean toward me. An awkward pause, then Allyn said, "How about you? Are you in the band?"

"Cheerleader," Emma G said, meeting Allyn's eyes, then looking away. "I mean, junior cheerleader. This fall will be my first year." The two girls examined everything in the room but one another. Emma G lifted the top of Allyn's bathing suit from the floor. "Your mama lets you wear a two-piece?" she asked.

"It's not my mama I have to worry about," Allyn answered.

Emma G cocked her head. "How is your daddy?" she said. "I haven't seen him in years. Same as always?"

"Same as always, only more so," Allyn said, and at that, Emma G gave her a genuine smile. Emma G lifted a paperback from Allyn's bedside table. "You reading *Of Mice and Men*?"

"I'm supposed to. It's on our summer reading list," Allyn said. "It seems kind of sad though."

"You got that right. I liked *Grapes of Wrath* better."

"That's kind of long, isn't it?"

"It's good though."

"I read *The Red Pony*," I announced. "That was sad too."

"Remind me to give you a medal for that," Allyn said. I became the next thing the two girls found to look at. "What are you doing in my room, anyway? Shut the door on your way out."

When the girls were little, my mother read stories with Allyn at one side and Emma G on the other. If my mother felt threatened that Emma G picked up on the words faster than Allyn, she never revealed it—something at which she was adept. Bit once told me that Emma G knew how to read before any of her friends in Baker Bottom. "I give your mama some credit for that," she said. Beyond reading to the two girls, my mother had taken to giving Emma G books she had previously donated to the library when we were done with them—a practice that had begun after Bit saw her carrying a stack of them out to the car and asked if Emma G could have them instead.

After that, my mother began to quiz Bit about the books Emma G was reading and to follow Bit's reports of Emma G's progress in school. When we dropped Bit off, Bit sometimes sent her daughter out to speak with my mother. Emma G would come to the car window, and my mother would ask, "What did you think of *Lord of the Flies*? I felt so sorry for Piggy!" and Emma G would stand on the rutted road beside our car and talk to my mother about books. Instead of sending Bit home with just the unwanted books, my mother began giving her books she thought Emma G would like.

When Bit decided to move Universal Gourmet into the McAllister kitchen, the reverend was happy to have us, but Tucker Gran less so. The first day Bit saw Tucker and Julia go into Julia's room and close the door, she knocked on it. "Miss Julia?" she called. "Y'all can't be in there with the door closed if the reverend ain't here." Jamie and I heard some muffled laughter from inside the room, some back and forth between Bit and Julia. Then Julia opened the door.

Tucker's voice spilled out from inside her room—"Are you kidding me?"—but after that Julia left her door open. The next day, we were cooking pigs-in-a-blanket when Tucker came in the kitchen and said, "Hey, Bit, I left my track shoes in the car. Would you go fetch them for me, please ma'am?"

The "please ma'am" got under Bit's skin. "No sir," she said.

"Excuse me?" Tucker was a big guy, and he moved an inch closer to Bit.

"Can't you see I'm busy here?" Bit said.

Tucker snorted, but he went out to his car himself. Julia watched this interaction from the kitchen door. "You see?" Bit said to her. "Just say no. He won't like it none, but he'll hear it."

Bit taught Julia how to fry an egg and boil rice. "Bake everything at 350," she told her, "and wait for your oven to heat up before you put your dish in there." She won over Julia just as she had won over Jamie and the reverend. Returning a pot from a previous evening's meal, Julia said to Bit, "I want you to show me how to make that one." My mother took in this new relationship between Bit and the reverend's daughter; I could see that it pleased her.

Meanwhile, Big M paid for every hour Bit spent in the McAllister's house, and though he expected nothing in return from McAllister, he did not let our family forget it. If McAllister tried to thank him, my father put him off. Gratitude was annoying. To thank a man for doing the right thing insulted him, because it suggested he would have considered doing something else.

For me, the move to the McAllister house meant a further loss of status. Already, I was the low-ranking member of Universal Gourmet, but at least, in my house, the domain was my own and Bit my family's maid. At Jamie's house, I was the guest, and in no regard was Bit's status inferior to my own. The move transformed Bit. Once inside the reverend's doorway, she took charge, and if she noticed, as I did, the kitchen's small size, its scorched counter and poor lighting, she did not mention it. Instead, she set about rearranging it. Jamie's mother had organized her kitchen with the glasses stacked tall to small, the dishes arranged big to little, and the pots aligned by size, every handle facing left. I found the symmetry pleasing, but she had managed to put what a cook seldom uses (a blender or mixer) in places easy to reach and what a cook often uses (bowls and trays) in places difficult to reach. Bit examined the shelves and asked, "Your mama, is she left-handed?" She pulled out the trays, took down the bowls, blender and mixer, and gave each a new home.

Rob McAllister came into his kitchen midway through the process, and I recoiled. My father would never allow a maid to walk into his house and rearrange things, but McAllister simply looked around the room with a bewildered smile. "What's going on here?" he asked. Bit explained her thinking, showing him why the bowls should be beneath the counters and the blender above the refrigerator, a kitchen logic unknown to men and boys. "Bit," he said, "you amaze me."

Bit cooked enough at our house for both my family and the McAllisters, but even so, when she crossed the McAllister threshold, she was pressed for time. Once she had rearranged the kitchen to her liking, she streamlined our duties. Bit mixed, I wrapped, Jamie baked, I washed, he dried. We could have given lessons to the UAW on automated assembly. Our Chief Executive Officer blossomed in this new setting. She even allowed herself a discreet fashion flourish, a tiny pair of yellow rosebud earrings that appeared only when she entered the reverend's kitchen. She never wore them at our house, and I never saw her put them in or take them out, but there they were, a present she must have bought for herself with her share of our profits. I felt uneasy about those earrings, and I couldn't resist calling her out, almost as a way of keeping her close. The Bit I knew, the one who made my bed and cooked my meals, did not wear jewelry. "I've never seen those," I said. "Where did you get them?"

Her hands immediately went to her earlobes, hiding them. "Oh, these old things?" she said. "I must have forgot to take them out."

Naturally inclined to laughter, she laughed more often in the McAllister kitchen, and though the reverend could seem intimidating, she found that when she teased him, he teased her back. If he drifted into the kitchen, drawn by the smell, and stole a still-warm pig from one of her trays, she'd say, "It's good, ain't it?"

"Bit," he answered, "it is exquisite!"

"I don't know what that is, but you owe me twenty cents!" I watched them laugh, the way Bit closed her eyes and covered her mouth. I loved that.

Cooking pigs-in-a-blanket became more Bit's enterprise than ours. She never failed to count her cut, her expression all business when Jamie placed the bills in her hand. No maid ever won a promotion, and few earned a raise. My father paid Bit our neighborhood's prevailing wage. Generosity toward the Negro did not count as a cardinal virtue among the white families in LaSalle. My mother tried to help Bit by sending her home with food (the "tote" Bit called it) and by slipping her a few extra dollars at Christmas. Conveniently, Allyn and Emma G wore close to the same size. My mother gave Bit clothes that Allyn grew tired of, and more than once, I heard Allyn complain that my mother had given away something Allyn really liked. "Oh, hush," my mother said, "You haven't worn that blouse in a hundred years, and I know Emma G will like it." Bit never turned down a gift until Emma G reached her teens. One day, looking through a pile of Allyn's blouses my mother had left out for her, Bit took one from the stack and handed it back to my mother. "She won't wear this one," she said. "Nothing pink."

My mother examined the blouse and said, "But I think it's very pretty, and Allyn has barely worn it."

"No pink," Bit said.

The smell of baking dough and the sound of Bit's laughter filled the reverend's house. He never helped roll a pig or wash a tray—that would have been beneath him—but he liked to hang out in the kitchen and talk with us. I had known Jamie's father for years, but I had never seen him relax. That summer, I came to know him better. I realized that when Carol was in the house, Jamie's father seemed to live in his tiny study. Now, with her gone, he stretched his long legs beside the kitchen table. I knew he missed his wife. At least I knew he should miss her, but I noticed his relief as well. Carol made sure the living room rug bore the even swirls of her vacuum, and she layered magazines with the precision of gears in a watch. With her gone, open books and half-filled ashtrays littered every surface, and Julia's hairbrush and socks lay on the coffee table. Bit picked up, but she could not do everything, and McAllister never complained. After work, he wanted to relax, and I suspect Carol never allowed that.

One day, Bit had us moving at peak production, with me wrapping pigs and Jamie drying bowls. Bit was washing a still-hot baking sheet, the steam billowing up from the sink and practically scalding her face. McAllister wandered in, no doubt musing on something he had just read or was trying to write, and he set a full ashtray next to the sink. "That ain't no place for that," Bit snapped. I froze. Those were sharp words.

McAllister saw the ashtray as if for the first time. "You're right, Bit," he said. "I'm sorry." He picked it up and left the room. Bit tried to apologize, but he was gone.

On another day, we were working in the kitchen with Jamie's father lounging at the table, and Jamie was trying to get me to eat a pig with grainy mustard. I told him I did not like specks in my mustard. He said they were just seeds, and I should try it. I told him this mustard was the wrong shade of yellow. Back and forth we went. Jamie never stopped trying to get me to eat what I did not want. McAllister was smiling and watching, when Bit said quietly, "I'm sorry, Reverend, but I think I needs to use the bathroom."

In our house, there was a toilet for Bit off the laundry room, but the McAllister house was much smaller than ours, and it had only two bathrooms, one off the bedroom where Jamie's parents slept, and one in the hall, which Jamie and Julia used.

"Just use the one in the hall," the reverend said.

"Are you sure?"

"Don't give it another thought."

In *Leaving the Boat*, Rob McAllister describes a maid he came to know. He calls her "Bet." *Bet was a kind-hearted woman,"* he writes, *"with a ready laugh and innate goodness that appealed to all who knew her, black and white. It would have been easy to dismiss Bet for her fractured dialect and simple ways, but she had a kind of earthy charm not uncharacteristic of women of her race, and the more I talked with her, the more I came to feel that the bond between us was genuine. In listening to what she said and noticing what she took care not to say, I came to appreciate some of the challenges she faced. She worked long hours for low wages, though she was fortunate to have found a family invariably kind to her. Her primary concern was for the welfare of her daughter, now sixteen years of age, a bright, spirited adolescent, who could be, as all adolescents are, worrisome.*

Bet took pride in her daughter's academic achievements and wanted her to stay in school. I think she valued learning because she had so little herself. In my conversations with Bet, I grew aware of our tendency to conflate the fruits of education, namely, a good vocabulary and a trained mind, with intelligence, which is innate and cannot be taught. Bet had a good brain, but her ability to express herself was limited to earthy epigrams, colorful truths she strung out like laundry on a line. "There's no undoing what's done been done," she might say, a tautology expressed with such conviction, it struck one as profound. She punctuated each conclusion with a laugh so infectious one could not help but laugh along. It served as a good reminder for a man in the profession of making sermons. Her laughter was more convincing than words.

Bet feared that her daughter would have to find work as a domestic. She made some claims about what her daughter was reading and accomplishing in school that, frankly, I found difficult to believe, but I promised her I would do what I could to help her, and I assured Bet that, if it became necessary for her daughter to take work as a maid, I would help her find a "nice" family. Bet understood all too well that a girl in her prime takes a risk when entering a strange household. In some houses, even a difference in race is inadequate protection from unwelcome advances.

Bet worried for her daughter, wishing her to live a better life than her own. Beneath Bet's sunny exterior, I discovered a grim and fatalistic point of view. Like Bet, I had grown up in the segregated south, and though my experience was the inverse of her own, I understood the hard side of Jim Crow. In the abstract, it bothered me. Indeed, those concerns led to my controversial article, but those reservations would have remained more abstract than real if not, I think, for my conversations with Bet. Through her, I saw the evils of our system on a more personal level.

I once asked Reverend Butters about Bet, and he smiled at the mention of her name. "If only I could bottle Bet's energy," he said. He noted Bet's role as a long-standing member of the Caring Circle and praised her for her regular visits to the elderly and ill. She served as a judge in the Easter fashion show and sewed robes for the Christmas pageant. With regard to her romantic life, he compared a few male members of his congregation to bloodhounds. They scented her single status, and Bet did not treat them coldly. She was fun to be with and appreciated their advances, but she was fiercely protective of her daughter and cherished the memory of her husband. None of her suitors, and there were several, measured up to her exacting standards. She teased them, laughed with them, shared the occasional glass of beer or gin after work, but never considered any deeper relations. She devoted mind, body, and soul to the promotion and protection of her daughter.

Through Bet, I came to appreciate the faith of outcasts. The spiritual fervor of the dispossessed far outranks the careful reasoning of the privileged. Bet no more chose to believe than she willed her heart to beat. I may have surpassed her in the social hierarchy, but the Lord applies standards of His own. All my spiritual speculations pale in comparison to the brilliant heat of her innate faith.

In retrospect, McAllister should have spent less time worrying about Bit's daughter and more about his own. One day, Jamie and I were heading out for the afternoon shift change at the mill when I returned to his bedroom to fetch our change wallet. Alone in Jamie's bedroom, I was startled by the sound of Bit's and Julia's voices, as if they stood behind me. Remembering the vent in the back of Jamie's closet, I bent down and saw that it was open. I crouched at the door of the closet and listened.

"How long, you say?"

"I don't know. I'm not really good about keeping track. I know it hasn't been this month. I'm trying to remember last month, and I just can't, you know? So much has been happening with Mama gone and Daddy in trouble at church."

"All right, hush now. Crying about it won't make it better. We need to talk to your daddy."

"You can't tell Daddy. Nobody can know, especially not Daddy. What if someone in the church found out? He's already in trouble, and if word gets out that his daughter, that I—"

"All right, now. That's enough of that. I'll talk to him with you, you and me together. Stop this, now. You going to make yourself sick getting so upset this way. If you are in that way, you need to start thinking about your health, about that baby's health."

"There won't be a baby. I can't have a baby, Bit."

"Ain't nothing you can do about that now."

"Yes, there is. I know there is. You have to help me."

"Help you how? What you talking about, girl?"

"Find me someone. Someone that will help me get rid of it."

"I can't do that."

"You have to. You have to! If you don't find me someone, I'll have to go somewhere else, or I'll have to do it myself."

"Don't you be talking that way! Don't you go be hurting yourself!"

"I will, Bit! I swear I will! If you won't help me, I'll do it, and I'll do it soon!"

"You need to tell your daddy. That's what you need to do. Besides, I don't know no doctor like that, no white doctor anyway."

"He doesn't have to be white."

CHAPTER 14

MOST of us are not much good at keeping secrets, but I kept Julia's secret. I suppose I could have told Allyn. She would have relished this salacious gossip about a girl who occupied the pinnacle of LaSalle High, but I liked Julia, and in those years, Allyn was as much my rival as my ally. She always kept secrets from me, clamming up if I lurked too close to one of her endless phone conversations. Now I knew something that she didn't, and I gloated over my advantage.

Julia was in an awful fix. Without exception, LaSalle High kicked out pregnant girls. I suppose they set a bad example, these teen brides, home changing diapers while their friends went out to movies and basketball games. That was no life for a vivacious girl like Julia. Beyond that, she knew that if word got out that she was pregnant, her father would not preach another sermon in LaSalle. Julia had her reasons for confiding in Bit, but she'd put Bit in a terrible position. If Bit got caught helping Julia, all the blame would fall on her. My father would fire her, and no other family would ever hire her. She might even face criminal charges.

Just say no. That's what Bit had said to Julia about Tucker Gran, and she could have given herself the same advice. Julia's problem wasn't Bit's problem, and Bit had every reason to walk away from Julia. But she didn't. Maybe she felt loyal to Rob McAllister because he'd dared to enter her church. Maybe she sympathized with Julia, a girl in trouble with no mother at home. I suspect she was stalling, trying to make up her mind. I knew better than to reveal to Bit that I'd overheard her conversation with Julia. No need to poke a brooding bear.

I couldn't imagine approaching Jamie's father—even Jamie was off limits. I wanted Jamie to be down at the mill with me, selling pigs-in-a-blanket, not dealing with yet another problem at home. Had I been one year older or one year younger, I might have gone to my mother. She was the problem solver in our family. She knew how to listen (a skill that never mattered much to Big M), and once she heard about a problem, she promptly looked for a solution. But I was at an odd age, in the waiting room for adolescence. I didn't want to talk to my mother about Julia. I didn't want her to know that I knew what an unwanted pregnancy was or how it came about. The little I knew about sex embarrassed me, and to discuss Julia's situation with my mother would have pained me. I was old enough to know better, but I clung to a childish hope that the problem would just go away.

My life continued along its normal course. When I was away from the McAllister household, Julia's secret seemed less real. We belonged to a country club even though our house had a pool. Allyn preferred the pool at the club to our own pool, because she saw her friends at the club and that included boys. When she breezed through the kitchen in a new two-piece swimsuit, my father said, "I hope you're not planning to wear that at the club," and Allyn answered, "No, Daddy, I'm wearing it to the movies downtown." She left before he could answer. My father wanted me to go to the club for lessons in tennis or golf, because he wanted me to be part of a team, and he believed in character-building competition, but he backed off once Universal Gourmet got rolling. Jamie and I had a business to run.

The other boys I knew were hanging out in their own backyards and their friends' houses, and when they went to the club, they walked the golf course, played tennis, and swam in the pool. Jamie and I ventured into a different world, the mills downtown. The other boys ordered Cokes with maraschino cherries from the Black club waiters, who wore white coats with their first names monogrammed at the breast. We sold pigs-in-a-blanket to doffers and weavers coming off the second shift, their hair filled with lint.

The mill buildings defined downtown LaSalle, looming in big brick mesas at river's edge. We craned our necks to read the name at the top of a mill tower: The Swallow Spinning Company. A painted bird soared from one edge of the sign, depicted on a white background with the brick showing through. Pigeons circled above in silhouettes, the clatter of their wings barely audible. If we stood close and turned our heads, the windows seemed to march in rows down the building's long façade, a lesson in perspective, each window whited out. The air issuing from an open door felt warm and moist because of the industrial humidifiers used to protect the cotton. We set up our table on the far side the parking lot, well away from the factory security guards. The asphalt radiated heat. The mill thrummed. The looms ran night and day, shaking the ground. A whistle shrieked at shift change, and the emerging workers appeared anonymous and small beneath all that brick. They crossed the lot slowly, as if crawling to escape the mill's enormous shadow. Then one would call out and wave, and I recognized him as Cal or Phil or George. Relieved to be finished with work, happy to see us, he laughed in anticipation of Jamie's ever-changing pitch.

They spoke a language of their own. They talked of spooling, spinning, and creeling the drawing. They worked on carding floors and in slasher rooms. When Jamie asked George what kind of work he did, George told him, "I run the roving through the slubbers." Jamie and I never saw the inside of a mill. The words the workers used, the sound the looms made, and the edifice of brick-on-brick conveyed a sense of mystery about what went on inside.

One day, as we were peddling toward the mill with sacks of pigs, a policeman stopped us. "Y'all can't go this way," he said, holding up his thick hands. "Broadway is blocked off for the demonstration."

"What demonstration?"

"What rock you been living under?" he said. "This is the so-called protest where all the coloreds get to come tell us how awful we is. Opportunity of a lifetime."

"We've got to see this," Jamie said when we'd left the policeman behind. We skirted a couple of blocks north, made sure the officer was out of sight, then turned back toward Broadway.

I had seen better parades. Black men led the group, but women marched as well, and a few whites I didn't recognize. The men wore coats and ties, the women somber dresses, their march a glum affair, no singing or talking, just the scrape of their feet on the street. Reverend Butters led the way in his white shirt, gray jacket, and narrow tie. His solemn demeanor remained composed, though some whites along the sidewalk jeered at the marchers. I looked for Tucker Gran but didn't see him. A sizable police contingent blocked the hecklers from the marchers. As Butters passed us, he acknowledged Jamie with a barely perceptible nod.

The demonstrators carried signs, black block letters on white pasteboard that read, "I am a Man!" and "Equal Rights for All." Some wore sunglasses, and the women carried large purses. The policemen sweated through their blue uniforms and stiff hats. Most wore aviator sunglasses, which gave them the look of merciless wasps. They reminded the marchers to keep moving, and when a white boy in his late teens yelled at the marchers, calling them "spearchuckers" and telling them to "go back to Boola-Boola," a cop lumbered to his side and stood next to him, hands on hips, until the boy backed down. When one woman, exhausted by the heat, sat down on the sidewalk, her feet in the gutter, her head resting on her knees, an officer nudged her with his toe and told her to move on.

I didn't see the rock until it was in the air, a lump of broken concrete coming over the head of a policeman facing us. It hit the asphalt near Reverend Butters, breaking into pieces, and he jerked back, jostling the man next to him, who caught him by the shoulders. Then everyone craned their necks, trying to see the thrower, and the policeman turned, wading back into the group of kids behind him. Butters' hat had come off, and I could see his bald head wet with sweat. A woman handed him his hat, and he paused to thank her, tilting his head, his manners still impeccable. He squared his hat, straightened his jacket, and continued down Broadway.

A small group of teenage girls, out of place among those solemn adults, brought up the rear. I realized one of them was staring at me. It was Emma G. She saw me before I saw her, and rather than turning away, she gave me a fierce look. "Don't you tell her, Little!" she called. "Don't you say a word!" She kept me fixed in her minatory gaze as they walked past, and I cringed beneath it. One of the cops turned his wasp shades on me, this white boy who seemed to know one of the marchers. "Let's go," I said. Jamie and I turned our bikes away. We arrived late at the mill, and by the time we had our table set up, we had missed the shift change.

"So, Emma G is a rabble rouser!" Jamie said, laughing. "Her mama is not going to be happy about that! Are you going to tell her?"

"She said not to."

"That's not what I asked," Jamie said. "What do you think Bit will say if she finds out?"

"I don't know," I said honestly, trying to decipher it. I knew about Tim Butters because I had watched him preach. Bit heard the same sermon. Butters had talked about women who washed and cleaned all day but could not take a seat on the bus. I tried to remember how she had responded, but I had been watching Butters, not Bit. Then something else struck me, an altogether different event that had made a strong impression on me. I saw it now in a new light. I said to Jamie, "Emma G is the reason we boycott Patterson's Department Store."

"Hold on. What? You've never told me that! Who boycotts Patterson's?"

"We all do. Mama won't let us shop there."

"Who is 'we'? Not Big M, I bet."

"Big M goes where Big M wants, but not me and Allyn. I haven't been inside there in years."

"But why? What does it have to do with Emma G?"

"This was a long time ago. If I was there, I don't even remember it, but Mama and Allyn have both told me this story. It was around Christmastime, and Mama decided it would be fun to take Bit and Allyn and Emma G shopping together. She thought it would be a real treat for Emma G. Well, as soon as they got to Patterson's, she realized it wasn't such a great idea, but by then, it was too late. There was Santa Claus on his throne, ho-ho-hoing away, and these girls wanted nothing more than to sit on his lap. Emma G and Allyn were both begging to go see him, and Mama kept saying things like, 'Let's go look at the toys instead' or 'What's this over here?'"

"And where is Bit?"

"Bit is right there with them. She's holding on to Emma G, and Mama has got Allyn, but the more they say 'no,' the more these girls want to go see Santa Claus. Emma G manages to wriggle away from Bit, and she runs over and tries to climb up on his lap. That's all she wants to do, just sit on his knee and tell him what she wants for Christmas, but this old Santa isn't having it. She climbs up, and he pushes her off. She climbs up again, and he pushes her off again. Mama and Bit hurry over, and while Bit is trying to pull Emma G away, this Santa grabs Allyn and pulls her up on his lap. He's desperate to have a white girl on his lap, any white girl, so that Emma G can't climb up. My mother is not about to let him use Allyn that way, so she grabs Allyn and snatches her off his lap, and Allyn starts crying, and Emma G is already crying, because Bit was trying to pull her away, so there they are in the middle of Patterson's store with "Jingle Bells" playing nonstop and both these girls hollering their heads off. Mama and Bit had to drag them out of there. Not a fun trip."

"Did your mother talk to the manager?"

"Mama is not the talk-to-the-manager type. She's more the get-a-headache and spend-four-days-in bed-type. She never talked to anyone but us about it, and that was years ago. We haven't been back to Patterson's ever since."

"And what about Bit? Does she boycott Patterson's too?"

"Yep," I said. "She doesn't go there either."

That was not true. When Jamie asked, I realized I had seen Bit use a Patterson's shopping bag to carry home her "tote," but it was a better story if Bit joined the boycott. In retrospect, I think my mother was more traumatized than Bit. This man was paid good money to play Santa Claus, but he refused to allow a brown girl to sit on his lap for one minute in his sorry little life. Store policy, no doubt. My mother's shame turned into a cold fury. I know she was angry with herself for putting Bit and Emma G in that situation. As for Bit, she was mad, but I bet she wasn't shocked. For her, it was just another day in the Jim Crow South. Why wouldn't old Saint Nick be yet another bigot?

And Emma G? One does not forget getting shoved off Santa's lap. Ten years later, she marched with Timothy Butters. "Don't you tell her!" she called to me. I remembered her in church, how Butters' words galvanized her, and how she recoiled when her mother touched her.

After we left the mill, I felt a headache coming on as our bikes climbed the hill near my house. The sun flared through the treetops and bits of silica in the asphalt sparked up at me. I dropped my bike in the yard and vomited on the lawn. Bit rushed out, saying "What in heaven's name?" and I brushed past her holding my head, desperate for my dark room.

Minutes after I crawled into bed, Bit came in with a bowl and a cool washcloth. "Look at you," she said softly. "You still has your shoes on, you poor thing." She pulled my shoes off then sat on the side of my bed, and I sank toward her, her weight pulling me down, but it was good to feel her there, her close soft thigh, her cool, soft hands, and she gently stroked my cheek with the damp cloth, saying "Look how hot you is, you poor thing." No one in the dark room but Bit and me. It was the way it used to be, just the two of us, and she was stroking my face with her cool cloth, whispering to me, her voice rich and soothing. I began to fall asleep, cared-for and floating, lulled by her presence. I did not tell her about Emma G, because I did not want to ruin this moment. If I had told her, it would have upset her, and she might have left me. That was the last thing I wanted. I wanted her to stay.

That is my last, most vivid memory of Bit nursing me, but there were many. I can still feel the cool press of her hands, the rough, damp cloth she laid across my forehead, the way she brushed my hair back and spoke softly, allowing me to relax and drift, safe in her care. Always Bit and never my mother. My mother was sympathetic, but she had her own headaches to deal with. She never touched me the way Bit did. She kept to herself.

CHAPTER 15

"Do you remember that time Mama took you and Emma G to Patterson's, and Santa wouldn't let her sit on his lap?"

"I remember," Allyn says.

Several years have passed since I last visited Allyn's house, but I can picture her sitting on her porch, cradling the phone, studying her bird feeder. Sometimes, when we talk, she will interrupt, saying out of the blue, "There he is!" Meaning the woodpecker, an aggressive male with a brilliant slash of red that makes him her backyard celebrity.

"Christmas was never the same after that," she says. "Every other child in the world was worried about whether Santa Claus was real or not, and I was worried about what I would say to the son-of-a-bitch if I ever caught him in our living room."

"I've always felt proud of Mama for boycotting Patterson's."

"I guess, but her little boycott didn't exactly bring them to their knees. I don't think anyone ever noticed, except for you and me. Typical Mama. She throws a boycott but doesn't tell anybody."

"But at least it shows she had her principles."

"Which she managed to keep private. I don't see what good it does to have these lofty ideals if you keep them to yourself. You remember what Mama was like. When she wasn't sick, she was worried about getting sick. She may have been mad as hell about the way they treated Emma G, but she didn't do anything about it. That would have involved a level of conflict her delicate constitution couldn't tolerate."

"She stood up for Rob McAllister in the church, with the elders."

"A lot of good that did him." Allyn sighed. "Why are we talking about this, anyway?"

"Remember how you told me that Emma G is going to speak at the memorial for Tim Butters? That got me thinking about her and Bit and how we grew up, with segregation and all. I know it's an accepted fact these days that we were pure evil, but back then, it was just the way things were, you know? Do you ever wonder how Mama thought? I know she didn't join the demonstrations or anything like that, but at least she supported Rob McAllister."

"You're stretching, Little!" Allyn half sings the words, teasing me. "Remember, you're talking to me now, your sister. I lived there too, and I know what it's like to tell someone that you grew up in LaSalle. It's like confessing that you have some really sweet memories of growing up in Nazi Germany. No one is going to understand, Little, and you can't change the way it was, the way we were. You're never going to remake Mama into some kind of civil rights champion. That's not who she was."

"I sent a check for the Butters memorial."

"Of course you did. How big of a check?"

"Enough."

"Jesus. You and your gifts."

"I told them I wanted her name somewhere in Courthouse Square. In Memory of Elizabeth Nickerson."

"Just her?"

"Just her. Daddy would not want his name anywhere near a monument to Tim Butters."

"Maybe not, but it seems perverse to make a gift in memory of only one parent. Why her, anyway? It's not like she cared about civil rights."

"I'm a rich old white guy, Allyn, and I want my mother's name on the plaque, OK?"

"No need to get all huffy about it."

"I'm thinking of going, and I want you to go with me. I'll buy your ticket. It'll be fun. We'll drive by the house, eat some Macon Road barbecue, and go see Emma G speak."

"I don't think I want to see Emma G speak, or rather, I don't want her to see me. I'm not ready to face Emma G just now."

"When will you be ready?"

"How about never? Look, Little, be realistic. No matter how much you give, Emma G is not going to see you as one of the good guys, and if you try to remind her of that story about Santa Claus, she's not going to tell you how much it meant to her that Mama boycotted Patterson's. She's not going to have anything nice to say about any of us."

"But you and Emma G were friends!"

"That's just what you and I tell ourselves. Another pretty memory of growing up in Deutschland. We weren't really friends. Daddy couldn't stand her for one thing, and she saw that. We both did. Neither of us were old enough to understand, but when Daddy was in the room, Emma G always went very quiet. When I got older, I came to understand that it wasn't anything that Emma G had done, but she embarrassed him. Think about it. He and Mama were still a relatively young couple trying to make new friends. None of those friends let their daughters play with colored girls. You can try to act like we did it because Mama was somehow ahead of her time, but Daddy certainly wasn't. He hated having Emma G in our house, and he couldn't wait to get her out of there."

"So, Emma G becomes a civil rights activist because of Big M? How ironic is that?"

"That's not what I'm saying, although he did provide her with the opportunity to experience humiliation firsthand, not in the obvious way, like getting dumped off Santa's lap, but in a roundabout way everyone understood, Emma G better than most. But that's not why she marched. You need to give Tim Butters some credit. You saw him speak, not me, but you said he had her pretty stirred up. Even that isn't the whole explanation though. I knew Emma G, and I also remember what it was like to be a teenaged girl. I can tell you why she marched."

"Why?"

"Because it was sexy. She did it because it was the cool thing to do. She was sixteen years old, the same age as me, and at that age, you couldn't care less what your mother wants you to do. All you think about is your little group of friends. They were bored, they were drunk on hormones, and they wanted some excitement. When they got a chance to sneak out of school and go protest, I bet they were champing at the bit. You have to hand it to Tim Butters. Everyone remembers his oratory, but he was strategic as well. When he couldn't get enough adults into the streets, because they had to work or because they were worried about losing their jobs or because they didn't believe LaSalle would ever change, he recruited the kids. It was brilliant. He needed bodies, feet on the street. He didn't care how old they were, and those teenagers had nothing to lose! For them, the whole thing was a giant holiday, until it wasn't."

"But isn't that sort of a demeaning way to look at it? You're taking this great social movement and reducing it to hormones."

"Because I remember what it was like! She was Black, and I was white, but we were both adolescents. If I had been Black, I would have marched. You want to know the truth? I was jealous of Emma G. I mean, here she was, taking it to the streets to bring about societal change, and what was I doing? I was trying to get up enough courage to wear a two-piece to the country club. Compared to hers, my life was completely frivolous. She was out there with the adults, shaking her fist and marching, and I was sitting poolside watching Randy Wade tie a knot in a cherry stem with his tongue."

"Randy Wade. Didn't he turn out to be gay?"

"That's a different topic."

After our call, I allow myself a bit of brooding. I must admit to a stagnant quality in my relationship with Allyn that I can usually, but not always, push aside. She will forever be the big sister, the one who knows so much more than I do, and who deigns, on occasion, to enlighten me. Her take on Emma G is not exactly flattering, and I do not appreciate her snide remarks about my mother's "delicate constitution," but she is my sister, and I love her despite herself. Despite myself. We may not see our past the same way, but she is the only person I know from a time and place that is slipping beyond the horizon.

CHAPTER 16

AFTER publishing the article that nearly cost him his job, Rob McAllister chose his sermon topics carefully. He kept his unique style, mixing in snippets from John Donne, Niebuhr, and Groucho Marx, but the essence of his message conformed with that of the other ministers in town. Every gesture of charity is worthwhile, he reminded us, no matter how small. He encouraged us to be alert to God's presence in our everyday lives, telling us that our struggles with doubt strengthen our faith. And he avoided the subject of civil rights. The collection plate began to fill again.

But Tim Butters smoked him out. By putting demonstrators in the streets, Butters forced each of the ministers at the four major white churches to address the issue of segregation. For the Baptists, integration led to miscegenation, thus perverting God's division of the races, and they wanted no part of it. The Episcopalians and Methodists vowed to keep politics out of the pulpit. A few Presbyterians, under McAllister's leadership, qualified as liberals—a relative term—and agreed to make mild gestures of goodwill, such as donating canned vegetables to the Council's annual food drive.

McAllister told the session of elders that his conscience would not allow him to denounce the demonstrations, but he promised no more surprises. He explained a hundred times how the release of his article had been botched, and, in the privacy of the session meetings, he continued to press his message of racial enlightenment. Our church board, like our town council, was split. Some saw the protests as a plain violation of the law and wanted to see Butters and his followers arrested. Others believed that, by taking to the streets, the radical minority had exposed just how weak their movement was. They could barely muster a quorum. Both sides agreed that McAllister should do nothing that would embarrass our congregation.

One member of the session thought it might not be such an awful thing to allow one or two well-mannered Negroes to attend our services, if only at Easter and Christmas. That was my mother. She reasoned that, if Black people came into our houses to cook our food and care for our children, why would we shoo them away from church? What harm could come from putting a few Black fannies on the pews? There was plenty of room in back.

In his book, McAllister gives the maid "Bet" credit for helping him see the problem of integration in less abstract terms, but I give my mother some credit as well. She would not have described herself as integrationist, segregationist, liberal, or conservative. She simply responded to the people around her. Some she liked, and some rubbed her the wrong way. She knew a few Black people as good company, much better company than at least one member of the session, Mimi Hurd, who wore her phi beta kappa pin to every meeting. I knew from Allyn that Mrs. Hurd had fired her maid for stealing liquor without asking if her teenage son might have been the guilty party. She often spoke of the need to protect our congregation's "integrity."

The session of elders consisted of nine members, four men and five women. My mother charmed the men and impressed them with her good sense. She made friends with all the women but one, and when they disagreed with her, she listened respectfully. At each meeting's close, she chatted about children and recipes, allowing the conversation to cool. My mother stood up to Mimi Hurd, which none of the men on the board had the gumption to do. Even Rob McAllister deferred to the church's largest donor, but when Mimi lectured the group on the need to preserve the purity of our race, my mother said, "Oh, for heaven's sakes, Mimi. We're people, not baking flour."

I will not maintain that my mother stood before the board and argued for integrating the congregation. Allyn would not let me get away with that, and I have no evidence for it. She was, as Allyn said, not confrontational. I like to think that, had I been an adult in 1960s LaSalle, I would have marched with Tim Butters and refused to attend a segregated church, but my closest proxy is my mother, and she did not do that.

My mother and father grew up in the same town, drank water from the same river, and learned their multiplication tables at the same elementary school, but they did not think the same way about race, maybe because my father was a few years older, or because he grew up on a farm, whereas my mother grew up in a nicer home close to the county courthouse. My father saw Sonny Coleman's body dragged through the streets, and he cared for Brother. Knowing that, you might expect him to sympathize with the Black man's plight, but other people's plights never really troubled Big M.

He pretended to be tougher than he was. Even his thick hide was thin in places, which meant that he saw social change as a form of personal criticism. When he was a boy, Black men knew their place. If we were to change that by, say, sharing a water fountain or showing a man a modicum of respect, that would imply there was something wrong with the way my father was brought up. To reject the social mores of south Georgia during the depression meant rejecting his teachers and parents, who they were and what they believed. His great grandfather fought for the Confederacy and damn near died for the cause. Our ancestor had defended our home from the Yankee invaders, and my father revered him for that. If I were to write Big M's biography, I would name it *Staying in the Boat*.

My parents maintained a pragmatic relationship, as I suppose most married couples do. The buildup of time wears away the romance, grinding off the shine with hours of grocery shopping and paying the bills. The daily reality of keeping my father fed and scraping his scraps into the Dispose-All could not compare with the mythic childhood and saintly father my mother remembered. Big M did himself no favors when he issued empty threats to put down his foot, by god, and fire the help, but he managed to keep in my mother's good graces by adhering to a single principle: She never doubted that, where our family's welfare was concerned, her husband, Morris Nickerson, would do the right thing.

My father's mother endured the burden of her years by describing in unceasing, monotonous detail every pinch, pull, and pain she felt. My uncle Bob got so fed up, he bought her a house in town just to get her out of the farmhouse. My father regularly made the hour-long drive from LaSalle to Cemochechobee, sometimes taking Allyn or me, often traveling alone. He delivered a case of gin on every trip. When I went along, we sat in my grandmother's stuffy bedroom with its old bureau the size of a cast iron bank safe and listened to her gripe about her ankles and shoulders and everything in between. She swore the maid was stealing her gin, and the maid reliably pulled my father aside and threatened to quit. My father, who could appreciate a nice ironic gesture, pacified the maid by giving her a bottle of gin. When they diagnosed my grandmother with gastric cancer, my father could have parked her in a nursing home, but instead, he arranged for a woman to sleep at the house. Bob refused to help, saying he had done enough, but my father kept after him, until Bob agreed to visit her. She died as my uncle napped in the chair beside her bed. While she was alive, I never connected this old woman with the person who squeezed my father's hand as Buford King dragged a corpse past their Cemochechobee church.

My mother never regarded the four years she spent at a small women's college in south Georgia as a "higher education." She was aware of what she did not know, and she always carried a small spiral notebook and a ballpoint pen to church. Whenever McAllister dropped a striking reference, she wrote it down. Consulting her notes, she found a copy of *Walden* at the library, read all of it and liked parts of it. *Mere Christianity* became one of her favorite non-fiction books, and *Zorba the Greek* one of her favorite novels. She sent *Zorba* home with Bit for Emma G to read. Kierkegaard was a nonstarter. She decided to let McAllister wade through the muck of the thicker tomes and to rely on him to drop the best quotes into his sermons.

After a service, when McAllister was shaking hands with his exiting congregation, if my mother asked about a passage, he might say, "Oh, that was Camus," and suggest one or two titles. He enjoyed being her mentor, just as she enjoyed being his student. "How goes it with *The Plague?*" he asked on the following Sunday. "The beginning put me off a bit," my mother might say, "but I haven't given up on it." When she finished it, she gave her copy to Emma G, who sailed through it, unfazed by the author's opening description of stepping on a rat. She loved it, and mentioned Camus to one of her teachers, who then told her to read *No Exit*. She liked that as well and mentioned Sartre to my mother, which led to a minor victory. The next time McAllister brought up Camus, my mother told him, "Camus is good, but I prefer Sartre."

Rob McAllister was inches taller than my father and two years younger. One grew up in the peanut fields, the other near the steel mills of Birmingham; one served as a Marine, the other as a naval officer; and one worked in a cabinet shop, the other as a man of the cloth. My father had a keen, measuring intelligence, while McAllister was bookish and idealistic. They respected one another, but warily, each aware of the gulf that separated them. My mother loved one as a husband and venerated the other as a mentor. Allyn saw how my mother responded to McAllister's lean good looks. I saw how her mind reacted to his. My father respected my mother for her common sense, but it never occurred to him to discuss a book with her. McAllister did just that, nurturing ideas and interests that extended the boundaries of her world.

In *Leaving the Boat*, McAllister avoids naming names, even giving Bit a new one, but one board member he describes as "my champion, confidante, and friend." The word "confidante" intrigues me. My mother had been friends with McAllister for years and had invited the minister and his wife to dinner at our house several times until it became apparent that Carol was always either "not feeling well" or "had a previous engagement." Now, with the church in turmoil and Carol away, my mother's relationship with Rob McAllister deepened.

People gossiped that the minister's wife seemed to be spending quite a long time in treatment, and my mother must have wondered about it as well, but she committed herself to McAllister's well-being. She spent hours bucking him up, lingering in his office after a meeting of the session, or staying for coffee after bringing Bit to his house. I would see them sitting on the couch between those dragonware vases. I heard her tell him, "Mimi just talks to hear herself talk" and "You have more friends on that board than you know." Every visit to the McAllister house ended with the same question, "How is Carol?" McAllister assured us she was fine or "coming along," but offered nothing more.

Late one afternoon, my mother came to pick me up and give Bit a ride home. It was already late, and my mother was in a hurry, as was Bit. She picked up her tote and walked outside to wait in the car. We paused at the kitchen door, and when my mother asked about Carol, almost as a passing courtesy, McAllister surprised us with his answer. "She's coming home Thursday," he said. My mother started, a shift in posture so subtle I might have imagined it. She stepped back into the house and hugged him. Then, holding his hand, she said, "Oh Rob, I'm so happy for you."

He smiled down at her, bathing her in his warm, blue-eyed gaze, holding her smaller hand in both of his, and said, "Elizabeth." Nothing more, just her name. They stood that way, her hand in his, as Jamie and I looked on. "Well then," my mother said, and she turned and brushed by me, in a hurry to leave, to get in the car, to take Bit home and give my father his dinner.

CHAPTER 17

I tried to feel relieved that Carol McAllister was coming home. Julia's secret and Bit's dilemma troubled me, and I struggled to convince myself that Julia's mother would find a solution, though I could not have said what that solution would involve. I was aware of the mechanics of reproduction, but I had not yet felt the thrum of its engine. I shared a house with Allyn, but menstruation mystified me, and though I understood adults did, indeed, copulate, I assumed they did so only rarely, with the door locked, the curtains pulled shut, and the covers pulled high. The thought of Julia McAllister, my own minister's daughter, engaging in carnal relations with Tucker Gran, a creature barely one generation beyond the simian border, unnerved me. I knew Julia was dealing with an unwanted pregnancy, but I grasped very little of what an abortion involves, so the references to finding a doctor or Julia 'doing it herself' perplexed me. I counted on Carol McAllister to arrive home and sort out the mess, a calculation that required me to forget how Carol's frailties cordoned her off. Julia would never ask her mother for help she could not provide.

The night before Carol came home, my family gathered at our kitchen table for one of my favorite dinners, spaghetti and smothered steak, covered in cheddar cheese. My mother served my plate just the way I liked it, with white space between the spaghetti, salad, and roll. "Rob says her drinking is just a symptom," she told the table. "She's trying to treat her mental problems with alcohol."

"Me too," my father said, pouring himself another glass of Chianti.

"Poor Carol," my mother said. "I've never seen a person so anxious. She's pretty and smart, and Rob and the children are so good to her, and yet, she's so nervous around other people, she can barely leave the house."

"Rob must have known what he was getting into when he married her," my father said. "These quirks don't just bubble up out of nowhere."

"If that's the case, then why would he marry her?"

"Why," my father said, his face impassive. "Red hair. Blue eyes. Nice figure. Could it be that our spotless minister took one look at this girl and decided it was God's will that he take her as his wife, the sooner the better?"

"Carol does have a nice complexion," my mother admitted, primly.

"A woman like Carol McAllister shouldn't be sitting inside all day, nursing a gin and tonic. She's smart and fine looking, but she acts like we're all out to get her. I don't understand it."

"Rob says it runs in the family. He worries about Jamie. Carol's father had to be institutionalized, not for drinking, but for emotional difficulties. He had these episodes. It got to the point where the family couldn't control him. Rob mentioned a suicide a couple of generations back. Apparently, Carol's family was very prominent in Birmingham back in the day, old coal money or something, but by the time Rob came along, every last dime was gone, Carol's father had been put away, and she was living with her mother in a house that was falling down around their ears. Rob rescued her from all that."

"Oh, so this was an act of charity, and the nice complexion had nothing to do with it."

"Why do you always have to think the worst of everyone?"

"I'm usually right."

My mother rearranged her silverware, containing her irritation. "I think Rob thought he could help Carol," she said. "I'll grant that Rob likes to see himself doing the noble thing. That's why this trouble at the church is so hard on him. He doesn't want to be the one who needs help. He wants to be the one doling it out to others."

"Doling it out doesn't sound like much of a higher calling to me."

"OK. That was a poor choice of words on my part. Look, Rob is not perfect. He would be the first to admit that, but he also says you don't have to be good to do good."

"Convenient," my father said tersely.

My mother stood suddenly and began clearing the table. "I knew there was some reason I don't like church," my father added, but she did not answer his parting shot. This little tiff amounted to an argument between my parents. Once my father's snide remarks took on a sharper edge, my mother withdrew into a silence that walled the rest of us out.

That night, when I was in bed, my mother came into my room and closed the door, so Allyn would not hear us. "I don't want you to think too much about what I said about Carol's father and the rest of her family," she told me.

I pretended not to know what she was talking about, but my mother always kept a step ahead of me.

"Rob has told me there is a history of mental illness in Carol's family, but that's all it is, history. He's never seen anything in Jamie to make him think Jamie has inherited any sort of problem from his mother."

"But how can you tell if someone has it?"

"Little, I'm sorry I ever said anything. Don't worry. Jamie is as healthy and happy as any boy I know."

"But how can you tell?"

"Goodnight, Little."

She left without kissing me, which was unremarkable, because we were not a kissing family. Uncharacteristically, she shut my door. She had never done that before. I always slept with the door open. But either because she was distracted or because she wanted to stop my questions, she closed it. I suppose I could have gotten up to open it and returned the world to normal, but I didn't. I enjoyed the mildly sinister feel of this unexpected privacy. I lay in bed in my still room and watched the beguiling patterns shift on the ceiling as branches moved outside my window. I had considered Carol McAllister's mental illness another remote feature of the adult world, as irrelevant to my life as a mortgage payment, but now it crept closer, threatening to invade my friend's health. This idea titillated me. Maybe my mother didn't know me so well after all. She thought I would worry about Jamie, but in fact, I savored the idea of this secret vulnerability. It allowed me to feel superior.

I should have had reasons enough already. My house was bigger than his. We had a maid, and his family did not. His mother had been sent away. His father was at risk of being fired. In every respect, my status should have been superior to Jamie's, and yet he always seemed to have the upper hand. When we went to the mill, the workers wanted to talk to Jamie, not me, and Bit treated Jamie as her partner in Universal Gourmet. I thought about what my father said about Carol McAllister, how she was pretty and smart but afraid to leave the house. Some days I hated going to the mill. Just hearing another linthead talk made me cringe. In the early days of Universal Gourmet, when we were still collecting dimes for watermelons, I noticed how Jamie's mother arranged his coins on his bureau, with quarters in stacks of four and dimes in stacks of ten. A stack of twenty nickels makes a fragile tower, so she had arranged them in a crescent beneath the other coins, overlapping as evenly as her magazines, each coin heads-up. I liked the arrangement so much I did the same with my coins at home. Maybe I was the crazy one, not Jamie.

We were ready for Carol McAllister when she returned. Bit had suggested we fix her a nice dinner, and my mother agreed. Bit was lighting candles on the McAllister table when we heard Rob and Carol's voices in the driveway. "Ain't this something," Bit said, taking her position by the sink, proud of herself, wiping her hands on her apron. My mother and I stood beside the set table. McAllister stepped into the kitchen with his arm around his wife, and she looked fragile, but not crazy, her hair neatly done, her lipstick precisely applied. When Jamie and Julia hugged her, she closed her eyes. Then my mother hugged her, and Carol touched only the tips of her fingers to my mother's back. I wondered if I should shake her hand, but she did not look at me, so I hung back.

Carol said, "I didn't expect to find you here, Elizabeth." The Carol I remembered was perpetually nervous, with eyes that never settled on anyone or anything. This new version moved slowly, careful with her feet, as if the kitchen floor were ice, and she feared falling through. "And Bit's here too," she said. "How are you, Bit," not asked as a question but as a statement delivered in monotone.

"Miss Carol," Bit said, smiling.

Jamie's mother didn't seem to smell the roasting potatoes or see the candles on the table. She studied the cabinets and shelves, her gaze above our heads. "Why is the blender there?" she said. She reached up and moved its handle right to left.

McAllister touched her shoulder. "Bit did some rearranging for us while you were gone," he said.

She walked to the kitchen counter and opened a cabinet, studying the interior. We all watched as she looked inside. "I don't understand," she said, her voice flat.

"I was just trying to help out," Bit said, "putting things where they belongs. If you see anything you don't like, you just tell me, and tomorrow, when I come in, I can fix it for you."

"I think it's much better this way," Julia offered.

Carol turned to Rob. "Bit is coming here tomorrow? Does Bit work here now?"

McAllister smiled. "We should be so lucky. No, I'm afraid I haven't been able to pry Bit away from the Nickersons. She just comes in for an hour in the afternoon to help the boys."

"Help the boys," Carol said, turning to Jamie. "Help you with what?"

"With our business," Jamie said. "Universal Gourmet. Little's dad got tired of us cooking in their kitchen, so now we do it here. It's great. Bit has figured out a system and rearranged things, so that we can cook and box the pigs really fast. Wait until you see us go!"

Carol turned to McAllister, her mechanized sequence continuing: turn, look, speak. "In my house?"

"The boys needed a kitchen, and ours was sitting here unused. It has worked out well for everyone."

Now she turned to Bit. "So, you just came into my kitchen and re-arranged things."

"Like I say, Miss Carol. If there is anything you don't like, you just let me know."

"I don't like any of it," Carol said, the words delivered in the same monotone with which she had greeted Bit.

"Well, I do," Julia said, her eyes defiant in the candlelight. "I think it's much better this way." I had been watching Carol, not Julia, but now I saw her blazing eyes.

McAllister moved toward his wife. "We can sort all this out tomorrow when Bit comes in," he said. "Look at this nice dinner Elizabeth and Bit have fixed for us, and candles too! This is wonderful. Thanks to both of you for doing this, and you too, Little. It makes such a difference."

"I don't want to sort this out tomorrow. I don't want Bit touching my things."

"Carol," McAllister said.

"Jesus," Julia said. "Bit, I'm sorry. Don't listen to her. She's crazy."

"Julia!" McAllister said sharply, as if by simply saying their names he was going to control his wife and daughter.

"It is my kitchen, Julia," Carol said, dead calm, answering her daughter's rage with a tranquilized gaze. "I don't want Bit here. I can have my kitchen whatever way I want."

"Of course you can, *mother*." Julia spat the word as if it were an insult. "We will put everything back the way you like it, because it is your kitchen and your house, and the rest of us just happen to live here. And tomorrow, you can come into my room and refold my underwear and wash my comb and pull every single hair, one by one, out of my brush. Won't that be fun? Just like old times."

"Enough of this, Julia," the Reverend said.

"This family," Julia said, "is incredible. How long has it been? Literally, one minute, and already she's doing this! Here, let me help!" Julia pulled open a cabinet and began banging the pots around, lifting lids and slamming them down, wrenching handles right to left, clattering and crashing, a dreadful noise, and yelling above the clatter, "Not like this! Like this!" Clang! Banging down a lid.

"Stop it, Julia!" Jamie yelled, tears streaming down his cheeks. He did not want me to notice, but I did. He was miserable, openly crying.

Carol noticed as well, and though she had retreated from the clatter, eyes closed, now she seemed to regain her composure, if one can call a lifeless glare composed. "See what you've done? You've upset Jamie. Why do you have to be this way, Julia?"

"Julia didn't do anything," Jamie said. "Bit either. There is nothing wrong. Everything is fine. Let's just have supper."

"I am going to bed," Carol said.

"But, sweetheart," McAllister said, "Bit has made this nice dinner for us, and look, Elizabeth has brought flowers and candles."

"I don't want Bit's food," Carol said. "You and Elizabeth can eat it." Then she turned to Bit. "I don't want you here," she said, and she left the room.

Jamie turned away from me, hiding his wet cheeks.

"Rob," my mother said.

"She's had a long day," he said, turning away from my mother, watching Julia as she fled the kitchen, not following her mother through the living room, but out of the house. We heard the car start and race away, too fast for their narrow street.

My mother, Bit, and I piled into our car with Bit in back. "Never in all my life," Bit said. "Did you hear the way she talked, saying she didn't want me to touch nothing? What's wrong with me touching her things? Who she think she is?"

"I'm sorry, Bit," my mother said. "You shouldn't have to hear that. Carol didn't mean it. She's not well." As breaches of the code go, Carol's transgression was flagrant, and my mother felt ashamed. One of her roles was to protect Bit, and she had failed.

"She's crazy is what she is! Crazy as the day is long! Who she think she is, talking about me that way? Did you hear her? *I don't want Bit here, neither!*" Bit said, imitating Carol in a puffed-up voice. "Why take it out on me? Somebody ought to set that lady straight. Teach her how to act when others are just trying to show her a little bit of kindness. And here, her husband is a preacher too! What you think he think? He knows better than to act that way. You know he does!"

"Let's just sleep on it, Bit," my mother said, working hard to pacify Bit. I had never seen Bit so furious. Add that to the fact that I had never seen a girl talk to her mother the way Julia had, and I had never been in the presence of anyone who had acted as robotic as Carol did. I was ready for the world to return to normal, but Bit wasn't having it.

"Sleep on it? I ain't sleeping on a damn thing! That woman won't catch me inside her kitchen ever again. No ma'am. If she wants to keep all her pots and pans lined up like they was in a dollhouse, that's her own damn business. I'm done with it, all of it, her, him, the whole mess."

"But Bit," I said, "what about cooking the pigs? We have to go there."

"No, we don't neither. Not me. You don't know nothing about it, Little. You don't know a thing about how I feel, and you got no business trying to tell me what to do. I don't take orders from nobody. I do whatever I want."

We pulled to a stop in front of Bit's house. I saw Emma G come to the window and look out. Bit opened the car door.

"Let's just sleep on it, Bit," my mother insisted. Carol McAllister had revealed something vulgar my mother was desperate to hide.

"You can sleep on it all you want. I done made up my mind." We knew Bit was not slamming the car door at us, but it slammed nevertheless, and inside the car, it made a mighty bang.

We sat in the silent car, my mother with her eyes closed. She gripped the wheel so hard her knuckles were white. "That woman," she said, "What is the appeal of that woman?" It confused me. That woman? Carol? Bit's rage had shaken me, but my mother was responding to something else.

Back at our house, I went to my room and sat on the edge of my bed. I thought of Carol pointing to the table with its silverware and lit candles, saying to her husband, "You and Elizabeth can eat it." And I thought of Bit. I had never seen her so angry. The stricken look on her face when Carol said, "I don't want you here!" I thought back to the time, years ago, when I made Bit walk behind me. Her stern look then, how she had pointed her finger at me, and said, "That ain't no way to treat a person, especially not me." I thought of Bit as family, but we were white and she was not, so we bore responsibility for protecting her. It was utterly nonsensical, this paternal obligation I felt toward a woman who served as my surrogate mother. I sat alone in my room, trying to sort it all out.

CHAPTER 18

Later that week, Carol called my mother to apologize. My mother said she sounded better, more like her old skittish self, constantly clearing her throat. She told my mother that I was Jamie's best friend, welcome in their house anytime. She thanked my mother for preparing such a lovely dinner and expressed regret that she had not sat down to enjoy it. "I think I was just frazzled to be back in my own house after being away so long." She said Bit need not bring any more meals. Now that Carol was home, she could take care of the cooking and cleaning herself.

A couple of days later, I became disoriented by the smell of Julia's perfume in *my* house. Julia McAllister smelled better than any girl on the planet. Ask a man to describe his first erotic experience, and he might recall a scene in a movie, how Kim Novak looked in her black sweater, or some encounter with a sister's friend, when she blew an errant strand of hair from her eye. For me, the scent of Julia's perfume, heavily applied, marked that beginning. I stood in the hall and wondered if Allyn had decided to wear Julia's perfume, which would have been ridiculous, Allyn trying to be Julia. Then I heard Julia's voice and realized she was in our house.

Here was high-school royalty, cheerleader, beauty queen, "pinned" girlfriend of the magnificent Tucker Gran, come to visit Allyn, of all people, a lowly sophomore who did not even make the junior cheerleading squad. If Allyn could have vacuum sealed and padlocked her door while Julia was there, she would have done so. Allyn suffered enough just sharing a house with a person like me. She was not about to endure the added torture of having me enter a room where she made conversation with Julia. After Julia left, my sister parked herself in front of the television, her face glum. I asked why Julia had come.

"None of your beeswax."

"What did y'all talk about?"

"Hey, Little, do you see that box on the cabinet there with the pictures on it? That's called a TV, and I'm trying to watch it now. Go away."

"I was just wondering why Julia was here. She never comes here."

"Why don't you go ask Bit?" Allyn heaved an exasperated sigh. "Julia McAllister couldn't care less about seeing me," she said. "She kept asking if Bit was here, and before she left, she went and found Bit folding laundry and closed the door behind her. God knows what that's all about."

I knew what Allyn did not. A rare occasion that tempted me to needle her by hinting at what I knew. I didn't though. I understood enough about Julia's condition to appreciate that her situation was grave, so I held my peace. She would not have come to our house had she not felt desperate.

Julia's unexpected visit fit into my theory that Bit was stalling her. The blowup with Carol gave Bit an excuse to stay away from the McAllister house, which meant she could stay away from Julia. But Julia followed her. Realizing she couldn't escape, Bit had to decide how to handle this white girl. She knew helping her was crazy. If they were discovered, everyone would see Bit as the villain and Julia as her victim. No one trusted colored people. Bit knew all this. She wouldn't have wasted her time wishing for a fair hearing. But denying Julia put her at risk, too. Julia was asking her for a favor. When white people asked for favors, even when they were careful to say "please," they weren't really asking. Can't say no. Can't say yes. Bit was in a bind and stalling, I felt sure.

I found her in my parents' bathroom, scrubbing the bathtub. She had rolled the bathmat to cushion her knees, and I faced her wide bottom and the raised veins twisted in knots on her calves. She had slipped off her flip-flops, and I saw her pale heels and the wrinkled folds beneath her arches. As she scrubbed, she grunted into the reverberating tub, attacking the turquoise stain around the drain. "Hey, Bit," I said, doing my best to keep it casual, "Was Julia McAllister here?"

"Not that I know of," Bit said. She didn't look up from her work.

"I thought I heard Julia talking to Allyn."

She rocked back on her haunches, breathing heavily. "Can't you see I'm busy here?" She tossed the soapy brush into the tub with a clatter, still without looking at me. I could see a damp half-moon beneath her arm, and her breast was heaving.

Bit never cooked another pig-in-a-blanket in Carol McAllister's kitchen. She'd had enough of that lady. But with her decision, Universal Gourmet was finished. We'd lost our product, our production facilities, and our chief executive officer. Having minted a boys' fortune with her help, Jamie and I couldn't go back to the demeaning business of slicing watermelons for dimes, so we folded my mother's table and returned it to the garage. I was happy to stay home from the mill, to float in the pool rather than to stand in that hot parking lot. Though he didn't admit it, I think Jamie was relieved as well. Most good commerce tends toward mind-numbingly repetitive work. If a widget sells for twenty cents, one must sell lots of widgets, widget after widget, again and again. That kind of monotony did not suit Jamie's restless soul. Had our glorious enterprise not collapsed on its own, Jamie would have eventually gotten bored and killed it.

The fall of Universal Gourmet hurt Bit more than us. She'd lost the most reliable cut she ever had. But she didn't waver. She'd sacrificed her income to preserve her pride. She came back to our house for her full nine hours, as broke as ever, with no way to get by but by folding and washing and cooking and cleaning. She climbed the hill in the morning and took the late bus home. Every day, Allyn left her wet swimsuit on the bathroom floor, and Bit picked it up. She swished out the toilet and wiped hair from the sink. She said *no ma'am* to my mother and *no sir* to my father. She wore a uniform. She came and went by the garage door.

While I sat at the table for lunch, she stood at the sink eating a chicken wing. She looked out the window and did not share her thoughts.

With the end of Universal Gourmet, I wanted and expected life to go back to normal. Jamie's mother was back home. Life at church seemed to be under control, and we were no longer obligated to go to the mill. We were safe to return to our own lives, an ordinary boy's life, sitting by the pool with Bit serving us pineapple and mayonnaise sandwiches. It wasn't quite the same as it had been, though. Bit often acted preoccupied and irritable. We could all see it. She said little and smiled less.

Beyond the green enclave of our backyard, Tim Butters' demonstrations gathered strength. With the help of a local DJ, Hollerin' Hen, Butters transmitted cryptic messages to his teenaged followers that local law enforcement could not figure out. They would learn later that when Hollerin' Hen played certain songs, like Sam Cooke's *Chain Gang*, it was a call to arms. The demonstrations grew so large and the kids so animated, Bit must have known that Emma G wouldn't be able to keep away. Bit could hardly stay home to keep an eye on her, though. She had a job to do at our house.

My mother began driving Bit home just to buck up her spirits. She told Big M that she was protecting her from the demonstrations downtown. What if Bit's bus blundered into a clash between demonstrators and police? Bit had enough on her plate without that. Big M agreed, though grudgingly. He complained these demonstrators were making life difficult for everyone. Driving Bit became part of my mother's routine. One day, not long after Julia's mysterious visit, my mother felt a headache coming on and told Allyn to take Bit. She told me to go as well, "to keep Allyn company."

We climbed in the car, me up front, Bit in back. "You'll have to show me how to get there," Allyn said.

"Don't you know where I live?" Bit said. "You been there with your mama plenty of times."

"I wasn't driving, though. I know where you live, but I don't know how to get there."

"You tickle me, Allyn," Bit said. "Go down the hill and go right like you was going to the shopping center. You know how to get there, don't you?"

Allyn smirked at Bit in the rearview mirror. "Yeah, I've figured that one out."

"I expect you did," Bit said, smiling.

As we passed the shopping center, Allyn said, "Hey Bit, you remember how you and Mama used to take me and Emma G shopping here, and then, we would stop at the bakery and get gingerbread men?"

"Sure, I do. If your mama needed to shop, sometimes we brought you girls along to get y'all out of the house. You two sure did love that gingerbread."

"I ate mine from the feet up, but you told Emma G to bite the head off first, so he wouldn't have to suffer."

"I said that?" Bit was pleased with her own wit.

"You think Emma G remembers that?"

"I expect she does."

In Baker Bottom, shotgun shacks lined the unpaved, unlit road. A ditch ran on either side beneath sagging wires, and the houses were no farther apart than a length of clothesline. Most shacks sat close to the ditch, with one or two warped, unpainted steps leading up to a narrow porch. Some were tidy, with curtains in the windows, the porch posts painted, clay pots of Creeping Jenny resting on the railings. Others looked abandoned, their windows broken, a rusted padlock on the door. Squat brick pillars supported the bowed floor joists, the space underneath weedy and dark, a haven for rodents. As Allyn pulled to a stop at Bit's house, I saw a cat hunkered beneath her steps, its fur ghostly in the gloom.

"That's Mister Kitty," Bit said. "He be wondering where his supper is."

"Hey, Bit," Allyn said. "Is Emma G home?"

"She sure enough better be."

"I'm going to say hello," Allyn said, opening her door.

"No, honey. Let's don't do this now. Let's do this some other day."

But Allyn was already at the porch steps. "Give me one minute, Bit. I just want to say hello." Bit hurried behind her, and I did not want to be left in the car alone, not in Baker Bottom, so I followed them up the steps, through the door, and into a single room painted a stark canary yellow. I saw a pair of overstuffed chairs at one side, our old couch at the other, a lace doily beneath a pale green radio, a lamp I thought my mother had thrown out, a Mason jar of water with a few pansies, and a framed photograph of a Black man with a broad, if posed, smile. I had never laid eyes on Bit's husband or even thought about him, and it surprised me to see his young, handsome face so prominently displayed, evidence of a loss Bit had never mentioned to me. A pastel Jesus hung on the wall above one of the chairs, his palms pressed in prayer, his blue eyes upturned to a yellow beam of light. A naked bulb with a pull chain hung down from the ceiling above a braided jute rug.

Emma G emerged from the next room back, her bedroom or her mother's, and she was barefoot, her hair in pink rollers. She'd been expecting only Bit, and her large eyes widened with surprise. She moved sideways, placing one hand on the rounded back of the chair, her features caught in the stark glare of the overhead bulb. She looked older than Allyn, almost like a grown woman, her blouse tight around her breasts.

I knew we should not be there, but once Allyn had barged inside with me in tow, we could hardly wheel around and leave. "Hey, Emma G," Allyn said, her voice artificially bright. "We were just dropping Bit off, and I thought we'd come say hello. You were at our house. Now I'm at yours!"

"Hey."

"I always loved that blouse," Allyn continued gamely. "It was one of my favorites."

Emma G did not look down at her blouse, but her hand rose to the collar, touched it, and dropped away. "Thank you for that," she said.

"Oh, don't thank me, Emma G! You look good in it, better than I ever did!" Allyn forced a laugh Emma G did not return. "You'd look good in anything though. You always have. I remember when we were little, and Bit used to tie your hair in pigtails with yellow ribbon, remember that? I begged Mama to let me have pigtails too, because I thought yours looked so cute, and I told her I wanted yellow pigtails just like Emma G." Allyn floundered, trying to fill the room with words.

"Well, thank y'all for driving me home," Bit said. She had not closed the door, and she did not invite us to sit down. She stood at the door, holding it open.

Emma G's eyes shifted, and I caught a spark of curiosity there. She looked out the window at the car then back at Allyn. "You drive?" she said.

"I got my license last month."

"Last month," Emma G repeated.

"You know, Emma G, if you ever want to go somewhere, and you need a ride, just call me and I'll come get you."

Emma G lifted her face, her chin tilted as I had seen Bit's sometimes tilt, and her eyes settled on Allyn. "And take me where?"

"I don't know. Like if you need to go to the store or something. We could go get gingerbread!" Allyn offered cheerily.

"Then what? What are we going to do at the store, you and me?" Emma G asked, her voice low and cool. "Try on bathing suits?"

"I don't know," Allyn said. "But I guess so, if you need one."

"You think so? Because I'm not so sure what the nice lady would say if you and I went into Patterson's together and I asked to try on one of their bathing suits."

"Don't start now, Emma G," Bit said.

"Maybe if I told her I wasn't sure about the size. You think that would work? You think if we went in there together, just the two of us, and I explained to the lady that I needed to try on a suit because I wasn't sure about the size, you think she would show me to the dressing room?"

"I'm telling you, we don't want to hear this now," Bit said, speaking to Emma G in a way she never spoke to us.

"Hear what, Mama? Allyn came in here offering to take me to the store. I'm just trying to work out the details." I heard the defiant timbre in her voice and remembered Bit telling my mother *I got one of my own.*

"Maybe we better go," Allyn said.

"How about on a date?" Emma G said, cocking her head now. "You think we ought to double date together?"

"Well, maybe not a date."

"You go on dates, don't you, Allyn? What about tonight? You free tonight?"

"Not tonight," Allyn said. Allyn had never been on a date in her life.

Emma G touched her curlers. "I go on dates," she said. "My boyfriend's father lets him borrow his car sometimes. If I need to go somewhere, David takes me. That's my boyfriend, David. He takes me wherever I want to go. You have a boyfriend, Allyn?"

"Not yet," Allyn said.

"Oh. Not yet."

"Enough of that," Bit said. I thought she was talking to Emma G, but then she said, "Both of you." She was still standing at the door, holding it open. As we walked past her, she was looking at Emma G, her eyes hard, and as soon as we were on the porch, she closed the door behind us. I had never been kicked out of a house before.

We drove through the deepening twilight of Baker Bottom then accelerated on the four-lane, relieved to be out of there. Home safe in our driveway, Allyn turned off the car without saying a word. I followed her inside and saw the closed sick-room door, the gloom of another headache already pervading the house.

The image of Bit's yellow room with its stark lighting lingered in my mind, as did the image of her standing by the door. In that setting, her uniform looked more like a theatrical costume than clothes, an outfit she wore to come into a house so different from her own. Bit's shack felt alien and grim to me, the stern figure at the door nothing like the warm presence I found in my kitchen most mornings. The Bit I thought I knew was playing a role, which meant the rest of us were acting as well, though I couldn't say who it was we were supposed to be.

Our impromptu visit had threatened Bit and infuriated Emma G. Bit knew how we lived. She had figured out how to fit herself into our lives. But her life away from us—a life I suddenly realized I knew nothing about—was her own business. I had always assumed I knew Bit inside and out, but now I wondered. Did she ever sit on her porch, scratching Mister Kitty's ears, and gossip and laugh with friends? What did they talk about? These men she sometimes saw, did she ever embrace and kiss them? It seemed impossible. That green radio, did she ever listen to it at night, sipping a glass of gin, resting her aching legs, nursing thoughts of her own? And what were those thoughts? I did not know.

CHAPTER 19

"Hey."

"Hey, yourself," Allyn says.

"Do you remember the night we went into Bit's house because you wanted to say hello to Emma G?"

"Ugh. Do we have to talk about that? Not my finest hour."

"I never understood why you did that."

"Because I was a stupid teenager. Who knows what I wanted? This was just after Julia McAllister's visit, when I was so excited to have *the* Julia McAllister coming to see me, only to find out she couldn't have cared less about me. The only other girl who bothered to visit me in my room was Emma G, and we know why she was there. But even Emma G made me feel bad about myself. She was a cheerleader, and I wasn't, and she was clearly way ahead of me in the whole blossoming into womanhood business. My teens were some pretty miserable years. I was sick of all these other girls being better than me. Not that I thought about it—thinking is not something I did much of at that age—but I had this need to find at least one girl I could feel superior to. I guess I went charging into Bit's house because I knew my room was nicer than Emma G's, and I could lord that over her, somehow. Well, I got what I deserved."

"Emma G was pretty tough on you."

"Emma G was bad enough, but what I really dreaded was seeing Bit the next day. I knew she wasn't going to let me get away with what I'd done. I just didn't know how bad it was going to be. Not as bad as it could have been, I guess. I mean, once I started crying, she backed off.

And then when I apologized, she actually gave me a big hug. My bet is that she was a lot tougher on Emma G."

"Why? Emma G was just defending herself!"

"Bit came down hard on Emma G about everything. If Emma G took one breath at a time, Bit found something wrong with that. We all knew how smart that girl was, and I think that frightened Bit. It's one thing to have some dimwitted daughter you let grow up to be a maid. But it had to be an awful responsibility for Bit, seeing all that brainpower and knowing that if Emma G ended up working in some white lady's house, she'd be miserable."

"Did you know," I say, "that Bit wanted Rob McAllister to help Emma G get a scholarship to Tuskegee? Emma G's teachers had mentioned a scholarship to Bit, and they offered to write a recommendation, but you know how Bit was. She always had an angle. She got it in her head that a recommendation from a white minister would really stand out, so she went to work on the reverend. He'd be sitting in the kitchen with us while we were making pigs-in-a-blanket, and the whole time Bit would go on and on about how well Emma G was doing in school."

"Did he agree to help?"

"He was skeptical, I could tell, but it was like Bit had figured out another cut. Once she found her angle, she worked it."

"You got that right. She must have pulled Mama into it as well. Mama always loved Emma G, and she told me more than once that Emma G belonged in college. She told Bit she had to keep Emma G out of trouble. Her worry was that if Emma G got involved with the protests, she'd hurt her chances of getting admitted. She leaned on Bit, and Bit leaned on Emma G."

It's just like Allyn to get a new piece of information and then act as if she knows more about it than I do. It's in her DNA to feel superior to me. Not only does she claim to remember every hour of our childhood, she pretends to understand the motivations of everyone we knew. In the presence of such omniscience, it pleases me to give her a little poke now and then, so I say, "Do you ever wonder what Mama thought about Rob McAllister?"

"Mr. Blue Eyes? How can you even ask that? She adored him!"

"Adored him how?"

A beat passes, maybe two, then Allyn says, "Oh Lord. My little brother has officially gone off the deep end. This is Mama we're talking about! Yes, she adored him, but no, she did not adore him in that way. I can assure you that would have been way beyond her emotional range. She shied away from anything that distressed her aching head. For her, filling the birdfeeder was enough excitement for one day."

"You make her sound like an invalid."

"Well?"

There is no use trying to inform, persuade, or argue with Allyn. She is the Oracle. Once she has taken a stand, no matter how extreme, she will stick to it. Years ago, I learned how to skirt around her opinions, a skill that has helped keep our relationship intact.

Rob McAllister drew so many of us into his orbit: Bit, who wanted him to help Emma G; my mother, who was defending him in the session of elders; and me, his son's best friend, a minor moon. Within his own family, McAllister no doubt enjoyed his son's adoration and learned to tolerate his daughter's willful ways, but Carol he could not manage. She did not so much live in their house as take shelter there. She refused to enlist as his disciple in the grand cause of civil rights. His book barely mentions her, and when it does, she's referenced as "my wife," a background player, nothing like the troubled soul I knew who filled that house with so much anxiety and gloom. She did not fit into his story, because he could not change or inspire her. Bit enlisted him to play the Great Patriarch, sweeping her daughter to safety, but for his wife, he was obligated to play a lesser role, and even in that, he failed her. The Rob McAllister I thought I knew was well-suited to act the hero, but not the nurse.

I never mounted an open rebellion against my father (yet another way in which I take after my mother), but I committed a minor heresy by falling under McAllister's spell. I cannot imagine Big M ever writing a book. He lived each day as it came to him, finished one, had a couple of drinks, and moved on to the next. Let the reverend play the tortured soul. My father had a business to run and a family to raise. I was his sensitive child, worried about risks Big M barely noticed, refusing to touch the unfamiliar foods he gobbled down with relish. On our family nights out at The Fisherman's Net, I watched in horror as he ate raw oysters by the dozen, each lathered in chili sauce and horseradish. Allyn once described herself as "the son our father never had." I inherited my mother's slender build and bookish ways. I think it bothered Big M that Jamie was taller and more athletic than I was. My father couldn't change my build, but occasionally, he pulled another page from his catalog of Things All Boys Enjoy. One day, not long after Allyn took me into Bit's house, he decided we should shoot some rats.

"Good news!" he said. "Winn Prather's seed barn has burned to the ground."

"Why is that good news?" I asked. "Is he going to need new cabinets?"

"Anytime you have an old barn like that with so much seed lying around, you're going to have lots of rats. You can try to trap or poison them, but there are so many, it won't do you much good. Rats in barns are as common as laces in shoes. Did I ever tell you how me and Brother used to yank rat tails?" Regardless of how I answered, Big M was going to tell it again, a story I had heard a hundred times. "We couldn't have been much older than six or seven. Me and Brother, or Brother and I, I should say, crawled up under the corncribs, and there were rats above us in the cribs eating corn. We could see their tails hanging down through the slats. We'd grab one and pin the rat's hind-end down on the bottom of the crib. God, that was fun! I'll never forget sitting under those cribs in all that dust and shade, with Brother smiling and holding this squirming pink tail and saying 'Lissen to him squeal!'"

My father laughed, transported by this memory of his bucolic youth.

"We're going to yank rat tails?" I asked.

"No, Little. A man of my station in life does not spend his days yanking rat tails. We're going to do a little target practice. You can never get rats out of a barn, because they have so many places to hide, but now the barn has burned down, and the corn has spilled everywhere. The corn will bring the rats out, but there won't be anywhere for them to hide. If Winn is going to get rid of his rats, today is the day to do it. That's why he's calling us. He wants us to meet him out at his barn and help him shoot rats."

We put a .22 rifle, a single-shot .410, and a pump sixteen gauge in the trunk of my father's car. I asked if I should bring my BB gun, and he said no. He told me to change into shoes with better soles because it might get slippery. At the barn, we met Mr. Prather, and his son, Tom, a boy of about Allyn's age who looked like he aspired to be the next Tucker Gran, linebacker for the team. What a clunk. Mr. Prather and Tom held their guns broken open, the barrels slanting over their forearms toward the ground. Tom wore an army green t-shirt, cut-off jeans, and hunting boots. A carpenter's nail belt sagged around his big waist, weighted down with shotgun shells and boxes of .22 rounds. Mr. Prather smiled and shook my hand, thanking me for coming to help him out, but Tom ignored me, his close-set eyes giving him a look of perpetual, mild confusion.

I had not been inside many barns, but the ones I knew, apart from Brother's elevated barn, rested on the bare ground. This one had been different, with a basement about three feet deep. We climbed the small rise behind where the barn once stood. From there, we could see that the floorboards had burned away, the corn had poured down into the hole, and rats were gathered there, dozens of them.

Tom started us off. His .22 rifle whistled each time he pulled the trigger. The first rat bounced back from the direction of its nose, a head shot, and the next two writhed and shrieked, both gut shots. With each report from the rifle, rats scattered and collected, like a school of fish. Tom did not slow his work for the crippled or the floundering. No rat got more than one bullet. He progressed methodically, more like a mason laying brick than a boy shooting rodents.

My father handed me his .22. "Here, Little," he said, "You try one."

"Which one?" I asked.

He laughed. "Your choice," he said.

I fired. A little puff of ash rose from the ground, and the rats scattered.

"Try again."

Another shot and another puff of ash. Meanwhile, Tom had shot two more.

"Don't close your eye," my father said. "Don't even aim. Just look down the barrel of your gun."

I fired another round into the ground.

"Choose your rat. Don't look at all of them. Just look at one. And when you choose one, you don't want to look at the whole rat. Just look at his nose or his eye. Don't squeeze until you see the rat's eye."

I fired again, scattering a half-dozen rats. "They won't stay still," I said. Three more shots, raising puffs of ash. Off to my right, Tom was laying a foundation of rat parts, gelatinous piles of guts, fur, and tails.

"Try this instead," my father said. He slid three shells into the sixteen gauge and handed me the shotgun. Heavier than the .22, this gun delivered a broad pattern of shot, and its weight stabilized my aim. I found a rat, forcing myself to concentrate on the black, liquid glint of its eye, and I squeezed the trigger. The rat erupted into a red mist, bursting like a water balloon.

"Nice shot!" my father said.

"I think I need to sit down," I said.

My father took the sixteen gauge from me, saying, "The safety is off. Always remember to put the safety back on." I apologized and promised I would, then I found a place in the weeds to sit. He loaded another shell and studied the burned-out hole with his arms still lowered, finding his shot. When the gun came to his cheek and shoulder, his movement in no way resembled the mechanized sequence of Tom's shooting. He lifted the gun, gazed down the barrel, dipped his hips, and swung his shoulders forward all in a single gesture, surprisingly fluid for a man his size, kinetic in his concentration. He fired three times and rolled three rats, using the gun's recoil to bring the pump back after each shot. He loaded more shells, sliding the fat red cylinders into the gun's hot chamber in rhythmic strokes, found more targets with the gun still lowered, lifted, and fired. One rat bounced into the air, and another was decapitated midair, the shot sending it into a somersault. My father moved with such graceful ease, such unabated joy, that I couldn't help but wonder where he had learned to do this, whether on the farm or in the Marines. He killed with rhythmic ease, as if dancing a ballet, his movements as graceful as those of a dancer drifting across the floor in a bourrée. Then I realized he was, in fact, humming, making music of his work, and I remembered the words as he hummed the tune. *Pardon me, boy, is that the Chattanooga choo-choo?* Boom! Boom! Boom! The doomed rats leapt, pirouetted, and fell, a baroque display of blood and gore to which he seemed indifferent.

He remembered himself and turned to me. "Want to try again?" he said. "I don't want you to miss out on the fun."

I did not want to try again. I liked watching him shoot, and I was nothing compared to him. Besides, the piles of trembling gore and spattered fur sickened me, as did the rising heat and the smell of burnt, wet wood. Looking down into the pit, I did not know which I hated more, the living or the dead, but I could not tell my father this, so I picked up the .410. I tried to shoot as he did, holding the gun at my waist and lifting it only when I was ready to fire. I chose my target, a fat cannibal with a crimson snout, and I slammed the gun to my shoulder. Nothing happened.

"It helps to take the safety off," my father said.

"Oh, right," I said.

Tom abandoned his .22 and began to use his shotgun, once killing two rats with a single shot. The surviving rats thinned out, and it was getting hotter by the minute. I managed to shoot another, though it would not die. It squirmed and writhed in its pooling blood. I fired at it a few more times, trying to take its head off, but even with a shotgun, I could not hit it. Plumes of ash rose around the shrieking, suffering rodent.

"Say, Mo," Mr. Prather said, "Can I interest you in a cold beer?"

"I think you might," my father said, and, taking the .410 from me, he fired from the hip, finishing my rat. We walked back to Mr. Prather's station wagon. He had a cooler in back, and he fished out three beers plus a Coke for me. It impressed me that Tom was allowed to drink beer.

"Pull those chairs out, Tom," Mr. Prather said, and Tom set up folding chairs for us beneath a generous oak. My father pulled the pop top off his beer and settled into his chair. The beer and shade were luxurious in this heat, and we sat quietly for a while, enjoying the buzzing country air. Mr. Prather passed around a bag of barbecued potato chips, but I didn't take any. I only liked plain chips. My father took the bag from me, and I knew it irritated him I was no red-fingered guy like Winn's boy, Tom.

"So, Mo," Mr. Prather said, "You going to be marching on Saturday?"

"Wouldn't miss it," my father said, his voice thick with sarcasm. "And you?" Mr. Prather nodded his head and raised his beer can in a small toast. "Remind me, Winn," my father said, teeing him up, "What time do we start?"

Winn stretched and brushed off a pant leg. "Oh, I reckon we'll get going right around two o'clock. You see, that way, if we get started right at two, we can be sure we're shutting down every shop in town right around the busiest hour of the busiest day of the week. No sir, we wouldn't want anyone making a dollar downtown, not when they could be out watching us march instead."

My father raised his beer in another small toast, his lips pursed in a smile. My mother kept my father on a tight leash. Sitting here in the shade drinking a beer, having slaughtered some rodents, I could see that the leash was off. He relaxed.

Mr. Prather crossed his legs and continued to brush something from his knee, a piece of lint, a bit of dirt. "Of course, things will clear out well before that time. You know that, don't you, Mo? I figure it will be around twelve o'clock—high noon—when the stores empty out. No cars, no buses, and certainly no people. You won't find a stray cat downtown." He was looking away from us, declaiming to the empty, weedy field. "You know why that is, Little?"

I was surprised to hear this question directed at me. "No sir," I said.

"It's because these people are so upset about the plight of the noble Negro that they don't give a damn about the tailor, the clerk, and the shoeshine man." He turned to me, suddenly adamant, fixing me in his gaze. "You know what these people, these *activists*, hate most about our economy? It works. It's not supposed to work. They've read that it is repressive and unjust, and I don't know what all, and by reading that and only that and by talking to each other and never to anyone with a shred of common sense, they have come to believe it cannot work. So, when they get outside of that little bubble they live in and come to a place like ours with a living, breathing, functioning capitalist economy, and they see it working and not just working, *thriving*, it galls them. You know what that means, 'to gall someone?'"

"Not really.

"It means to stick in their craw." He slumped back in his chair and looked away from me. Tom snorted and took a pull of his beer. Locusts buzzed in the field, their music rising and falling with the passing of thin clouds. A mockingbird perched above us, claiming this tree as his own.

"So that's noon," Mr. Prather continued. "All commerce is paralyzed. Then around one o'clock, cars begin to appear. Not cars you've ever seen around here, and you sure as hell won't ever see them again. Out-of-state plates. Connecticut, Massachusetts, New York, Minnesota." He enunciated the names syllable by syllable, a string of refined profanities.

At the mill, Jamie and I had heard every form of vulgarity in the workers' lexicon. We understood that men talked that way when women were not around, indulging themselves in a casual incivility. Just so, Mr. Prather unwound, free of the need to keep his thoughts and words in check. No need to mollycoddle men and boys like us. Did he really believe anyone would drive from as far as Minnesota to join a protest in LaSalle? Certainly not. He clowned for us, and I could see that my father, released for an hour from his leash, enjoyed it.

"These cars will be filled with three types of people. You know what they are?" Mr. Prather held up an index finger. "Number one. Jews. Wherever there is trouble, you will always find Jews." A second finger. "Number two. Coloreds. Brought in from all over, as if we did not have enough of them already. And last, but not least, number three," a third finger popped up, "There will be liberals. You know what a liberal is?"

"Sort of."

"A liberal is a communist in training. A liberal is a person who knows nothing about LaSalle, Georgia, but what he's seen on a road map, yet somehow feels compelled to come down here and tell us how despicable we are."

Tom, enjoying himself, fiddled and scratched between his legs. I suspect the beer had gone to his head. My father was smiling, his eyes half-closed. Winn Prather was relieved to say out loud what he really thought. My father had heard it all before, thousands of times in a hundred different ways, and he did not object. The beer was cold, the shade fine, and he felt good.

"So that's one o'clock," Mr. Prather continued. "These folks will get out of their cars and begin milling around and talking. Mill and talk. Mill and talk. You know why they have so much time to stand around and talk? It's because not one of them—not one!—has a job that requires them to get into an office at nine o'clock and stay there until five. No, sir. These are people with a higher calling in life. They're too important to work. They can't be bothered to work. They're so busy coming down here to mind our business for us that they don't have time for any business of their own. Once they do get around to marching, they will go down to the courthouse and demand what they damn sure are never going to get. Then they will drive away, and we will never hear from them again, praise be to Allah. And you know what will come of it?"

"No sir."

"Nothing! Not a goddam thing! We'll go back to living our lives just like we did before, and just the way we will until the end of time." Mr. Prather poured the last few drops of his beer onto the ground, then crushed the can, no longer amused, suddenly irritated. "These people," he said, looking over at my father. "Can you believe these goddam people?"

My father finished his own beer and squinted into the sun. "No, Winn, I cannot," he said.

Riding home in the car, I could not get the image of the rats and Tom Prather out my mind, his close-set eyes, the way he clawed at his privates. He could shoot better than I could, but not as well as my father, not even close. Still, he must have killed twenty rats, and his father let him drink a beer with the men. A few weeks of basic training to burn off the baby fat, and Tom could be a Marine. Is that what my father wanted for me? I would never get there, I knew, because I could not stand people like Tom Prather or Tucker Gran. Better to remain as I was. My mind wandered back to the rats. The crows had descended before we left, plunging their beaks into the gore. One tugged out the intestines of a still-convulsing rat. Some sport. I tried to think of someone besides my father and the Prathers who would have enjoyed it. Not Jamie. Tucker Gran, certainly. Maybe my old playground nemesis, Larry Williams. I tried to imagine Rob McAllister joining us on the rat shoot, or sitting beneath the tree for Winn Prather's harangue, but I could not conjure up an image of the reverend holding a gun, and I knew his presence would have held Mr. Prather's monologue in check.

Something in these ruminations inspired me to provoke my father. We were driving west, and he rested one hand on top of the wheel, the visor pulled down to shade his eyes. "Hey, Daddy," I said, "Why was Mr. Prather talking so much about the marches?"

"Oh, that was just Winn being Winn. He's one of those people who is going to tell you what he thinks, whether you want to hear it or not."

"Did you agree with him?"

"I expect he was pulling your leg for my benefit. Once Winn starts sawing the violin, he's not so much giving you his opinion as he is just getting carried away with the lovely sound of his own voice. I do agree with him though that these protests aren't doing a damn thing to help the LaSalle economy. I think it's time for the good Reverend Butters to go back to teaching the gospel and let some of these agitators go somewhere else."

"What would you do if someone you knew joined the march?"

He turned to me with a smirk. "You thinking of joining?"

"No sir, but I mean really, what if you did know someone?"

"Like who?"

"What if Bit did?"

"Bit! Bit has more sense than that. You won't see her go within a hundred miles of that march."

"What about Emma G? They say a lot of kids are marching." I felt a mild thrill in asking this, the titillation of having a secret my father did not know.

"I would never allow that," he said. "I can't have her doing something that would reflect poorly on our family. Bit knows that too. She's not going to let Emma G do something crazy."

"But how would that reflect on our family? Emma G doesn't even work for us!"

"Her mother does. If Bit can't control her own daughter, and if I find out that Emma G has been out there making a fool of herself, Bit knows what I'll do. It would be awful, and I certainly hope it doesn't come to that, but I'd have no choice. What if someone like Winn Prather found out that my maid's daughter was out there marching? He'd never let me live it down."

CHAPTER 20

My father had threatened to fire Bit once before, when she was using our kitchen for Universal Gourmet. My mother hadn't taken him seriously, but Bit had some sixth sense to move us out of his way even though she hadn't heard the threat, personally. She knew better than to test my father. In this case, Bit hadn't seen Emma G marching or heard my father's menacing words. I suppose I could have warned her, but since Allyn and I had already crossed a line with Bit, I wasn't going to stick my nose into her private life again. I had to trust her to know how to handle my father. She had lied to him about her cut from Universal Gourmet, and she had lied to me when Julia came to our house, so I trusted her to lie again if circumstances required it. I tried to reassure myself that my father would never actually fire Bit. Down deep, that's not who he was. Besides, my mother wouldn't let him.

I raced over to Jamie's house, but he had no interest in my crisis. "Seems like everybody is talking about marching these days," he said wearily. "It's the thing to do."

"But Jamie," I said. "Daddy might fire Bit!"

"So, your dad fires Bit. Worse things have happened."

"How can you say that? This is Bit! We have to protect her, Jamie!"

"What do you want me to do, pound on Bit's door and tell Emma G I refuse to allow her to march? Is that what you want?"

"It just seems like we ought to do something."

Jamie's bedroom was barely large enough for his bed, two bookshelves, and a bureau. We sat on his bed, and Jamie leaned against the wall, rocking his head slowly, thumping it against the wall, not hard enough to hurt, but enough to make it clear he was distracted. "What would your mother do," he asked (thump), "if your father fired Bit?"

"She'd give him hell." I was new to the use of profanity, but the depth of my feeling seemed to call for it.

"Would she leave him?"

"Leave him?"

"Yes, you know, leave him, as in, to go away (thump), get out of the house (thump), take his children and move elsewhere. Because that's what my mother says. She says, if Daddy joins the march, she'll leave him, and she'll take Julia and me with her."

"She'd never do that."

Jamie gave me a cold look and did not answer.

"Then we can't let your father march either."

"But I don't want to stop him. I think he should march. We've talked about it a lot. It's practically the only thing he does talk about these days. Reverend Butters has been calling him, encouraging him to join them. Butters says it would make all the difference to have a minister from one of the big local white churches demonstrating with them."

"I heard that all the people organizing the march are from out of town," I said. Winn Prather's monologue had stuck inside my head.

"That's not right. There will be people from the outside, but this is Reverend Butters' march. People from Atlanta and up north have been volunteering to help, but he's put them off until now. This demonstration is going to be much bigger than all the others, big enough to fill Courthouse Square. That's why it's so important for Daddy to march, too. Reverend Butters says that when folks start complaining about outside agitators, they need to see Daddy there representing the white citizens of LaSalle."

"But that's crazy. No one supports the march." (Mr. Prather again. I could not dislodge him from my brain.) "He'll just get himself in trouble."

"You sound like my mother."

"But she wouldn't really leave, would she? Maybe she's like my father. He says he would fire Bit, but I'm not sure."

"You know what? I can't spend my time worrying about your father and Bit. Big M is going to do what Big M does, and I can't do anything about it. My mother is not in good shape. You don't get that, because nothing ever goes wrong in your family, but in my family, it does. In fact, things go wrong all the time. I thought Mama was better when she came home, not that first night, but after that. It did her good to go into the kitchen and put everything back in its wrong place. She must have spent an entire afternoon wiping down the Venetian blinds, one by one. Even the cords. She got a bowl of soap and water and washed each cord. She untied the plastic pulls and soaked those and dried them, then tied them back on. She knows it's crazy, but it helps her calm down. But then Daddy started talking about going on this march, and Julia started driving her nuts."

My stomach twisted at the mention of Julia's name. "What did Julia do?"

"Something is up with her. It's almost like she's sick or something, but if my mother asks about it, Julia snaps her head off. Julia is not like me and Daddy. We just stay out of Mama's way, but not Julia. She fights back. They were arguing, and Mama told Julia she didn't want her to be a cheerleader this fall. You know why? Because Mama thinks boys look up her skirt when she cheers. You should have heard Julia. She started yelling that Mama belongs in a mental institution and that we should have left her there. She said we were happier when Mama was locked up. Most times, when Julia says stuff like that, Mama just goes in her room and closes the door, but last night, she was drinking. When she's been drinking, it's bombs away over Tokyo."

"I thought she wasn't supposed to drink."

"That's what I'm trying to tell you. People don't always do what they are supposed to do. She promised us she'd never take another drink, but then she started again, and Daddy threatened to take away her car keys, and she said he was making her his prisoner. It was awful. After Julia stormed out, Mama was yelling at him, and my dad, he never does that. He never raises his voice at anyone, but he did last night. She yelled at him, and he yelled back. He ended up sleeping on the sofa bed in the living room."

I tried to imagine Rob McAllister's imposing frame stretched on that rickety bed with the bar that pushed into your back. I couldn't do it. I idealized Jamie's father as the scholar in his study, not the husband exiled to a couch.

"Where are they now?" I asked.

"He's at church, and she's probably in the bedroom with the door closed."

"I know what that's like," I said. Jamie gave me a skeptical look. "I do. My mother stays in her sick room all the time with her headaches, and it's awful. We can't go see her or talk to her or make a sound."

"Your mother is nothing like mine," Jamie said. "Not even close." He began rocking again, thumping his head against the wall. I told him I was leaving, but he didn't seem to care. Stepping into the narrow hall, I turned to the closed door of his parents' bedroom, creeping closer so I could listen. No sound of a TV or radio. I imagined Jamie's mother lying in bed, staring out at a birdfeeder no one had bothered to fill. I moved on through the living room, past Jezebel, curled on the couch, who watched me pass with those green eyes.

Carol was waiting for me in the drive, standing beside my bike. She wore a turquoise bathrobe with pink hearts, a pair of green gardening gloves, and flip-flops, the polish on her toenails chipped and brownish red. She had pinned her hair back in odd clumps. Without makeup, her features looked washed out, almost plain. "Hey, Little," she said. "I've been admiring your bike. It's a Schwinn, isn't it?"

I told her that it was.

"Schwinns are nice. I had a Schwinn when I was a girl. It was a blue bike with a white stripe, and I always dreamed of riding it to the ends of the earth." She laughed to herself. "Or, at least, away from Birmingham. I've always been fond of the name, the way it sounds, Schwinn. Schwinn,

Schwinn, Schwinn. I'd like to swim in my Schwinn." Standing close to her, I could see the delicate veins around the blue irises of her eyes. Her pupils seemed very small, screwed tight. "Don't mind me," she said. "Half the time I don't know what I'm saying. Swim in my Schwinn. It's just nonsense. Don't listen to a word I say. No one else does. Do you ever feel that way? That no matter how much you talk, no one ever listens? Even when I yell my head off, which I know you're not supposed to do, particularly if you're the minister's wife, but even when I do, even when I scream at the top of my lungs, no one hears me."

She held a damp washrag, and as she spoke, she wiped my bike with it, the fenders, the seat, the handlebars. "You hear me, though, don't you? I've noticed that about you. When Rob is talking about some book he's read, or Jamie is going on and on about God knows what, you just sit there and listen. You pay attention. That's what I like about you, Little. I bet you're a good student, aren't you?"

"I guess so," I said. I knelt beside the bike and held out my hand for the rag. She passed it to me, and I began wiping each spoke of the wheel. "I like it when the spokes are clean," I said. "The way they sparkle when the wheels turn."

"I like that, too," she said, standing back, and I knew that it calmed her, watching me polish the spokes of my bike. I was on my knees, focusing on the spokes because I did not want to look at her. One by one I cleaned them, sliding the rag from rim to hub, digging out the grime at the hub. I felt her watching me. "Does anyone ever listen to you?" she asked. "I bet some people do, not your father, of course, but maybe your mother. Bit sometimes. And Jamie. I think if you told Jamie that his father shouldn't join the march, he would listen to you. If you told Jamie, and he told his father, his father might listen to him. It's like with his bike, you know? Your bike is nicer than Jamie's bike, and that worries Rob. He wants Jamie to have whatever he wants. If I want it, it doesn't matter, but if Jamie wants it? That matters."

The rag was dirty, which meant she had been waiting for me for a while, polishing my bike. I knew she would not have begun with a dirty rag. "Will you do that for me, Little?"

"Do what?"

She knelt next to me on the driveway, taking my arms in her gloved hands. No adult had ever looked at me that way, her face so close I could feel her breath, her blue eyes pleading, the pupils tight as nail holes. She begged me to help her. She wanted me to talk to Jamie so he would talk to his father. I promised her, only to get away from her, saying the words so she would back off and I could get on my bike. I knew Jamie wouldn't listen to me, but I had to promise, just to escape.

In his book, McAllister writes: *My wife and I discussed the matter. We both knew that I was inclined, perhaps even compelled, to join the protest, but how could I justify doing so when the consequences were potentially disastrous? I reasoned that I owed my congregation an unambiguous expression of my feelings on the race issue. A single article was not enough. How could I take the pulpit on Sundays and exhort my parishioners to follow their ideals when I was practicing just the opposite? Compromise here would represent a subtle form of fraudulence.*

We discussed the matter, he says. Nothing of the fact that his wife was institutionalized or that her views on the status and rights of Black people bore no relation to his own. No mention of his night on the couch. In his version of events, no adult goes down on her knees and begs a twelve-year-old for help.

I did not consult with the session of elders, because I was determined to make this decision on my own. If I chose not to march, I wanted the session to see it as just that, my choice, not as a concession. If I marched, I wanted them to see it as a public demonstration of brotherhood, not as a gesture of defiance. I knew even our moderate members would counsel against joining the demonstration. They wanted me to restore the harmony of our congregation, not to open a fresh wound. By their logic, the right time to demonstrate is always tomorrow and never today.

I suppose I agree with McAllister that my mother would have urged him not to march, but she never would have lectured him on the need for 'harmony in the congregation.' *Think of Carol,* she would have said. *Think of Julia and Jamie.*

I knew I was breaking a cardinal rule by going into the sick room, so I did what I had seen Bit do. I took off my shoes. I tried to open the door without making a sound, and I must have succeeded, because, as I stood in the dark room near my mother's bed, I heard her slow breathing. It unsettled me, the sound of the air going in and out as she slept. An alien sound, somehow removed from the person I knew.

"Mama," I whispered, "are you awake?"

I heard her stir. The room had a dank smell. "What do you need?" she asked.

"How do you feel?" I feigned sympathy to cover my transgression.

"Tell me what you need," she said.

"I'm worried about Bit, Mama. I'm worried Daddy is going to fire her. He told me he would fire her if Emma G was in the march, and I saw Emma G marching once before. Jamie and I did, one day when we were going to the mill. She told me not to tell Bit, and I haven't. I haven't told anyone, but I don't want her to get Bit fired, so you need to drive over there and tell her she can't march. She'll listen to you if you tell her."

My eyes adjusted to the light. I could make out my mother lying on her back, one arm resting across her eyes. I thought she was going to tell me to get out. "I can't go there tonight," she said at last, "I'll talk to Bit in the morning. How about that?"

"But what if Bit can't stop her? Emma G was marching when she knew Bit didn't want her to. What if she marches, and Daddy finds out, and he fires Bit?"

She took slow, careful breaths, as if to keep her stomach settled. "Come sit next to me," she said. I went to her bed and sat at the edge. I never did this. Sometimes, when I was sick, Bit would come and sit on my bed with me, but I never sat on my mother's bed. We knew she was to be left alone. I tried to sit on the bed without putting my weight down, because I did not want to disturb her or make her shift. I knew how important it was for her to stay still. "Your father is not going to fire Bit. You know how he talks, but you're old enough to understand you shouldn't believe everything he says. Don't listen to what he says. Watch what he does."

"But I'm worried, Mama."

"You have to stop this, Little. You can't let everything worry you the way it does. I'll talk to Bit in the morning. She is not going to let Emma G do anything that will get either of them in trouble. Bit has a good head on her shoulders, and Emma G does too." Her hand came down to rest beside her hip. "Have you had dinner yet?"

"Not yet."

"Then go find Allyn, and you two get dinner, or find Daddy, and he'll get you something."

"I'm sorry, Mama."

"Just go. Go get something to eat."

The next day, my mother emerged from her bedroom, a bit unsteady, but vertical, and that night, she joined us for dinner. At the table, she said, "That big demonstration is planned for next week, so I told Bit just to stay home that day. I was worried about her riding the bus, and I don't want to drive anywhere near that crowd." I understood that, if Bit stayed home, she could keep Emma G from marching.

My father plopped more mashed potatoes on his plate. Then he turned to me. "This is exactly what Winn Prather was talking about. I have to pay Bit to stay home and do nothing."

The phone rang, and though we knew my mother was not feeling well, we expected her to answer it. "Well, hey Bob," she said, "I'm surprised to be hearing from you at this hour." She listened and said, "I see. I'm so sorry to hear that. Well, here he is, then," and held out the receiver for my father. "Bob has some news," she said.

Seeing her expression, my father said, "I'll take it in the bedroom." My mother waited until he picked up, then she returned the receiver to its cradle. She came to the table without looking at us, her face gray from her headache, her eyes tired.

"What does Uncle Bob want?" Allyn asked. "He never calls."

"There has been an accident. Brother was inflating a tractor tire, and apparently, it over-inflated, and the tire exploded."

"Is Brother okay?"

"Bob was out in the field when he heard the explosion and by the time he got back to the shed, Brother was already dead. Bob thinks he must have died instantly." Allyn returned my sickened look. Neither of us had experienced death before, and we reeled at the shock. I remembered riding in Brother's truck, the way he rested his hand on the gear shift. Probably, he had never noticed that, how his own hand looked, the fingers loosely curled, and now he was gone. "This is going to be hard on your father," my mother said.

Allyn's eyes filled with tears, and she protested, "But I loved Brother!" She began to sob.

My mother took Allyn's hand and squeezed it. "I know you did. We all did. Brother was a kind man." Then I began to cry too, and that embarrassed me. I wiped away tears that would not stop. We sat at our familiar table and wept, Allyn and I, the two of us brought together in this unexpected grief. My mother patted each of us on the back, looking unwell. I felt that I had known Brother and experienced his goodness and now shared the poignancy of his loss with my sister. As tragedies go, this was a mild one for us, but the mildness made the sadness sweet. I cried while knowing that Brother's death would not change my life.

My mother began to do the dishes in her pink gloves, and Allyn even helped a little. After they were finished, my mother stood at the sink and looked up at the clock, peeling the rubber gloves from her hands. "Your father must be off the phone by now," she said. "Bob has never talked to anyone for more than five minutes. Why don't you go check on him, Little?"

He was not in the bedroom, so I went outside. I found him beside the pool. The last light of the long summer evening reflected off the water, illuminating his pale face. He looked into his open hands, brushing the backs of his fingers across one palm and then the other. I didn't know what to say, so I sat next to him without saying anything. Sometimes, when I was younger, the two of us would sit by the pool in the evening and gaze at the trees in the vacant lot behind our house, finding, in the dark, leafy branches, the shapes of faces and monsters. I would point to a tree, describing what I saw—a snout, a mouth, the extended claws —and he would peer at the tree in question, then jump suddenly with fright in a way that never failed to draw a laugh from me. I was too old for that game now. I sat beside him and waited. Looking up, I saw the bats were beginning to feed. It had always frightened me when I was in the pool at night, the way they appeared to be plunging at my head. But they seemed harmless now, strange and hungry little things. Shadowy, mysterious, yet somehow peaceful. Venus was rising over the dark oaks.

"We used to fish together," my father said in the hushed voice one sometimes will use when light is leaving the sky. "His mother gave us some chicken livers for bait, and we'd go catfishing. I never have the time for fishing now. I suppose I could do what other men do, and fish for bass, but that doesn't appeal to me, sitting in a boat with a three-dollar lure. What do you think my friends would say if I told them that I wanted to take some chicken livers down to the riverbank and catch catfish? They'd think I had lost my mind."

He spoke slowly, brushing his fingers, occasionally looking up at the looming trees. He was finding his way, not expecting me to answer.

"Isn't it odd how you can know things? Nobody ever told me that grown men like me don't fish for catfish. Boys do, of course, not you, but other boys, and coloreds do, because they like to eat catfish, but not men like me, though I still enjoy a fried catfish when I can get one. There was never a day when I decided to stop. That was a running joke between Brother and me, that when I was done with all this," he waved his hand vaguely, a gesture that encompassed the pool, the yard, the sky, "I would move back to Cemochechobee, and we'd spend our last days fishing to-gether. He always said he knew I'd come back, and I'd play along, because it was pleasant to think that way, to imagine that we could go back to the way we were, not boys anymore, but old men, and somehow just the same.

"We brought the fish back to Brother's mother. Her name was Ruby Mae, and she would say, 'Look at this fine mess of fish you boys caught,' and she invited me to dinner, and I didn't think anything of it. I sat right there at the table with Brother and the rest of his family, and we ate catfish. Best meal I ever had." My father coughed and cleared his throat.

"No one ever told me to stop going there, but the older I got, the more jobs Daddy gave me. No one can ever tell you how much work it is to have a farm. You just have to live that life to know it. Same with Brother. His daddy worked him from sunup to sundown. We both got so busy, we didn't have time for fishing or anything else."

It was getting darker by the minute, the bats more difficult to see, the stars emerging as if rising from the depths. "This is going to be a difficult thing for Gladys," he said. Gladys was Brother's wife, a lighter skinned woman who hung back when my father was around. Brother's children never seemed to interest my father much. He couldn't remember their names, or even how many Brother had, whereas my mother asked after each by name and knew their ages too. "Gladys can't have an extra dime living the way they do, and she still has those children to raise. She'll have to find another place. Brother's family has been in that house ever since my grandfather bought that farm. For all I know, Brother's folks came with the package. Bob isn't going to force them out. He's not that hard. But he won't want them living there with no way to pay rent or help with the farm work. He won't have to push. Gladys, she'll know."

The cadence of his words was deliberate, as if he were crossing a stream on stones. "I'll take care of her though. Brother would have known that I won't let his wife and children go hungry. He was a proud man. I bet you didn't know that, did you? Living out on a farm that way, the way he does, or did. You would never think he was proud, but he was. Proud of his wife, of his children, proud of his work. That's what made him so valuable to Bob. Any job Brother took on, he took pride in it. If he was going to fix a tractor, that tractor was going to stay fixed, by God."

It was dark now, my father's features obscured, but I could sense him shaking his head, could feel it in his words. "Brother was the product of a different era. People these days don't understand that. All this talk about dignity, as if a man like Brother didn't have any, because of where he lived and how he acted. He had plenty, though. He earned it through his work. That farm is Brother's farm. Bob owns it all right, but Brother ran it, and I don't know what Bob is going to do now that Brother is.... Well, it won't be the same."

The chorus of night bugs and frogs pulsed from the bushes and trees, their music thick in the humid air. "Are you going to the funeral, Daddy?" I asked.

"No." The night air felt sultry and dense, the thrumming bugs everywhere and close. "That's no place for me. Gladys would rather be left alone to remember Brother and grieve for him in her own way without having to deal with someone like me. Bob told me where they took his ... took him, and I'll call down there tomorrow and pay for the arrangements. Your mother will send some flowers."

I had never seen my father weep, and I cannot say I saw it then. It was dark, and I looked away. But I heard him. An awful sound.

CHAPTER 21

O<small>N</small> the day of the demonstration, Big M worked at the shop, as always. The kitchen seemed empty without Bit there. My mother sat in the living room with a book. The day before, she'd gone to Cemochoechobee, where she ate lunch with her mother, and afterwards attended Brother's funeral, sitting in the back. I announced I was biking over to Jamie's house and left before she could ask any questions. When I arrived, he was waiting outside.

"Is he going to march?" I called.

"He still doesn't know," Jamie answered. "He said he was going to the parking lot where the demonstrators are gathering, wants to see who shows up."

"Maybe you could stop him. Maybe you and I could find him and persuade him not to do it."

"Why would I do that? I want him to march."

"But what about your mother?"

"I'm going now. If you want to come with me, come, but I'm not going to try to stop him."

On our bikes, we headed for what served as the temporary town library while a new, air-conditioned library was under construction. The books from the old library had been moved to the upper floors of the First LaSalle Trust and crammed onto metal shelves on the second floor. The reading room, with its long tables and periodicals, occupied the third floor, where tall windows overlooked Courthouse Square. In the old days, this served as a dining hall for the bankers and their clients, a clubby room with a high stamped-tin ceiling and overhead fans.

A small group of women stood at the tall windows, looking out, their faces awash in sunlight. One of them, older than the rest, with loose folds hanging beneath her chin, invited me to stand in front of her. "Come look, honey," she said. "This is history being made!"

It did not look like history to me. People milled about on the street below us. From our elevated vantage point, the men looked like a collection of bald spots, wandering beneath the bank's facade. No one looked up at us. They smoked and murmured amongst themselves, clusters of people spooling and unspooling in the relentless heat. The sound of an occasional laugh or conversation wafted up to us, and we watched their heads turn as a figure approached.

"You see that one there?" a woman at the next window said. "The one with the walkie-talkie? He's one of the organizers, but I think he's trying to stay incognito." Jamie had squeezed in next to me and poked me in the ribs. I knew he was tickled by the way she talked, how she said "in-cog-NEE-toe."

"I just hope no one gets hurt," another said.

"There's a few of them that deserve to get hurt. If we had us some police with a little bit of gumption, they would have made them feel some hurt a long time ago."

"Oh look, something's happening," the lady behind me said. "Watch close, now. This is history. Happening right here in front of your eyes."

The man with the walkie-talkie started to herd people back down Broadway, away from the courthouse. "Where are they going?" I asked. "What's going on?"

"The police have said they can't march into Courthouse Square, but the marchers have said they're going there anyway. The protesters want to stand on the steps to give their speeches, but the mayor says that the courthouse is a symbol of law and order, and we have to protect it from the protesters."

"Look at this," the woman at the next window scoffed. "They can't even organize a walk down Broadway, and they want us to give them the vote!"

Broadway gradually cleared. Down to our right, Sweet Papa's statue guarded a vacant square. For a few long minutes, I stood in a room of women, looking down on an empty street. The fans above our heads struggled to stir the heavy air. Pigeons pecked at scraps in the gutters. Buildings and trees cast their sharp shadows, the sun brilliant and high above them. Across the street, I saw people peering out from office windows, their faces in shadow while ours were bathed in light.

"Look now," the woman behind me said, "Here they come. Isn't this exciting?"

Turning to look up Broadway, I saw the marchers come down 6th Street and turn toward us. Like an army executing a maneuver, the marchers on the far end trotted to keep up, while those near the axis of the turn barely moved. The size of this crowd dwarfed the one we had seen before, when half the demonstrators had not yet graduated high school. This procession commanded respect, its progress solemn and determined, more people than a shift-change at the mill, many more, a walking congregation that filled Broadway. The leaders began to sing, and the marchers took up the song, their voices distant and small, the words a slow dirge.

> *We are not afraid*
>
> *We are not afraid*
>
> *We are not afraid someday*
>
> *We are not alone*
>
> *We are not alone*
>
> *We are not alone someday.*

No hecklers lined the sidewalks, and not a single policeman stood at the curb. The street and sidewalks had been abandoned to the marchers, as if this army were marching into a city from which everyone had fled. A man emerged from a doorway across the street, a white man with a camera. He ran into the middle of Broadway and began taking pictures as the marchers came on, a slow tide, and he backed away from them, snapping photographs.

As they approached, I recognized Reverend Butters in front, and behind him a tall figure with a shock of white hair.

"I knew he would," Jamie said quietly, not wanting the women to hear. "He had no choice. He belongs there."

I have returned to this image of Rob McAllister so often I no longer trust my memory. In my mind's eye, he's taller than the rest, his plume of hair a brilliant flag, his proud features practically carved in granite. I still see him as a boy would. I know he didn't lead that march. He followed Butters. And not one member of our congregation followed him. But on that day, I was convinced I saw a hero, and in that year, in that place, the only hero I could see was white. I watched as the reverend made his way down Broadway, each step an outrage. Our congregation had almost forgiven him for his article, and here, he answered their forgiveness with an act that would make our Presbyterian fold the laughingstock of every Baptist, Methodist, and Episcopalian in LaSalle. My own father, not to mention the likes of Winn Prather and Mimi Hurd, would think it ridiculous for a grown man to carry on this way. But I didn't see it like that, and the years since have proved me right.

They finished their song and continued down Broadway in silence, the leaders' arms locked, somber men in pressed pants and jackets, most wearing hats, McAllister just behind them, dignified in his white shirt and narrow tie, the women dressed in shades of navy, gray and black. But for the signs, this march looked like a funeral procession. *Jobs Now!* one sign said. *Equal Rights for All*, read another.

"Well, it's about time," the woman at the next window said. She was looking toward the courthouse. Police emerged from its double doors, descended the steps, crossed the square and formed a thin line, hardly an impediment to the oncoming crowd. The police wore peaked hats, sunglasses, and short sleeves. They carried batons, but the officer in front, the chief, did not. He had a great pot belly, a wide black belt, and no gun that I could see.

"Oh no," Jamie said.

I had been focused on Jamie's father, following the marchers' progression down Broadway. When I turned toward the courthouse, I saw what Jamie saw, what the marchers could not see from down on the street. Courthouse Square stands at the intersection of Broadway and Main. The marchers were north of Main, heading south. From our high windows, we saw a line of paddy wagons and police cars creeping up Main toward the square. They emerged from alleys, garages, and side streets where they had been hidden. The lead truck stopped a half block back from the square, shielded from the view of the marchers by the bulk of Patterson's department store.

"I have to go," Jamie said. I moved to follow him, but he stopped me. "Keep your eyes on Emma G," he said. "Don't lose sight of her."

"Emma G?" I said, and then he was gone, pushing through the women past the elevator and down the stairs.

I turned back to the marchers, my stomach churning. I searched the crowd until I found her happy, uplifted face. She stood with a bunch of kids, and unlike the solemn leaders, they were smiling and waving up to the windows, like Santa's helpers at the Christmas parade. I should have followed Jamie down to the street to warn her, but what good would that do? Emma G would never listen to me. I was paralyzed. The chief moved forward, his hands raised to stop the marchers, and Butters halted before him. When the reverend stopped, the congregation compressed, those in back still moving forward, those near the front crowding in to listen. I saw Emma G pressing in to hear, but I could not find Jamie.

I couldn't hear all of what the chief said, or what Butters said in return. The chief began with his hands outstretched, palms up, trying to turn Butters back, but Butters shook his head, pointing toward the square. Then he knelt on the hard, hot asphalt. The chief stepped back, his arms folded across his wide waist, his head cocked to one side. As Butters began to pray, the chief's arms came down, his elbows rose, and he clinched his fists on his hips. McAllister stood just behind Butters, his head bowed, and Emma G stood farther back in the crowd, craning her neck to watch. "Almighty God," the reverend intoned, profession-ally projecting his words, "our Father who art in heaven looking down on us today, I beg of you to hear my prayer." Then he began in earnest to ask, offer, praise, and preach. As the reverend's address dragged on, the chief glared down at Butters' shining head, the hands he raised in prayer. The chief had to be roasting, the sweat seeping into his eyes and pouring down his back. The dark rim of perspiration that ringed his blue belly slowly expanded as the reverend's voice rose, fell, and rose again. By go-ing to his knees, Butters had neutralized the chief and all his men. They could hardly handcuff a man while he was beseeching God. When he finished, if ever he would finish, they might swarm in with their batons and beat him silly, but for those long, sweltering minutes, he held them hostage, florid in his righteousness. They stood in the radical heat and watched him drone on, his devout humility a more effective form of ar-rogance than spitting in their faces. He prayed for the demonstrators, for the town council, for the governor and state legislature, for the police chief and all his deputies, asking the Lord to remind them they were all His children, Black and white, bound to serve Him with peace in their hearts and love in every gesture. The cops, I could tell, were just itching to beat his head in.

Had I known the prayer would last so long, I could have rushed down to Emma G and pulled her away from the crowd. I could have at least warned her, but each passing minute felt like a minute too late. As the prayer dragged on, I kept thinking I should have left then, or then, or then. One minute before, two minutes before. I should have bounded down the steps and forced my way through the crowd, hollering Emma G's name, but instead, I squandered the opportunity, too timid to act.

Butters rose at last, a bit stiff, and a man next to him gestured to-ward the square. The chief shook his head and held out his arms, as if he alone could hold back all these people. The marchers on the edges of Broadway slipped forward, hesitant at first, then hurrying, an appar-ent loss of discipline, not waiting for their leaders but moving into the square themselves. They flowed around the chief, giddily defiant, and poured into the square. The deputies moved forward to stop them, but there were not nearly enough, and soon the demonstrators had filled the square.

The chief scarcely seemed to notice, as if he had never intended to hold the protesters back. He snatched Butters' sleeve, not roughly, but with authority. With his other hand, he reached out and took hold of McAllister's sleeve. A full head taller than the chief, McAllister flinched, as if to pull away, then submitted, following Butters' example. Holding Butters in his right hand and McAllister in his left, the chief led them toward Main, his great blue belly parting the crowd.

By now, the people at the front of the charge had caught sight of the waiting paddy wagons and police cars, and they tried to retreat, but the vehicles lumbered forward, moving out onto Broadway to form a double line that blocked off any escape. Officers swarmed from the trucks and cars with clubs, and the deputies in the square wielded their batons to poke and herd the demonstrators toward the wagons. The marchers stumbled back and forth, uncertain what to do, unsure which way to go. Butters had been hauled away, and the other leaders vanished in the tangle of the crowd. The once solemn procession had lost its front and back, with no way forward and no retreat. People faltered and lurched, then pushed, and the clubs came down with fury. Women screamed, crouching to protect their heads, and men flailed and fell and cursed the cops. The officers swung and kicked, pulling the demonstrators by their arms and hair, grabbing, shoving, and swearing, all the frustration that had built up during Butters' long prayer now released in a sudden blast of rage. A woman fell hard on the street. A deputy took hold of her foot and dragged her, like a cowboy pulling a calf. She kicked at him, howling, her dress wrenched up around her hips, her girdle exposed. Two of the cops ignored everyone but the man they were beating, taking turns to pound his back, like loggers chopping a tree. He curled into a fetal ball, his arms wrapped over his head. In a knot of people near the middle, demonstrators knelt and held hands in a sudden, desperate prayer of their own. The deputies yanked them apart with relish, hauling bodies over the abrasive asphalt as if pulling branches to a trash fire. Other deputies (only a few, but I saw them, they were there) struggled to restore order. I even saw one grab another's baton in mid-swing. But in the main, it was chaos. The confused marchers had no minister to lead them, and the furious police had no chief to keep them in check.

I could not keep track of Emma G. I had seen her move into the square with the rest, then I had looked away when McAllister was arrested, and the vehicles moved to block off Broadway. When I looked back, she was gone, and in the melee, impossible to find. I searched the crowd, but everywhere I looked, I saw another travesty, another woman knocked down, another man bleeding, the police officers battering every head and back in sight.

The violence did not last long. Once the cops had clubbed down, handcuffed, and hauled away the true believers, those left behind looked bewildered and demoralized, folks who had agreed to march but had not signed up for a street fight. These people worked as waiters, maids and laborers, as gas station attendants, mill workers, yardmen, truck drivers, and cooks. With their leaders gone, they began to organize themselves with no help from the police, almost despite the police. The demonstration-turned-riot now turned into something patently docile. They fell into line, and even those who were bleeding waited for a place in the paddy wagons. They had mastered, through bitter generations, the humble art of submission. Moments before, they were racing into the square, giddy in their newfound freedom, but now the old ways returned, and they waited in helpless lines, some with proud faces still lifted, the women's cheeks streaked with tears, the men's mouths contorted with frustration and anger. One or two officers still swaggered among them, poking with their sticks, but most of the police responded as the crowd grew docile, as if learning from it, and remembering their duties. They formed a corridor of blue shirts and clubs and herded their captives into the vehicles that now moved in an orderly line. An ambulance was called for a woman who could not stand, and an officer waited with her for its arrival, smoking a cigarette.

I saw a Black man—he was hard to miss—in a white lab coat. He had grizzled hair and walked with the upright carriage of a professional, as if he were passing through Courthouse Square on his way to hospital rounds. Hands in his pockets, chin raised, he proceeded through the lines of batons to a waiting paddy wagon, his coat in the sunlight bright as a banner. Pausing but a moment at the steps of the van, he nodded to the deputy holding the door, and before he could catch himself, the deputy tipped his hat in return.

CHAPTER 22

WHILE the ladies waited for the elevator, I bounded down the steps two at a time. Out on the street, scraps of litter lay all around: a hat, a broken sign, a pair of sunglasses, pages of newspaper, a button pin the size of a fifty-cent piece, torn from a cop's shirt. I put it in my pocket, a memento I've kept for years. A Black woman sat on the curb and bawled, mucus streaming from her nose. Cops hurried back and forth, but they didn't look as if they knew where they were going. Three anxious teens passed me, calling a name. A man approached me and said, "You ain't seen her, has you?" I shook my head. A paddy wagon rolled slowly in reverse, lights flashing, crushed glass beneath its tires.

On the far side of the bank building, I found my bike, but Jamie's was gone. I headed toward the jail, not really knowing the way but figuring it out as I went. I discovered a street map in my head I didn't know I had. A few blocks from the square, I passed the same paddy wagon, now with a flattened tire. The driver stood helpless beside it, and I heard the people inside calling to be let out, thumping on the wall panels and door.

The old Pauly jail wore a sad façade of neglect, two stories of crumbling brick surrounded by a cyclone fence. Built in the same era as the First LaSalle Trust, our municipal drunk tank was much too small for all the demonstrators. They crowded the narrow yard inside the fence, and I could see them looking down through the bars on the second floor. I rested my bike on the sidewalk across the street. I expected a cop to shoo me away, but no one seemed to notice me or care. Young men lingered and laughed outside the fence, calling to those inside, but the flustered police left them alone as well. A pair of deputies guarded the gate, pulling it open as police cars arrived to deposit new admissions. A tall deputy climbed out from one car, unfolding to peer over the roof, his head swiveling atop his thin neck like a periscope. A cop at the gate studied his clipboard and waved him off. "Not here, Paul!" he called. "You take yours to Cusseta!"

"But I thought we was supposed to bring them here first, so we could have them processed," the cop named Paul called back. He sounded like a country boy working to remember his police vocabulary.

"Wasn't you listening, Paul? Cusseta! You take them to Cusseta!"

Back and forth they went, the deputy at the gate waving his clipboard, and poor, dogged Paul uncertain what to do. "This is a mess!" he finally announced to no one. He pulled away through the crowd, his siren adding to the noise. Seeing their captors' confusion, the people inside the fence had begun to relax. They smoked and talked. Some leaned against the fence, legs crossed, their fingers wrapped through the wire as they swapped stories with those on the other side. One reenacted his arrest, playing both cop and himself, repeating what the cop had said and what he said back to the cop, then laughing along with the men outside the wire. Only minutes old, his story was already changing, widening out. In the years since, countless retellings have polished the stories of that hour in LaSalle to a mythic luster. Each man and woman arrested there wears a badge of civil rights nobility.

A group of women were gathered in one crowded corner of the yard, and they formed an impromptu choir. *This little light of mine*, they began, *I'm going to let it shine!* The first verse sounded tenuous, as if they were testing the air, the second bolder, louder.

> *This little light of mine,*
> *I'm going to let it shine!*
> *This little light of mine,*
> *I'm going to let it shine!*
> *Let it shine! Let it shine! Let it shine!*

Others in the yard dropped their conversations and turned toward the singers, some smiling and laughing, clapping their hands. They began to join in, taking up the refrain, *Let it shine! Let it shine! Let it shine!* A cop emerged from the jail and yelled from the top of the steps, "You stop that singing right now, you hear me?"

A man answered, "What you going to do, arrest us?"

The yard erupted in laughter, and now they all joined in, full-throated and joyful. Up in the windows, I could see people laughing, clapping their hands, and singing along. Even I started laughing, caught-up in the silliness, and the cops at the gate frowned and tugged at their belts, angry little men in uniforms.

But I had not come for the show. Without Jamie there to make decisions, I didn't know what to do. Was I supposed to march inside and demand to see the reverend? I had to choose between going to Jamie's house or mine. If Jamie had not gone to his house, it would fall on me to tell Carol her husband had been arrested. I decided to go home instead and find my mother. She would know what to do.

I peddled home, not yet understanding that this day would make my hometown infamous.

Years later, people still remember the photograph of the smiling cop with the beefy lips and nose, his hat pushed back hayseed style, and the button pinned to his breast that says NEVER, as in never allow a Black child to swim in a public pool, and never let one ride the Ferris wheel at the county fair. Never allow a man, after five days' work, to take his wife into a restaurant and sit down for a nice meal. Never pay an equal wage. Never trust one. Never shake a Black hand. Never leave a white woman alone with a Black man. Never allow a voice or a vote or a scrap of hope. All the police had pins, though the town council and mayor swore they knew nothing of the source. One rumor named a local businessman, who joked that the expense ought to be tax deductible. Folks remembered that Winn Prather had fished and hunted with our chief of police since high school. Another rumor had it that the chief showed Mr. Prather how to set fire to a barn and leave no clues for the insurance adjuster.

With its history of more than a hundred years, a unique geography, and a few distinctive buildings, the mills among them, LaSalle deserves recognition for something other than a single hour of a single day. Yes, the town enforced a Jim Crow code, but nothing in our enforcement distinguished my hometown from dozens of others across the South. Those towns matched LaSalle cruelty for cruelty, but their police lacked the guile of our chief, and Tim Butters didn't preach in their churches. When a new acquaintance learns that I witnessed the LaSalle demonstration and mass arrest, they demand to hear my story. Retelling it so many times, I have come to understand what my listeners want: a lurid account, meaner cops, braver demonstrators, more blood.

I tell them of Butters' long prayer and of the sudden violence, and if they ask for more, I answer with the jailhouse story. But they never ask, and I never tell, how it felt to go home that day. Cycling from the jail in the old part of town, I saw how the crowded streets gave way to parking lots and newer structures with more glass and less brick, and how, as I crossed the river, the commercial buildings gave way to hills and houses where high-branched oaks shaded a different mix of people. I knew I would find my house at the top of the hill, a generous sycamore out front and in back, a bean-shaped pool. I'd find my mother in the living room, reading a book, Allyn in her bedroom, listening to records, and old Smoke asleep on the couch. No one marched down my quiet street or was arrested there. None of our neighbors bled or sang.

CHAPTER 23

I told my mother about the demonstration and how I had seen the police chief take McAllister's sleeve and lead him away, and how I had seen Emma G among the marchers before I lost her in the melee. "And you don't know where Jamie is?" she asked. I told her no. "We need to get to Carol," she said.

"But what about Emma G? Don't we need to tell Bit?"

"Emma G can wait," she said.

Jamie met us at the door. He told us he had come home when he could not find his father. After he told his mother what he had seen, she had turned without a word, gone into the bedroom, and closed the door. I have an image of Jamie standing alone in the hall, his father missing and his mother shutting him out. My mother gave him a long hug. "We're going to find him," she said, "Have you had anything to eat?" She led us into the McAllister's kitchen and fixed sandwiches for both of us. "You two hang tight," she said. "I need to talk to Jamie's mother." Sitting at the kitchen table, we heard her tap on the bedroom door and call Carol's name. No answer. We heard her turn the knob and step inside. I finished my sandwich, but after a couple of bites, Jamie pushed his away. I asked if he wanted to go outside, but he said he just wanted to wait for his dad to get home.

I knew Jamie was worried for his father's safety, but I kept faith that the reverend would soon walk through the door. Despite all I had seen in Courthouse Square and at the jailhouse, I told myself that the chief would never let McAllister come to harm. He must have led him away to protect him. I trusted my mother to find the reverend, just I trusted her to pry Carol McAllister from her bedroom. Sure enough, not long after I put my plate into the sink, Carol came into the kitchen and joined us at the table. I relaxed a bit, feeling reassured to know my mother was in charge.

She made coffee and poured Carol a cup. Carol sat pale and quiet, her long fingers forming a loose circle around the mug. Jamie watched her. My mother told him, "We called the police station, but we couldn't get through. We'll keep trying. Little says your father was taken by the police chief, so we know he's safe. That much is certain. It's strange he hasn't called, but since we can't get through, it may be that he can't call out either. We're just going to have to sit and wait. Little, tell us again what you saw. I think it would help Carol to hear it."

"Jamie and I saw him march down Broadway," I told them, "just behind Reverend Butters. We saw the police come out of the courthouse, and that's when Jamie went downstairs. I stayed behind because I wanted to see what happened to Emma G." I described Butters' endless prayer and the waiting cars and trucks. "It seemed like the police had planned the whole thing. They wanted Butters to try to cross into the Square, because once he did, they had an excuse to arrest him. They weren't trying to keep him out. They were trying to lure him in."

Carol shuddered, and I continued, telling the story mostly to my mother, because that felt safer. Jamie and Carol hung on every detail. "Those police cars weren't just from LaSalle. They were from all over. I could see the names of the towns painted on the doors. I bet the police have been planning this for weeks because they brought in paddy wagons from all over the state." The more I talked, the better I understood what I was saying. The mayor's prohibition, the thin line of police guarding the Square, the hidden vehicles, all part of a plan.

"Then I saw the police chief take Jamie's dad by the sleeve. He took him in one hand and Butters in the other. I saw him lead them toward a police car."

"Then what?" my mother asked. "Did you see him put them in the car?"

"No ma'am. Everything happened all at once. People were pouring into the square, and the police started...it got really confusing. I was trying to find Emma G, but I couldn't, and when I looked back, they were gone."

Another ragged sigh from Carol. She studied her cup, moved her spoon from her napkin, smoothed it, replaced the spoon. I had only made things worse. She hadn't said a word since coming into the kitchen, and I knew she did not want us there. My mother meant to help, but Carol hadn't asked for help. The last time we'd been in her kitchen, she'd practically thrown us out. It was humiliating for her to have my mother take charge. We sat in a smothering silence.

Julia came in. She saw the four of us at the table, and said, "What's wrong? Where's Daddy?"

"We think," Carol said, her words deliberate and flat, "he might have been arrested."

Julia, incredulous, laughed. "Arrested? For what?" Then, seeing our somber response, she sat down. "Tell me what's happened," she said.

"Why don't you tell her?" my mother said, looking at me. "You were there."

So, I told it again, a story I have repeated so many times it no longer seems real. Each time I tell it, I catch myself changing details to suit my audience, dialing my observations up or down according to my judgment of what the listener wants to hear. I had to tell Julia that her father was missing, possibly in danger, and I knew that Carol was attuned to the particulars, alert to any fact or nuance I might have omitted earlier. I spoke carefully, leaving out as much as I told. The clubs, the screaming, and the awful pandemonium in the square had no place in this version. I described a march, a prayer, a peaceful arrest, and how I lost sight of the reverend. Julia listened, her blue eyes gone gray, one hand resting on her stomach.

When my mother finally succeeded in getting a harried officer on the phone, his tone conveyed that the last thing he needed was one more hysterical female searching for someone who had no business getting mixed up in an illegal demonstration. My mother asked the officer's name and gave him her own, "Mrs. Morris Nickerson." She told him she was calling on behalf of the session of elders of the First Presbyterian Church regarding the Reverend Robert McAllister, who had attended the march as an observer. The officer told her that McAllister had been arrested, but he was not to be found in the LaSalle jail. No, the officer did not know where he was being held.

"So, he's still in custody?"

The officer didn't know.

"How can you not know where he is?"

The officer didn't know that either.

Nothing to do but wait. We sat at the kitchen table, five preoccupied souls without much to say. My mother asked Julia if she was looking forward to her senior year. Julia said she was. Carol unfolded her napkin, smoothed it, folded it, unfolded it, smoothed it, rolled it. My mother wiped her glasses, held them up to examine them, wiped them again. My mother looked from Julia to Carol and back at Julia. I couldn't tell what she was thinking, but just seeing her look at Julia put another knot in my stomach.

The wall phone rang and startled us. My mother and Carol looked at one another, and Carol said, "That must be him." When she answered, we heard a voice but not the words. Carol covered her mouth and placed the receiver on its hook, holding it there as if to keep it down. She was trembling, close to weeping, and my mother put her hands on her shoulders.

"Is Daddy okay?" Jamie asked. Carol separated herself from my mother, waiving her hand, palm out, in front of her face, a gesture I had seen once before, after the kitchen fire. She turned her back to us and gripped the edge of the counter. Then she washed her hands and dried them with a paper towel.

"These people," she said. "I don't understand what motivates these people."

"But who was it? What did they say?" Jamie asked.

Carol turned and looked at him. "It was someone who called to insult your father. Some hateful, horrible person."

"Don't answer next time," Julia said, her lips thin. "Let me do it. I know just what to say to them."

My mother moved toward Carol, but Carol warded her off. She looked the other way, searching the cabinets.

"I need a drink," she said.

"No, Carol. Please. Do you think that's a good idea?"

"Yes, Elizabeth, I do. I think it's an excellent idea, the only good idea anyone in this house has had for the past week. If you had heard what I just heard, you would want a drink as well." She filled her glass with ice, poured the gin and a little tonic. She took a long swallow and pretended to look out the kitchen window, but it was dark outside.

The phone rang again, and my mother picked it up before Julia could. She winced at what she heard. "You have no business calling here," she said. "You are very, very rude!" She slammed the receiver.

Carol raised her glass to my mother with a twisted smile. "Well, that should scare him off!" she said, and she smiled, imitating my mother's voice, "Very, very rude!" Julia laughed as well.

"It's all I could think to say," my mother said sheepishly.

Carol poured herself another and said, "Are you sure you won't join me?"

My mother sighed and said, "Oh, what the hell."

Carol poured her a gin and tonic. "I'm afraid I'm out of lime," she said. "But I don't drink it for the lime."

My mother took a tentative sip, then a longer one. "What did the man on the phone say?" I asked.

My mother cut a look at Carol and said, "I'll tell you when you're older."

"I bet I can guess," Julia said. "Did it sound like someone my age? It better not be anyone I know."

Carol bent down, a bit unsteady, reached under the sink, and pulled out an air horn. "Remember this?" she asked, showing it to Jamie and

Julia. Then, to my mother, she said, "I told Rob I wanted a gun for the nights when I was alone here with the children, but he told me ministers' wives don't own guns. He bought me this instead. He said the sound would scare a burglar much worse than any gun." She placed it on the counter beneath the phone and poured another drink.

"Oh, my God, the air horn," Julia said, shaking her head. "This family."

The phone rang and Carol answered. She said, "I'm having trouble hearing you. Can you repeat that, please?" Then she placed the horn to the mouth of the receiver and squeezed off a long, immense, industrial blast that sounded as if a train had crashed through the kitchen wall, its horn shrieking in our heads. When Carol at last released the trigger, the ringing walls faded to a welcome silence. We could breathe again, hear our own bewildered, returning thoughts. My mother mopped up her spilled drink. Julia started laughing.

"Way to go, Mama," she said, and her mother, returning her smile, raised her glass in a toast.

Carol refreshed my mother's drink and poured one for Julia as well. "Might as well," she said. "It's not like you've never had one."

My mother and Carol began to gossip about the session of elders. "Session of snakes is what they should call them," Carol said. She told my mother what Mimi Hurd had said once to Rob, and what Rob said back to her. My mother told Carol a story from years ago, when she and Mimi were organizing the attic sale for the Junior League. "It's pathetic that a woman that smart should be so dirt dumb," my mother said.

The phone rang again, and my mother gave Carol a mischievous look. "May I?" she asked, taking the air horn. We covered our ears, giggling. Smiling, she lifted the phone, raising the horn for us to see, the executioner's axe. "Hello?" she said, singing the word, sounding perky and full of fun, and then, "Oh my God. Oh, Rob, thank God, it's you!"

From McAllister's book: *They took me to Newfield. Why Newfield? Because Newfield is an hour's drive from LaSalle. An hour to sit in the back of a patrol car and ask questions the deputy does not answer. An hour to fear for my safety and for the safety of my family and fellow marchers. An hour to wonder where I am being taken and what will happen to me when we get there. An hour to pray, to find courage, to weigh my fears, which are merely temporary and personal, against the stern requirements of a higher cause. In Newfield, I am fingerprinted and photographed, locked in a cell with a half dozen demonstrators and one bewildered but lovely old soul who, due to a mental illness, regularly occupied a bunk at the Newfield calaboose.*

They held me for several hours, plenty of time to worry that my confinement might last days or weeks. They did not allow a phone call or access to an attorney. The deputy, the clerk, even the janitor ignored my questions. In a single afternoon, I had fallen from my status as an American citizen—surely the most prized privilege the modern world has to offer—to that of a prisoner stripped of his rights. Then I was released without an apology or explanation. I found my way to a pay phone and called my wife to assure her I was safe. With the dollars I had folded in my pocket, I bought my ticket for the bus ride home and two more for fellow soldiers in the cause.

Chapter 24

WHILE we sat in the McAllister kitchen waiting for a call, Bit and her neighbors swarmed into Mount Calvary Baptist. Clueless and alone, we waited for some figure of authority to give us the answer we needed, but the people of Baker Bottom gathered and gossiped, piecing together scraps of news. They cleaned scraped elbows and nursed bruises, talked, and wept and hugged one another. They exchanged a hundred rumors, interrogated the returning witnesses, and dispatched spies to linger outside the jail-yard fence. By the end of the evening, Bit knew much more than we did about what had happened and why.

Deputies drove the demonstrators to jails all over south Georgia. Butters succeeded in filling the streets and the LaSalle stockade with his followers, but our chief managed the overflow, and he sowed terror along the way. I experienced first hand the fear and worry of not knowing where Jamie's father had been taken, and even then, we had the comfort of our race. When my mother phoned the police station, she identified herself as Mrs. Morris Nickerson and did not hesitate to ask the officer's name.

The news Bit heard at church confirmed her fears. Emma G had been arrested. No one knew where she had been taken, and no one had seen her at the LaSalle jail. We were having breakfast when Bit came in the next morning. If she had planned to act brave, her resolve collapsed when she saw us at the table. She began to cry, and my mother stood and embraced her. "What on earth?" she said. "Come sit down, honey." She pulled out a chair and poured Bit a glass of ice water.

This was something new in their odd partnership, Bit sitting at the table with us, my mother serving her, then sitting close and rubbing Bit's shoulder. "Tell us what's happened, sweetheart," she said. In a story interrupted by tears, Bit told us that Emma G had disappeared into a paddy wagon, and no one had heard from her since.

"Incredible," my mother said. "They even arrested Rob McAllister!"

"I heard that," Bit said. "They took Reverend Butters too."

"Well, that's no surprise. Honestly, Bit, what did he expect would happen?"

Bit gave my mother a cold look and said nothing.

My mother forged ahead. "Have you called the police station?"

"Nobody down there is going to waste their time with me."

"I'll call for you then," my mother promised, still rubbing Bit's shoulder. "But I know they won't listen to me either. You know that too, don't you? I'll try, but I'm not optimistic. We're going to have to ask Mister Morris to help."

"I don't know about that," Bit said.

"I know you don't want me to, but we may not have a choice. Let me see what I can do first, then we'll decide." Mrs. Morris Nickerson placed another call to the LaSalle Police Department. She'd had little luck the night before, when she was calling to find the Reverend Robert O. McAllister. Now, she was calling on behalf of one Emogene Day, a colored girl from Baker Bottom. She returned to the table and said, "It's just what I thought. I'm going to have to call Morris."

"But Mama," I protested, "Remember what Daddy said? You can't call him."

"That was just talk," my mother said.

"What did your daddy say?" Bit looked at me, but I didn't answer. "Did he say he was going to fire me?"

"Um, I don't know," I stammered.

"I know just how your daddy thinks."

"You know how he talks," my mother said. "How he talks and how he thinks and what he does are all different things. He's not going to fire anyone."

"Ain't he? How do I know that? You call him, and you tell him they took Emma G, what's going to keep him from taking it out on me?"

"I am, Bit." The two women looked at one another. I trusted my mother. "I'm on your side, Bit," she continued. "You know that, don't you?"

More silence from Bit. She neither agreed nor disagreed. There was a way she had of allowing her face to go slack, utterly expressionless, so that no one could read her thoughts. She studied her glass of water, turning it in the morning sunlight. My mother left the table and called my father at the shop. Bit listened without looking up, still turning her glass. My mother hung up and said, "He wants us to stay put. He's on the way home."

Bit rose from the table. "Let me get these dishes done," she said. She knew she was going to be fired, I thought, and she did not want to walk out of our kitchen for the last time with dirty dishes in the sink. By the time my father came in, she had finished the dishes, dried them, and put them away. She was still at the sink, wiping the faucet and handles with a dishrag. She turned to face him, crossing her arms over her waist, each hand gripping a forearm, a grip so tight her fingers dimpled the flesh.

"Bit," my father said, greeting her, his face grim.

"Mister Morris," she answered.

No doubt my father had decided before he came through the door what he would say. He wanted to act on his own judgment before my mother, or even Bit, could change his mind, but something in Bit's face or posture weakened his resolve. He hesitated, looking from Bit to my mother then me. "I wish this hadn't happened, Bit," he said.

"Yessir," she said.

"It's not right, you putting me in this situation."

Bit tilted her chin a half degree, said nothing.

"What am I supposed to do now?" he said.

Again, no answer.

"You think I want to go down to the jailhouse and tell them my maid sent me there to find her daughter?" This sounded to me like part of a speech he planned to deliver, a long list of irrefutable grievances, and my mother, sensing the same, spoke up.

"No one is asking you to do that, Morris."

He turned to her. "Tell me again what they told you," he said. My mother began to answer, but he interrupted her. "Who was this you were talking to? He wasn't rude to you, was he?" I could see my father was angry, but I couldn't tell which way his anger would flow, toward Bit, the police, or somewhere else. Maybe he didn't know either.

"He wasn't rude," my mother answered. "Just a little short."

"And you told him your name?"

"Mrs. Morris Nickerson."

He turned to Bit. "You hear that? How do you think I feel having my name caught up in this mess?" Back to the grievances.

"Wasn't nothing I could do about it, Mister Morris." Her voice low, Bit wasn't confronting him, but she wasn't backing off either. I wanted to be anywhere but in that room. I wanted to dash out to the pool, swim to the bottom, and cling to the drain.

"She's your daughter, isn't she? You couldn't keep her home?"

"I tried, but she don't always do what I say." Then she added, "She can be like Allyn that way."

I thought he would fire her then. Bit had handed him the opportunity, talking back that way. He was in no mood to tolerate any suggestion of an equivalence between Emma G and our very own Allyn. His face flushed, and I saw my mother begin to rise, but before she could speak, he stopped her with a rueful laugh.

"You told her to stay home?" he said, his head cocked, studying Bit's face.

"I did."

"And what did she say?"

"She didn't say nothing, so I kept at her. I gave it to her pretty good, too. I told her I didn't want her getting caught up in all that trouble downtown. I told her it wasn't no business of hers, and you know what she said? She said, 'If it ain't mine, whose is it?'"

My father didn't answer. He stood looking at Bit, his face inscrutable. She held her position before the sink, arms pressed around her waist. Then he turned away. "She said that?" He laughed again, if one can call an incredulous, sighing sound a laugh. He shook his head. "They're something, ain't they, these girls?"

Bit nodded, detecting, as we all did, in his use of the vernacular, the "ain't they," the trace of a concession. "They sure is," she said.

So, the crisis passed. I realized he would not fire her and might even help her. But Big M could not bring himself to do so without humiliating her first. He walked over to the kitchen window and looked out across the yard. "I want you to listen to me, Bit," he said. "I'm going to ask you a question, and I want you to tell me the truth."

"I ain't never told you a lie, Mister Morris, not once in all the years I been working in this house." I cringed at this, knowing it wasn't exactly true.

"If I go down to the police station and ask where they've taken Emma G, I don't want to find out later that she's run off with a boyfriend or sneaked off to some girlfriend's house or done something foolish like that. That's why I need you to tell me the God's own truth. Are you absolutely sure she's been arrested and is still in jail?"

"I don't know where she is, and that's the truth of it. One of her friends saw how she got shoved in that police truck, and ain't nobody seen her since. I just has to find her and know she's safe."

"All right, then. Let's see what we can do. You need to step outside while I speak with Miss Elizabeth."

He sent me out as well. I went into the backyard and circled around the house to find Bit. She stood in the driveway, her back to our house. I hung back and watched her. She had no place to go, nowhere to sit in private. She stood on the concrete drive as the gathering heat of another day blazed up from the brilliant pavement. She did not seek the shade, but stood out on our empty drive, utterly alone. I thought that she was crying, but when she turned her head, I saw that her cheeks were dry. She wasn't weeping. She was thinking.

Then a car pulled up, and Allyn got out. She was wearing flip-flops, a bathing suit, and a shirt that was damp from her wet hair. She carried a rolled-up towel. As she crossed the drive, Bit held out her hands to her. Allyn gave her the wet towel and went inside.

CHAPTER 25

"I've decided you're right."

"God, I love the way that sounds! If I put Duncan on the phone, can you repeat those words to him? I think he could learn from your example."

"I've decided to tell them not to associate Mama's name with my donation after all. Her heart may have been in the right place, or at least, within a few hundred miles of the right place, but you were right. She didn't exactly lead the demonstration. I can't ask them to put her name near a monument to Tim Butters. I considered asking them to use Bit's name instead, but even that feels wrong, like I'm trying to rewrite history or leave my mark. I should be able to write a check without expecting anything in return."

"You're a generous soul," my sister tells me, "but I still don't understand why you're making a big deal out of this thing. They're getting rid of Sweet Papa. So what?"

"It's not about the monument," I tell Allyn. "I couldn't care less about that, but I can't stop thinking about Mama. She must have known that Rob McAllister was considering joining the march. Certainly, I did. Jamie talked about nothing else. She also had to know that Emma G was involved. When I told her I had seen Emma G at one of the demonstrations, Mama didn't seem surprised. But I never heard her express even the faintest interest in supporting the march herself. Why not? I know she had her headaches, and I'm sure Daddy would have pitched a fit, but why not do something? If these people are putting their safety on the line, why not encourage them, or at least, not discourage them! When she got wind that Emma G was demonstrating, she tried to convince Bit to keep her home. What was she thinking?"

"Mama loved Emma G."

"That's not the point," I say.

"Do you remember how Mama used to give books to Bit, so she could take them home to Emma G? Do you remember how Mama would sit in the car outside Bit's house and talk to Emma G about what she was reading? Do you know how many of her books Mama gave me to read? Zero."

Nothing I've said has made an impression on Allyn. I feel as if I'm close to something like an insight, but Allyn has wandered off on her own tangent.

"I used to tell her, *But I don't want to give this blouse to Emma G. I love this blouse*, and Mama would take it from me, anyway."

"You had a hundred blouses," I tell her dismissively. "You could buy any blouse you wanted."

"I can't remember a single moment of my early childhood when Emma G wasn't around. Why was she there? How on earth did Mama persuade Daddy to allow it? Mama adored Emma G, absolutely loved everything about her. Do you want to know the stone-cold truth?"

I want to say no, because Allyn's version of the stone-cold truth will be nothing more than her version, and I don't want to hear her twist our shared childhood into a shape I don't recognize, but I can't stop her. She might as well be talking to herself.

"Sometimes I hated having Emma G around. I wanted to live in my house with my mother and not share it with this other girl who ran faster than I did, learned to read before I did, and always spoke for the two of us. When you reminded me of the great Santa Claus debacle, I tried to go back and remember what happened, not the story we like to tell ourselves, but the actual sequence of events. I remember trying to hold Emma G back. How old were we? Six? Seven? Old enough for me to know that Emma G had no business trying to climb onto his lap. If I knew it, she knew it too. I didn't get mad at Santa Claus. I got mad at her. He was doing what management told him to do, what everyone expected him to do, but Emma G crossed the line. Everyone in that store stopped to watch the meltdown with me right there in the middle of it."

I want to stop her, to keep her from saying these things out loud, but Allyn keeps rolling.

"Mama saw how I reacted, and that embarrassed her. Yet another example of how I had let her down. I seemed to do so daily. You remember what she was like. She had this subtle way of conveying her disappointment without expressing it directly. She did it with Daddy all the time."

"No, she didn't."

"Those headaches gave her the excuse she needed to keep her distance from us. She obsessed on her poor, aching head, and exiled the rest of us to the wilderness. Do you remember that time you got sick walking home from school and wandered off and no one knew where you were? Have you ever thought it strange that Bit found you, not Mama? I mean, where was she? She was always disappearing into some world of her own."

"She could have been a thousand places. The store. The dry cleaner. Anywhere."

"Defend her all you want, Little, but you must admit we stayed on tiptoes around Mama. That's what made Bit so important. Around Bit, I felt like I could just be myself, which meant I could enjoy just being a kid. I remember sticking out my tongue at her, and Bit getting mad and shaking her finger at me, and me just laughing and doing it again. You could do that with Bit. If I had stuck my tongue out at Mama, she would have gone to bed for three days."

"You make it sound like she wanted to have those headaches. They were awful."

"I wouldn't wish those headaches on my worst enemy, much less my own mother, but Mama used her migraines to her advantage. We always tell ourselves what a great mother she would have been if she wasn't sick all the time, but being sick was a part of who she was."

"She couldn't help it, Allyn." I'm ready for this conversation to end.

"Did you ever see Mama and Daddy kiss? I never did. Not once. Don't you find that a little peculiar? I spent years making excuses for Daddy as the tough old Marine until I realized it wasn't just him. What kind of wife puts up with a husband who never brings her flowers or kisses her or does anything romantic? I think in some perverse way she liked that about him. She decided early on that he was never going to measure up to her saintly father, and that served as her excuse to push him away."

Where Allyn found this version of our childhood, I do not know. I almost say, "Not Bit. She didn't keep her distance from Bit," because I've always thought of my mother and Bit as friends. She let Bit bring her daughter into our house, and she and Bit confided in one another. But then the image of Bit riding in the backseat comes to mind, one of the hundreds of ways in which we kept Bit separated from us. I want to say, "Not me. She didn't keep her distance from me," except then I remember stepping into her sick room, and how it felt like trespassing.

"Are you still there?" Allyn asks.

"I'm here," I say. I don't want to argue with Allyn. I can't argue with her. I want to keep my sister close for however many years remain to me. "I'm going back to LaSalle," I tell her, "and I want you to come with me. I still have Bit's old shoebox, the one we found with her comb and ribbon. Do you remember? I'm going to give it to Emma G to remind her of how well we knew her mother, to reestablish that connection between us. I want you to be there for that."

"No thanks," Allyn says. "But, hey, *bon voyage.*"

After the call, I scroll through the website for the Tim Butters Memorial Fund, looking for a way to let them know not to use my mother's name, when I discover a donation made in memory of Dr. Amos Swift. The black-and-white photograph shows a smiling African American man in black horn-rimmed glasses and a white lab coat. The coat catches my attention. Another page on the website offers oral histories of the day of the demonstration. I find Dr. Swift's name there and watch a video in which his son, also a doctor, describes his father's role in the protest. "He wore his lab coat," the son says, "because he wanted people to know that the protesters weren't just teenagers or agitators from out of town. My father served the African American community in LaSalle as a prominent ob-gyn for decades. He wanted the town council to recognize him and to understand that the demonstrators included elite members of the professional community."

As a child, I never realized that LaSalle had a Black "professional community," much less elite members. I saw only the maids and cooks and yardmen. When Julia said to Bit, *he doesn't have to be white*, I didn't know what an abortion was, but in the years that followed, I thought of their exchange in lurid terms. I envisioned a procedure that was horrific and unsanitary, performed in the back room of a shack that sold groceries and gas by day. Julia McAllister never gave birth to Tucker Gran's child. For decades, I have imagined her pregnancy ending in some unspeakable way, but now I understand that the procedure could have been performed by a surgeon like Dr. Swift. This minor revelation comforts me by saving Julia from unnecessary suffering and aligning with my memory of Bit. The Bit I knew never would have put Julia's life in danger. If she helped Julia, and I suspect she did, then it's my guess she took her to a professional.

CHAPTER 26

MY father knew a couple of members of the LaSalle police force, and with their help, he learned that a paddy wagon had deposited Emma G in Ogletree, seventy-five miles southeast of LaSalle. An officer called to arrange her release but only into my father's custody and subject to a fine of fifteen bucks. My father came home from the police station ready to roll but for one catch. He wasn't sure he would recognize Emma G, or that she would know him. Allyn and my mother could not go with him, because, my father said, a jailhouse is no place for a lady, and Bit was not invited. He announced that I would be riding with him.

I jumped at the chance, eager to see the inside of a jail. Furthermore, I was beginning to develop a few of my own ideas about application of the code. I'd shot rats with Winn Prather and heard Tim Butters preach. I'd watched the police swing their clubs in Courthouse Square and heard the prisoners sing. I won't make any grand claims of enlightenment—I was just a boy—but I had figured out where my sympathies lay.

I was also beginning to develop a few ideas about my father. Just as my mother had predicted, he did not fire Bit, but he needed supervision. The time had arrived for me to "make some cornbread." I knew he would get Emma G home safely, but I did not trust him to do so with her self-worth intact. I felt no strong connection to Emma G. Her prickly personality rubbed me the wrong way, but I loved Bit, and I had watched as she, a proud woman, endured humiliation to win my father's help. They formed a strong-willed pair, Bit and my father, natural antagonists within the confines of our house. If the roles had been reversed, had my father needed help, I doubt if Bit would have lifted a finger on his behalf. Only my mother stood between them. Since she couldn't manage my father on the trip to Ogletree, that role fell to me.

My mother placed a cooler on the backseat of the car. Before we pulled out of the drive, they spoke through the open window. "Funny, isn't it?" my father said. "While your friend the reverend is writing articles and getting himself arrested, I'm the one driving over to Ogletree to bail this girl out." We were out of the drive before my mother could answer.

The Ogletree police station and holding pen appeared to have fallen into even worse condition than the LaSalle stockade. The old brick was crumbling, the mortar rotten, the bars scaly, the door hinge rusted. A poor and mean-looking place. Inside, a picture of our smiling, segregationist governor hung on the wall beside a series of "Most Wanted" posters. My father dropped a stamped piece of paper on the clerk's chipped and beaten counter.

The clerk examined the form. "She work for you?" he asked.

"Her mama is one of mine," my father said. "You got her?"

The clerk snorted. "We got her all right. Her and a half dozen more just like her. How many you want?"

They brought Emma G out in handcuffs. I was stupefied to see her bound this way, so I didn't realize my father was looking at me. The clerk hesitated. "This is her, ain't it?" he asked.

My father waited. "Hey, Emma G," I said.

She lifted her brown eyes but did not answer. She looked sullen and tired, a twisting strand of hair hanging near her cheek. "That's her," my father said.

He signed some papers and pulled a ten and a five from his wallet. The clerk unlocked the cuffs, and Emma G rubbed her wrists, eyes lowered. They passed a clipboard to her, and she signed her name. She followed us out the door without a word. On the street, she turned to walk away. "Hold on," my father said. "Where do you think you're going?"

She stopped, facing away, and threw her head back, as if she would wait to listen but would not deign to look at us. I knew she was trying to get her exhausted brain to work, wanting to be rid of us, rid of this town, this day, all of it. "I'm free now, right?" she said.

My father did not say what I knew he was thinking, which was, *Look at me when you talk to me, girl*, and I did not want her to provoke him. "Well, you're out of jail, at least," he said.

"So now I'm leaving." Her head was still tilted back, a wiry pigtail resting on her shoulder.

"You think you can just walk off? What are you going to do, call your mama? She's the one that sent me over here. You need to come with us."

Her head dropped forward, and she turned slowly, meeting my father's eyes with a look of drained defiance. "Where to?" she asked, her voice so low we could barely hear it. She was using her body, her voice, her eyes, to express her contempt.

My father dismissed it in kind. She was Black, yes, but she was just a teenager, and he was not going to let a little teenage pique get under his skin. He knew who was in charge. "I'm taking you home, Emma G. Your mama is worried half-sick."

"What if I don't plan on going home just yet?"

Now he looked away as she had, cast his eyes down the same street, and found there the same emptiness and litter. "You familiar with this town?" he asked, his voice thick with sarcasm. "You have friends here? Because if you don't know your way around, and you don't have any friends here, and if you don't have any money, you might ought to consider getting in the car with us. They can arrest you for vagrancy." He walked to the far side of our car and looked at her across the roof. "Hop in," he said.

Emma G looked inside the automobile. She was gathering her strength for one more act of defiance, but I saw it coming, and I cut her off. When she reached for the handle, I moved in front of her, climbed in the front seat, and closed the door. Too exhausted to argue, she climbed in back. Score one. Anyone who saw us driving out of town would assume we were taking the maid home.

Out on the two-lane, no one said a word. She sat behind me, so I could not see her, but I figured she was looking out the window just as

I was. She saw what I saw, the pine farm with all its trees no taller than a man, the occasional mailbox and house, a pickup baking in the drive, the old Baptist church set off the road with separate doors for men and women.

My father was a sociable man. Having wangled Emma G into the car, he couldn't allow this sullen girl to ride home in silence. No, my father needed to make small talk. The drive from Ogletree to LaSalle would take more than an hour, and, in his book, an hour passed in silence counted as an hour wasted. "So, Emma G," he said, "what did they give you to eat?" If he even noticed the resentment emanating from the backseat, it didn't faze him.

I thought she wouldn't answer, but she did. "Cheese sandwiches."

"What kind of cheese sandwiches? Grilled cheese?"

"One slice of cheese. Two slices of bread."

Another mile rolled past, and with it, the roadside carcass of a dog frozen in rigor mortis. My father persisted, "What about for breakfast?"

"They didn't give us any breakfast or lunch either. The cheese sandwich was supper last night." Emma G's voice was so low, I could barely hear her above the hum of the tires. I knew all she wanted to do was sleep, but she couldn't, not in a car with my father at the wheel.

My father looked over at me and said, "Reach in that cooler back there and pull out those sandwiches."

The cooler rested on the seat next to Emma G. She was pressed against the door and, as I leaned across the seat, we exchanged the briefest of glances, before her eyes moved to the window. It would have been easier to have her reach into the cooler than to have me lean over, but she didn't offer, and my father didn't ask. They were working through a standoff, and I was serving as the go-between and self-appointed keeper of the peace. I passed the ham salad over the seat to my father, and he held it back to Emma G, our communication triangular, obtuse. He looked down the road, holding the sandwich over his shoulder. She would have to lean forward and take it from his hand, a concession she wasn't prepared to make. "No, thank you," she said.

"Oh, go ahead and take it," he said, shaking the sandwich in its wax paper. "Your mama made ham salad because she knows you like it. Have one. We won't think any less of you." I took the sandwich from his hand and placed it on the seat next to her. My father told me to pass out drinks, and I pulled a Coke from the cooler. The opener was somewhere on the bottom, and I had to lean way over to look down into the cooler. Emma G sat right there next to it. Anyone else would have fished out the opener for me, but not her. She studied the roadside as I rummaged in the box. Days ago, she had said to me, "Don't you tell her." I had not told her mother, but she had no way of knowing that. She emanated the same distrust of me as she showed my father. I found the church key, opened the first drink, passed it to my father, and he held it over the seat for Emma G, our ornate relay continuing. "Take it," he said, "It won't kill you." Again, she did not move, so I took the bottle and handed it back to her, and she rested it on the seat beside her thigh. I had almost finished my sandwich when I heard the rustle of wax paper behind me.

We ate in silence. When my father finished his, he rolled down his window and threw out the bottle and paper. It made him feel better to have a sandwich and a Coke, and he shifted in his seat, ready for more conversation, one hand resting on top of the wheel.

"So, what else did you do?" he asked.

Maybe her mouth was full, or it could be she was debating the need to respond, considering the consequences of answering my father's persistent and irritating sociability with a hard silence. I held my breath. "Excuse me?" she said at last, though I know she had heard the question.

"What did you do while you were in jail when you weren't eating cheese sandwiches? Did they fingerprint you and take your mug shot and make you empty your pockets? I've never been in jail. Neither has Little, as far as I know. You've had a unique experience. Tell us what it was like." The low sun warmed my father's face. He sounded genuinely interested. I had watched him do this before with customers and contractors at the woodworking shop. My father liked other people, all sorts, and he liked to talk. He would meet a stranger and ask lots of questions.

"They interviewed us." Emma G said, "One by one, they took us into this room, one man in a uniform, a deputy, and another one wearing a suit and tie, an official of some kind. The official asked the questions, and the deputy wrote down the answers."

"What kind of questions?" Prodding her.

A deep sigh from the back seat, and then, "All about the march. How did I know where to go? Who talked me into going? Did my parents know? Who put me up to it? Things like that."

"And what did you tell them?"

"I told them it's my right to march. I told them to go read the First Amendment."

My father chuckled at that, looked out his window and rubbed his forearm, already rehearsing how he would tell this story later. I remembered Bit's report to us about her own exchange with Emma G, how the girl had said of the civil rights fight, *if it ain't mine, whose is it?* though I knew she would have said *isn't*, not *ain't*, this girl who read *The Grapes of Wrath* and knew the Bill of Rights. My father was stitching together his own observations, getting a sense of her rebellious character. She didn't intimidate him. He enjoyed a little feistiness. "What grade you in, Emma G?" he asked. "Tenth?"

"Going into tenth. Same as Allyn."

"What's your favorite subject?"

"Algebra."

"Algebra!" My father laughed out loud. "Allyn is no fan of algebra. No sir, she has no interest in x and its relationship to y." Before the summer came, my father and Allyn had been at war over algebra. He loved math and geometry, which were essential to all aspects of his work, from the sizing of drawers to the balancing of a three-legged stool, and he found it relaxing to work through a math problem. It frustrated him that Allyn froze at the sight of an equation, and her refusal to sit for his painstaking explanations drove him to drink (not a difficult thing to do). "What about the Great Americans project? Did you have to do that? Seems like Allyn spent most of ninth grade working on her Great Americans project."

"We had to do it in our school, too."

My father shot a quick glance at Emma G in the mirror. "Allyn did Lewis and Clark. She wanted to do Sacagawea, but her teacher told her it was just great Americans and not women or Indians. Who did you do?"

"George Washington Carver."

"George Washington Carver!" He laughed again and whacked his thigh. Emma G had not recovered from her cold fury, but for my father, this car ride was a hoot-and-a-half. "All about peanuts, right? How many peanut recipes did he invent? More than a hundred, if I recall. He was quite a man, George Washington Carver. Born a slave, right? What about his guide to character development? What was it, the eight cardinal virtues? Did you read about those?

"I memorized them."

"Is that right? Me too! Not in school. When I was in school, George Washington Carver wasn't exactly part of the curriculum, but when I was in the Marines, we played a game, trying to stump one another with the little scraps of things we knew, historical facts, things like that. Somehow, a bunch of us amused ourselves by quizzing one another on the eight cardinal virtues. Men do things like that when they're bored and cooped up together. Hold on now, let me see can I think of one. Oh, here we go: 'Be clean, both inside and out.' Remember that one?"

"Neither look up to the rich nor down to the poor," she answered. I noted this: as worn out and bitter as she felt, Emma G could not resist showing my father what she knew. Resent it as she might, she was beginning to engage with him.

"That's right! I had forgotten that one. How about, 'Lose without squealing'? That was my favorite!" It was not my favorite. I once struck out four times in a single little league game. When at last the game ended and I crawled into the car, holding back tears, my father had said to me, "Lose without squealing."

"Win without bragging," she said.

"You're good at this, Emma G!" He smiled, leaning forward for another glance in the rearview mirror. "One more! 'Be too brave to lie.'"

"Take your share of the world and let others take theirs." My father was right. Emma G was good at this, matching him virtue for virtue.

He smiled and looked out the window, reflective, lost in some long-ago contest. The conversation died out. "Take your share of the world," he mused, speaking as much to himself as to us.

"And let others take theirs," she answered, her voice one notch higher than it had been. Another ten miles, ten more minutes, then fifteen, and she stirred in the back seat. "Mr. Nickerson," she said, "I think I need to use the restroom."

"An excellent idea," my father said. "So do I." We pulled into a gas station, and he headed inside, leaving me in the car with Emma G. I waited for her to get out, but she did not. I heard her sigh and shift on her seat. I knew the best way to talk to her was to keep looking forward, to ask the question without confronting her.

"What's wrong?" I said.

"They won't let me go here," she said. I studied the gas station. There was no 'Whites Only' sign, nothing I could discern that would let her know she was prohibited from using this restroom. She saw something I missed. Maybe she just did not want to test it, or maybe she knew no gas station in rural south Georgia would allow her the privilege of using its filthy toilet.

My father returned, relieved, blissfully unaware of the circumstances. As we pulled out on the highway, I said, "Daddy, we need to find some other place for Emma G. She couldn't go there."

"Couldn't go?" he said, uncomprehending. Then, "Oh." He shot the briefest of glances at the rearview mirror. "Hold on, Emma G," he said.

We drove a few miles until my father pulled off on a red clay road leading back into some pines. We pulled over into the weeds, and my father left the car running while Emma G went back among the trees. Yet another humiliation for her, having to admit this personal need to my father, of all people, then having to hide and drop her pants back in the scrub pine. We were careful not to look at her when she returned, and we did not say another word until we arrived in LaSalle.

CHAPTER 27

Rob McAllister outshone his wife in any social setting, but she proved the more prescient of the two. Somehow, in all that musing and praying and searching of his conscience, McAllister lost count of votes in the session of elders. Carol never did.

After we delivered Emma G to Bit's tearful embrace (yet another embarrassing moment for Emma G), my father and I returned home for supper. I was looking forward to some TV time, but my mother told me to eat in a hurry, because we were heading over to the McAllister house. She had spent a day arguing with the church elders, all in vain. They'd decided to fire our minister, and she, as the sole dissenting vote, had been selected to deliver the news. She wanted me to go with her to provide support for Jamie. "I don't know how Carol is going to take this," she said. "I'm worried she might get hysterical, and if she does, I may need you there to help."

We rang the bell. When no one answered, we went around back and knocked at the kitchen door. Jamie let us in. His parents were seated at the kitchen table, empty coffee cups between them. McAllister stood to greet us, rising with effort, his bright eyes rimmed and heavy. "Come in," he said. "We've had a couple of calls and visitors that were not entirely friendly, so we decided to stay in the back of the house for a while. I'm glad you found us." He lifted the coffee pot, offering my mother a cup.

"Just black, please," she said. He poured her one, and she took a seat. "I've been at an emergency meeting of the session of elders."

"Oh?" McAllister said. "And no one told me?"

"The meeting was about you."

"I suppose that shouldn't surprise me. How is my friend Mimi these days?"

"It's not a joke, Rob. She's furious. They all are. Tell me something. How long had you been planning this?"

It surprised me how angry my mother sounded.

"I didn't plan the demonstration, Elizabeth," McAllister answered, unruffled. "I'm a foot soldier in this struggle, not a general."

"A foot soldier. Taking orders from whom? Tim Butters?"

"My own conscience," McAllister said. He and my mother were looking at each other in a way I had never seen. She had always revered McAllister, and he had responded with a kind of benign self-satisfaction, but not now. She was chiding him, and he was dismissive in return. Jamie sat still, watching. Carol studied her coffee cup, the vein on her forehead prominent. Julia came in, unkempt, her hair down, no makeup, no perfume. She pulled a chair to the table without saying a word.

"If you had been listening to my sermons, reading between the lines, my participation in the march wouldn't have surprised you," McAllister said coolly.

My mother put down her cup. No member of the congregation had listened more closely than she had.

"Every member of the session knows I've been considering this cause for a long time. Talking it over with Carol. Praying."

My mother glanced at Carol, who did not look up. Julia let out an exasperated sigh. "A lot of good the prayer did," she said, but no one answered her, and McAllister kept his eyes on my mother.

"You didn't bring this to the session," she said. "You didn't give us an opportunity to participate in your decision."

"I don't invite people like Mimi Hurd to tell me how to think and what to do," he said, schooling her. "What I decided wasn't church business."

"Really? Because it felt like church business, having our minister incarcerated. Seeing a picture of him in handcuffs on the front page of the paper. That felt very much like church business. Why didn't you tell me? At the very least, why not me?"

Carol stirred at this, looking from my mother to her husband, her curiosity roused. Julia too. Her sarcastic expression slipped away, and she leaned forward, genuinely interested.

"I didn't make my decision until the march had practically started," McAllister said. "I'm no fool. I knew some members of our congregation would object. I can give you their names. The truth is, I deliberated for a very long time. In fact, I was still debating with myself when I stepped out of my car and found Tim organizing his people. Even then, I thought I might turn back."

"But you didn't."

"I made a moral choice."

"You made a martyr's choice."

"I needed to see this through. I had come to a point in my life, in my spiritual maturation, if you will, when I had begun to wonder whether it was all just words. I read them, write them, speak them, all these pretty words, but what do they accomplish? We feel a bit better, I suppose, but so what? I needed to act. I'm supposed to be leading our church, not doling out feel-good pills. Believe me, I joined that march out of necessity."

"Necessity for whom?" my mother snapped, her voice rising. "Are people going to change their attitudes just because you managed to get yourself arrested? I'm certain you've traumatized Carol and Julia and Jamie, but I'm not sure what else you've accomplished. You got your picture taken. You've made a brave gesture. But that's all it was Rob, a gesture. You should have considered what comes next."

"Oh, we'll be all right," McAllister said, his voice calm, his demeanor patronizing. "I'm sure the board is red-hot right now, and people will be calling for my head, and they'll demand that I explain myself. There will be a lot of back and forth, phone calls and what not, but I'm confident of my position in the church. Trust me, Elizabeth. This will all blow over."

"I'm afraid you're wrong about that. The board has made its decision."

McAllister stiffened in his chair. Jamie said, "I don't get it. Decided what?"

"I believe Little's mother is telling me that my contract has been terminated," McAllister said. He put one hand on Jamie's shoulder and another on Carol's. Julia leaned back, arms crossed, her mouth open. "Effective when?" he asked.

"They've given you a week to clean out your office. They'll pay your salary through the end of the month."

"The end of the month!" Carol gasped. She pushed away McAllister's hand.

"This didn't have to happen," my mother said. "You should have thought of your family. They come first. You should not have left their welfare in the hands of those people ..."

McAllister stopped her. "Those people," he said, "are members of my congregation. Most of them are as confused as we are." He shifted in his chair, crossed his long legs, studied the floor. "This is a bit more abrupt than what I had expected," he said, "but so be it. We will just have to make do." We sat at the table as he examined the floor and thought. Then he said, "If I'm to be out by next week, who preaches on Sunday?"

"You do."

"Oh, beautiful," Carol said. The edge in her voice startled me. "The great man's farewell sermon. What an occasion that will be, another opportunity to wax eloquent." She rose from the table. "I'm going to bed," she announced. "I'm going back to that goddamned room, which I despise, every inch of it, every wall, every corner, the drapes, the bed, all of it. Have I told you that, Rob? I've loathed every minute I've spent in that room, but I will go there to be alone, without any of you bothering me, not even you, dear Elizabeth. If anyone tries to come in, or knock, or even stands at the door and listens, I will eat every pill in this house."

McAllister stood and said her name but did not stop her. She left us at the table. I looked away from Jamie.

A couple of days later, we returned to the McAllister house with Bit carrying a basket of fried chicken and potato salad. When my mother told her that she wasn't required to come with us, Bit said simply, "I want to." She gave Jamie a big hug, and said, "How you doing, honey?" I asked Jamie if I could borrow his copy of *Thirty Seconds Over Tokyo*. Borrowing a book seemed a way to keep him close. Jamie sent me back to his bedroom, and I was on my knees at his bookshelf, when his mother appeared at the door. She was wearing her turquoise robe with the pink hearts, her hair falling lank on her shoulders. "Oh hey, Little," she said, "I thought I heard you. What are you looking for?"

"A book Jamie said I could borrow," I told her.

"You and Jamie and your books! Jamie is just like his father that way, always with his nose in a book. I wish he would spend more time out-doors, doing the things boys are supposed to do, instead of reading all the time. It can't be good for him to read so much. It's bad for his eyes." Carol's own eyes looked unfocused. She was standing in the door, look-ing past me, gazing at Jamie's shelves of books. "Which one are you looking for? Not the pajama book, is it?"

"The pajama book?"

"Julia used to have a book about a girl in her pajamas. She loved that book! That was our little joke. I'd say, 'Go put on your pajamas, and I'll read you the pajama book.' The pajama book was our favorite."

I smiled and said, "Yes ma'am."

"I don't know what's happened to Julia. All she does is waste her time with that horrible boy. Something's up with those two. I tell her he's not good enough for her, but she's stopped listening to me. Everyone has. He came by the other day, and she wasn't even dressed! Can you imagine? She was wearing her pajamas! It's like no one can get out of their pajamas! I'm in my pajamas, you're in your pajamas, Rob is in his." She turned to look down the hall as if to make sure we were alone. "Is that Bit I hear? I hope she's not wearing her pajamas. She isn't, is she?"

I didn't answer. Carol McAllister giggled, a restless, unhappy sound. She looked around Jamie's room, inspecting the corners of the ceiling. "Don't mind me. I'm just talking nonsense. I know Bit is not wearing her pajamas. Bit probably doesn't even own pajamas. So, why does Julia trust her more than she trusts me? Why trust someone who doesn't even own pajamas?"

Another question I could not answer. She continued in a conspiratorial tone, "Have you ever seen the reverend's pajamas? Black with a white collar and cuffs. Very demure. Just the thing to show the world what a good man you are after you've abandoned your family, holy of holies and all that crap." She caught herself and looked at me. "Pardon my French. I'm just babbling. Babbling and babbling like the little bitty brook that broke the world. Because that's the whole point, isn't it? It's not to do good or to be good but to show the world and the elders and even Timothy Butters what a very, very, very, very good man you are, the best of men, the noblest of men, whereas your wife is, your wife is, well, she's just nothing. A speck of dirt. A mote. A crazy person you lock up in her pajamas."

She rubbed the door frame up and down, inspecting it, testing the grain with her palm. "In jail, they give you striped pajamas. Rob got thrown in jail. Did you know that? Probably not." She examined me, head tilted. "You're a sweet boy, Little, but you never seem to know anything. I think that's what Jamie likes about you. You're an innocent." She folded her arms across her waist, and her bathrobe shifted, falling open, dangerously close to showing me what I did not want to see. She was standing in the doorway, and I had no way out of this room.

"I don't think Rob liked jail. I think it disappointed him. Inside his cell, people couldn't see what a good man he was, and they made him stay there, eating that food they give the prisoners, the Brussel sprouts or whatever it is that prison people eat. He wasn't happy then, because when you're sitting in jail by yourself, you aren't reading Tolstoy, are you? Or typing. In jail, all you can read is the toilet paper. That's what I read when I go to jail. Some people read magazines, but I don't. If you look at the roll real close, you can see what's written there, stamped on it with the toilet-paper-making machine. It's nothing really, just the brand name most times and sometimes flowers, though I can't imagine why they put flowers on toilet paper. That's what I told Rob when he got home, after Jamie and Julia had gone to their rooms. I said you're just stamping flowers on toilet paper, Rob. Why does it matter what it says? You still use it to wipe your ass."

She leaned forward, her eyes defiant, and her breast fell from her robe. It looked like a water balloon. She straightened, slipped the breast beneath the robe, and cinched it tight, somehow unaware that she had exposed herself. Then she was gone. I sat on the floor, my back to the bookshelves, trying to breathe. One of the shelves cut across my spine, and I pressed into it, wanting it to hurt. I waited to hear her bedroom door click shut before I slipped out.

I found Bit at the McAllister's sink doing dishes. I stood close to her so no one else would hear. "Carol knows," I said.

Bit shot me a sideways look, chin lowered, the soapy pan in her motionless hands. "What you talking about?"

"She told me she knows something is going on between Julia and Tucker, and that Julia trusts you, but doesn't trust her. You have to be careful, Bit. She knows."

Bit turned to me, placing a soapy fist on her hip. "Knows what?"

"I heard y'all talking when you were in Julia's room. I heard you through Jamie's closet wall. She told you she was in trouble and said you had to help her, and you said you didn't want to, but she said you had to. I didn't tell anyone, but now Carol knows."

Bit's face grew hard. "You don't say another word about this, you understand? Not to me, not to Jamie, not to no one. You understand?"

I backed away from her. "Okay," I said, "I get it. I just thought..."

"Not never!"

CHAPTER 28

I had never seen our church so crowded, the women in their hats and cotton dresses, the men in their khaki and seersucker suits. Some faces I recognized, others I did not. Many of the men had sun-burned noses and hands, while their wives were carefully tanned. On our way in, I watched several men stamp out their cigarettes on the warm church steps. Those with hats removed them. Everyone knew someone, though no one knew everyone. An attorney handled the affairs of a businessman two pews down. The businessman's wife played bridge with a friend across the aisle. The friend's oldest daughter dated the son of a cash-strapped family near the altar.

They came to see their minister's surrender, the opposing factions side-by-side in the pews, solemn for the occasion, made bitter or proud by one man's self-inflicted wound, relieved or troubled to bear witness to his demise. We gathered again as we had every Sunday of my life, diverse in our attitudes and income, but uniform in race. The notion that our congregation should include Black people would have been considered bizarre, an idea that infuriated many and frightened most. Already, our minister had gone much too far. Our elders had made their decision in sober deliberations. We needed to regroup, slow down, protect ourselves.

Even Lutherans, Episcopalians, Baptists, Jews, and agnostics would watch his farewell. LaSalle's largest TV station, Channel 3, carried the weekly Baptist service, but the other station, Channel 5, carried our Presbyterian service. On this Sunday, many of those who had read in the LaSalle paper of McAllister's arrest chose to skip their own services and watch Channel 5.

I always liked how McAllister looked in his black robes with his tall frame and bright eyes. I admired his study, that tight, book-crammed room, the old typewriter perched in the center of his desk like a reliquary. I enjoyed hearing him string together words in a manner high-flown and fine. I had come to admire what he said and how he said it, the deft way he moved his congregation from restlessness to laughter, then silence. Though my mind often wandered in church, this sermon, his last, would command my attention.

Some in this audience would remain unmoved, whatever he said. They had come not to hear his explanation, but to take satisfaction in his humiliation. His participation in the demonstration shamed them, and now they would shame him in return. They felt the rest of the town laughing at us, the Presbyterians with their radical preacher. It incensed them that the session had allowed him this final say. Why not just pack him in a car with his nutty wife and send him on his way? He didn't deserve another hour of their time, and they intended to listen only as opposing counsel listens, not to understand, but to refute.

McAllister once joked to me that he spoke to our congregation "two ears at a time," by which he meant that each listener listened alone, a faction of one. He knew from private conversations that the consensus expressed on the church's front steps did not represent every parishioner's voice. Over the summer, with a surreptitious handshake or in a quick encounter in the parking lot, a few fellow Presbyterians expressed support for his article, and a quiet handful secretly celebrated his decision to march. He meant to speak for these people and for himself, to address supporters and detractors alike without having to worry about the collection plate.

We stood for the hymn, bent our heads for the prayer, sat and listened to announcements. *Please join us for an hour of coffee and fellowship after the service.* McAllister recited the familiar words, though we knew he would not attend. We rose for a hymn chosen by our minister.

Long my imprisoned spirit lay

Fast bound in sin and nature's night;

Thine eye diffused a quick'ning ray,

I woke, the dungeon flamed with light;

My chains fell off, my heart was free;

I rose, went forth, and followed Thee.

He took the pulpit, head bowed with its shock of white hair, his powerful hands gripping the lectern, his vestment falling in thick folds from his extended arms. If he felt ashamed, as so many hoped, his posture did not show it. He stood erect and allowed the silence to do its work, the slow seconds isolating the occasional cough, the thump of a hymnal returned to its rack.

"Why did I do it?" he began, and the question echoed from the walls of the hushed church. "Why did I join the march? Surely, I must have known where my decision would lead me. Anyone of right mind would understand that when I joined the other marchers stepping from Sixth Street onto Broadway, I could never return. If I could not guess that I would be arrested, I surely should have recognized that I was jeopardizing my place in this community and this church. So, why did I do it?

"Just a week ago, none of us would have imagined this Sunday would count as my last among you. We have travelled so far together, shared so many mornings in this lovely sanctuary. I had hoped to stay here until I retired. I dreamt that one day I would step down from this pulpit and join you among the pews, a fellow congregant, a disciple prepared to follow in the steps of my successor."

I felt he was speaking to me. I never imagined a Sunday would come when Jamie would leave. I accepted our friendship as a fact no less tangible than the bricks of the mill buildings. Jamie's father always would serve as our minister because he had served as our minister always.

"But now our paths diverge, because, some say, I have made our separation inevitable. Instead of leading this congregation, they say I have turned against it, and for this perceived betrayal, you deserve an explanation. After all, you have given me your trust, asked me to preside at the weddings of your sons and daughters, allowed me to speak at the gravesides of your parents. Hear me then, one last time, and I will tell you why I acted as I did.

"But first, what did I do? I stepped from Sixth Street onto Broadway. I joined a demonstration for equal rights. Nothing more. I did not urge members of this congregation to come with me on the march. I did not use this pulpit to deliver my political opinions. And I did not invite a Negro into this place of worship. I simply joined a demonstration. I walked, as one man, as a follower of Christ, with other men and women who also follow Christ. We walked together arm-in-arm because we believed that Christ would have us do so.

"And yet, in so doing, I embarrassed this church. Which church? The Organized Church? The church with its weekly collections and annual budget, its contracts with the printer, the plumber, the men who mow our grass and take away our trash? Or the Living Church? The church that knows no beginning or end, no walls, no ceiling, no floor, no brim or brink, no boundary or border? That Living Church endures without limits. It breathes when we breathe, catches each dying breath, and carries it to a newborn child. That church, I have not forsaken. That church, I have not embarrassed.

"I have not because I cannot. No man can. That church we cannot denigrate. It exists beyond us and within us, greater than any one of us, incomplete if it lacks a single soul. My membership in that church compelled me to act as I did. That church recognizes no race, no status, no differences among us. We worship its most exalted member, He who gave his own life to teach us humility. That church will tolerate no separation, no segregation, no petty distinctions rooted in race or wealth or family name."

McAllister paused, turned a page at his lectern. I looked across the aisle and down the pew. Some barely listened—he might as well have been speaking in Japanese—but he held others in his grip. One woman had slipped forward to the edge of her seat, her hand resting on the back of the pew in front of her, her face upturned.

"Why now? you ask. What changed? When the day of the demonstration came, what compelled me to join it?

"As I sat in my study preparing this sermon, I did as I so often do when searching for an answer. I began pulling books down from my shelves, looking in them for some key to what was written in my heart. I found a familiar volume by Leo Tolstoy and re-read these words, 'I sit on a man's back choking him and making him carry me, and yet assure myself and others that I am sorry for him and wish to lighten his load by all means possible...except by getting off his back.' And as I read those words, a sound beyond my study distracted me, the sound of a Negro woman coming into my house with a meal she had prepared for my family, a woman who once generously invited me into her church, knowing that I could never invite her into this one.

"That day, as I thought and wrote, she had been dusting chicken with flour, dropping it into hot oil. She has her work. I have mine. Her work sometimes involves caring for my own Jamie as well as his best friend. Meaningful work, nurturing a child, work as important as the labor of any person in this church.

"And how do we thank her for that work? We do not. What respect do we show her? Very little. We may feel some small degree of sympathy, some airy notion of how sweet we would feel if we lightened her load, but we do not, as Tolstoy says, get off her back. On the contrary, we have adopted in our speech, in our manners, in the very laws of this town, a system for humiliating her. We have denied her access to our restaurants, our churches, our schools, even our restrooms. We have given her a most precious responsibility, the care of our children, and we have paid her with contempt. This bargain we have made with the Negro."

I sat between my parents, my mother preternaturally still, her legs crossed, her fingers interlaced. I thought of the rhyme she recited when I was young, showing me first the church, then forming the steeple, then making me laugh by exposing her waggling fingers as the people inside.

Sitting next to her, her warm arm brushing mine, I could feel her breathe.
I watched as she watched, listened as she listened. I knew my father did
not like to sit, especially on a hard pew. He was turned away from me,
one arm resting behind Allyn's back. He was looking away from the
pulpit, his eyes raised to the stained glass, a subtle withholding of his
full attention.

"We force our colored neighbors to endure our contempt, yet we seldom acknowledge it. On the contrary, many of us here, most of us even,
would argue that we feel nothing but affection for the Negroes we know.
If a woman comes into my house to cook and sweep and care for my child,
I pay wages for that. I offer her a ride home when it rains. I advance
her a little extra if her stove gives out. I ask about her children, sympathize with her when hay fever season comes, laugh when she laughs, and
when she is troubled, I respond as a friend responds, with sympathy and
encouragement.

"But I do not get off her back.

"I may share with her the leftovers from my table, but I never invite
her to sit with me. When her feet have grown sore from walking, I may
give her enough for new shoes, but never in a lifetime enough for a car.
I may smile sometimes at the way she talks, how she says 'ain't' instead
of 'isn't,' or 'we is' instead of 'we are,' but I do nothing to provide her
children with a better education.

"I have paid for her welfare in nickels and pennies, meted out my ap-
preciation in portions appropriate to her race. An affection measured
inch by inch, ounce by ounce, cannot satisfy the Christian definition of
love. Instead, it languishes as mere sentimentality, feckless and wan,
more self-indulgent than useful. Once I recognized my professed caring as but a form of contempt, my false tenderness as a subtle type of
arrogance, I had no choice but to root them out."

The television signal spread through the city and neighboring counties, south to Chattahoochee and north to Harris. It crossed the river to
Alabama, carrying our reverend's words into Lee and Russell counties,
and passed through Baker Bottom, where second-hand sets captured and

held the gray, faintly granular image. The transmission passed over fields, creeks, and parking lots, playgrounds and closed repair shops, split-levels and pines and shotgun shacks. Some within the reach of the station's tower must have been perplexed by McAllister's words, others amused, and still others captivated. Beyond the country houses, the signal lost its strength, the image its definition, his sermon its syntax.

"Why did I do it? I did it because a living faith celebrates a continuous rebirth, and we should delight in shedding old skins. I did it because I aspire to an everlasting life that is not an outcome, but an ever-unfolding progression, each day a revelation. I stepped from Sixth onto Broadway, knowing I could never return. I sloughed off the useless integument of my old contempt and walked forth, a new man, to demonstrate for equal rights. Arm-in-arm, we marched, our voices joined in harmony, and when the policemen came with their clubs, they arrested us together, pushed us into their paddy wagons and police cars, and consigned us to cells we shared with pride.

"They held me for hours, but I would not have you think of my confinement as lonely, quiet, or dark. We were crowded together, too many for a single cell, surrounded by the echoing walls and bars, our lockup lit by the caged bulb above. No place to sit but the concrete floor, no bed but a shared bunk. No phone, no radio, no television, no access to the world beyond those bars. No faucet and sink where we could wash.

"We formed a different kind of union, a blessed gathering of the Living Church, voluntary captives united by our faith. The walls meant to confine us held us together instead. We rejoiced in a genuine communion, and when we were released, we rode home in the Greyhound together, the flat fields sliding past, acres of corn in their harvest prime. I felt a weary ecstasy on that bus ride, not to be leaving something, but moving towards it, not to be returning, but progressing, not to be restored, but transformed. *Ecclesiastes* tells us there is 'a time to heal, a time to break down, and a time to build up.' When I decided to march, I began to break down walls that imprison every member of this congregation. But I have not come here to heal. Healing requires acceptance, and if the status quo constitutes an unacknowledged crime, I can never accept it. No, now is a time to build up, a time to move forward. I ask you, I beseech you, and yes, I warn you to open wider the doors of this church.

"Let us pray."

In our church, as in most, the minister stands at the door and shakes hands with congregants as they file past, but we walked out through an empty door that Sunday, and McAllister's absence pained me. As long as I could remember, he had taken my hand once a week, bending to speak with me, his keen eyes and firm grip a brief exhilaration.

Beyond the door, husbands lit cigarettes for their wives, but with little of the laughter and sociability that followed a typical service. The men nodded to one another. Some of the women sighed and shook their heads. Their eyes conveyed a sense of having done a painful but necessary thing. My family had come in two cars, which we never did, and we left my mother on the church steps.

"I've got something to do that can't wait," she said.

"What is it?" I asked.

"Church business," she told me. She had a life of her own. I had come to appreciate that fact over the long summer, seeing her comfort Bit, hearing about her debates with the session of elders, watching as she tried to help our minister's family through their crisis. It still pained me to acknowledge that part of her life did not include me, but I was discovering in my exile the fresh pleasure of independence. I left her to her work.

CHAPTER 29

THE McAllisters packed their household goods, the old Royal type-writer, volumes of *Collected Sermons*, and the tacky dragonware vases. The reverend had not yet found another church, but Carol was not well, and the hateful calls and threats had not stopped. Someone had carved something vile on their front door, which McAllister covered in typewriter paper. They had decided to go to Birmingham and stay with Carol's mother. I went to help Jamie pack, and he kept trying to give me things. *You can have this. Did you ever finish reading this? Keep it. You can mail it to me.*

I wouldn't take any of it. I told him I was on my bike and couldn't carry anything with me. He laughed at that. He had seen me peddle with a watermelon. I told him that when my mother came to supervise the movers, I would come with her. I'd make sure his books and bike were on the truck. He would receive them in his new place, wherever that was, and could set up his room just the way he wanted. Soon, I would come visit and help him explore his new town—or next summer, when my family went to the beach, we would invite him to come down. We'd climb the dunes together. I imagined our future as a continuation of the years just passed.

Jamie had a knack for making small moments large. A walk in the dunes with him became an existential struggle, complete with burning eyes and bleeding feet, a spool of horrors unwinding from Jamie's lurid imagination. But our last moment in his bedroom, he kept small, though the event marked a turning point in both our lives. I sat on his bed while he ransacked his shelves and closet for something to give me. When

I stood to leave, he said, "I'll see you tomorrow." I knew we wouldn't be alone then. My whole family would come to wave the McAllisters off. Jamie and I couldn't say a real goodbye with our parents hovering around. If we were ever going to acknowledge what this parting meant for us, we needed to do it now. I wanted him to say more, but he didn't. He disappointed me. I couldn't wait forever, so I just left.

Jamie had grown quiet in recent weeks, no longer the boy who talked my ear off walking home from school. Both he and Julia inherited their father's magnetic charm, but his parents burdened him with problems he could not solve. As the manic energy of his beach days receded, Jamie became a more solemn and troubled soul. But maybe I'm overthinking it. Maybe he was just entering adolescence, and as always, I followed two clueless steps behind.

On the McAllisters' last day in LaSalle, we stood on their scorching driveway. My mother wore a sleeveless dress, her arms tanned from her time reading by the pool. Allyn wore shorts my father considered too short. Bit, in her uniform and flip-flops, squinted into the sun, hands on hips. When McAllister brought Carol out, she looked better than I expected, delicate but pretty in her sundress, her red hair pinned back. She wore sunglasses, and they provided a needed layer of protection, concealing her eyes from ours. We waited as if in the reception line at a funeral, except for Bit, who stood apart. Carol moved down the line, shaking hands with my father, then my mother and Allyn. I reached out to shake, but she took me in her arms and held me for what seemed a long time. I could feel the others watching.

"I'm going to miss you so much, Little," she said. "You and I, we always understood each other."

"Yes ma'am."

She stood back and examined me, mysterious in her cat-eye shades. "You'll come visit us, won't you, wherever we are? And come soon. I want you to still be Little when you come, not yet Morris."

"I won't ever be Morris," I said, and everyone laughed at that.

She gave Bit an awkward wave and climbed in the back seat of the car with Julia. Julia got out of the car, walked over to Bit, and hugged her. "Thank you, Bit," she said. Bit looked uncomfortable. I thought it risky for Julia to reveal herself this way. I thought for cover she should hug each of us. But her eyes passed over us, lingering only briefly on my mother, before she climbed back in the car. Jamie moved down the line, shaking hands. When he got to me, we didn't know what to do. It seemed odd to shake. Instead, he punched me on the arm, and I punched him back. Bit gave him a long hug, and when she released him, she sniffed and dabbed her eyes with her apron. "Just look at me," she said, apologizing. "Ain't this something?"

Rob McAllister gave my father a firm handshake, the cool Naval officer saluting the former Marine. Then he turned to my mother, took her hand and, bending close, told her she had been a wonderful friend to his family. "Yes, Rob," she said, "I think I have." He shook Allyn's hand then mine. He looked at Bit, cocked his head to one side, spread his arms, and said, "May I?" That got her fountains going. They hugged and Bit wept, rocking back and forth in his arms.

As their Chevrolet pulled out of the drive, I watched Jamie's face turn toward us and then away. McAllister slowed at the corner. I badly wanted Jamie to look back at me once more, but he didn't. We lingered there in the driveway, gazing down the empty street for what seemed like a long time, with nothing more to see.

"Well, Bit," my mother said, her voice resigned, "Let's get you back to the house, so we can start fixing supper."

"No ma'am," Bit said. She stood in the drive, arms folded, her cheeks streaked with drying tears. "I ain't coming no more, Miss Elizabeth, Mister Morris. Emma G and me, we leaving."

"Leaving?" my mother said. She took a step toward Bit then stopped. Something about Bit's stance looked unfamiliar, almost frightening. "Leaving to go where?"

"Newark."

"I don't understand, Bit. Newark, New Jersey?"

"Yes ma'am. I think that's where it's at. Either there or in New York somewhere. Emma G says she can get us there. I have a brother there, half-brother, I mean. My daddy had a boy with another woman before he met my mama, before he had us. Rennie. I been talking to Rennie, and he says Emma G and me can come stay with him until I find something."

None of us, not even my mother, had ever heard this family history. My mother lifted her hand, as if to take Bit's, but Bit did not move toward her. "When will you be back?" my mother asked.

"Never. We're leaving for good. I got to do it for Emma G. Her getting arrested, that was the last straw."

"You should have listened to me," my mother said. "I told you not to let her march."

"No, ma'am," Bit said, cutting her off. "Don't you go blaming me. This ain't my fault."

My mother studied Bit's face, and Bit glared back at her. "Did he talk you into doing this?" my mother asked. "Because if he did …"

"This ain't nobody but me," she said. "My choice. And I made it a long time ago. I just had to figure out the when and how."

My father stepped forward and rested a hand on my mother's shoulder, either to support or restrain her. "Bit," he said, "I don't know what's gotten into you, or who you've been talking to, but you need to listen to me. Newark, New Jersey is no place for you and Emma G. People up there, they're not like us. You're going to get up there, and you're going to be lonely." The image of Bit in her church returned to me. She had stood at the center of a circle of friends. She knew no one in Newark, was not even sure where it was. My father continued, "My advice to you is to go home, take a day off, think this thing over, and then we can talk about it when you come back tomorrow."

"I ain't coming back. I made up my mind."

"How are you going to pay for all this?"

"I been saving for years. Collecting my cuts. Universal Gourmet." Those two words exposed my part in a conspiracy to deceive my father, but Bit's announcement had baffled him, and he failed to notice.

"But you can't do this!" he said.

"I'm doing it right now, ain't I? Goodbye, Mister Morris, Miss Elizabeth. Bye, Allyn. Bye, Little."

Then I did what I should have done with Jamie. I applied a lesson I had learned in just the last few minutes. I crossed the drive and hugged Bit. Not what my father would have me do. More than my mother could do. Bit's arms folded around me, and I felt for the last time her warm, soft flesh. I could not believe that she would leave me. Despite all I had heard, my heart insisted that tomorrow I would find her in our kitchen.

"Look at me," she said, so softly the others could not hear.

"No," I said, squeezing her tighter.

She loosened her grip, put her hands on my shoulders, and gently pushed me back. I wanted the same tearful embrace Rob McAllister had received, but I didn't get it. "You have to let go of me," she said.

"But I want you here."

"You have a good mama. She won't never leave this family."

"But I want you here, too. You can't leave me!"

"I ain't leaving you. I'm just leaving, that's all."

"I love you, Bit," I said.

"Ain't you sweet," she said.

"At least, let me drive you home," my mother said, but it came out wrong, more like an order than an offer.

Bit gave her head a barely perceptible shake. She did not want fifteen minutes in the car, where she knew that my mother would try to change her mind. "I expect it's best if I just take the bus," she said. She turned before my mother could answer. We watched her walk down the street, a cryptic, almost comical figure in her flip-flops and uniform, the white string of her apron tied in a loose bow above her bottom, a minute yellow ribbon knotted in the back of her hair. I see her now as I did not see her then, no longer faintly absurd. Bit knew how to hold herself, back straight, chin tilted, in a way that conveyed her dignity.

CHAPTER 30

S HE missed it. All my life, I have cherished an image of the one person who saw and understood everyone and everything, but Bit's departure surprised her. I'll admit that my mother never described Bit as her friend, and in fact, the thought would not have occurred to her. Our perverse code forbade friendship, but she loved Bit as well as she knew how, and they spoke every working day. All the while, Bit was harboring a secret she never guessed.

My mother took pride in managing our household, which included overseeing Bit, helping with her bills, and sending her home with the tote; in short, treating Bit as well as any white woman treated her maid. We knew Bit did not trust Big M, even I saw that, but every member of our family assumed that Bit trusted and relied on my mother. She did not. My mother's gifts of second-hand books and Allyn's old blouses fell far short of ensuring Emma G's welfare, and the girl's arrest must have terrified Bit. When Emma G went missing, my mother couldn't help, and I saw how it galled Bit to rely on my father. Emma G's crisis gave Bit the gumption to make a change she had contemplated for years. She made it without asking my mother's help or even consulting her.

Though Bit's departure shocked me, I enjoyed the pliability of youth. I did not miss her as my mother did. I continued to mature. One less person treated me like a child. We never heard another word of Bit until, more than fifty years on, Allyn learned that Emogene would be speaking in LaSalle. I cannot describe Bit's remaining years. I can't conjure up the apartment where she and Emma G lived, the work Bit found, or even the bus ride north, first to Atlanta, then Washington, D.C., then New York, and finally, Newark. My version of Bit's life goes blank.

Jamie's father found a congregation in Ohio that deemed his arrest proof of his Christian character. In the months after the McAllisters left, I waited to hear news of Julia, but none came. I can't imagine that she arrived in a new town and solved the problem of her pregnancy before her parents discovered it. How would she know where to go? I convinced myself that Julia's abortion occurred before she left LaSalle, and that Bit must have helped her. I tried to reason that Bit left us because she wanted to escape before her crime was discovered. I could not and did not discuss Julia's situation with anyone. Call it another phase of my haphazard maturation. I learned to keep an ever-closer guard on my thoughts. I became even more like my mother.

I missed Jamie and tried to persuade my mother to drive me to Ohio, but we never made the trip. I sent him a few postcards. He answered the first, but not the others. That hurt my feelings, so I stopped writing, which I now regret. I don't know why Jamie didn't write. Maybe he just didn't get around to it. We never fell out with one another. I'll admit that I felt jealous of his relationship with Bit, the way she naturally took to him, and that I always deferred to him, whether we were selling watermelons or sharing some boyhood fantasy, but I enjoyed every day of Jamie's company. He took me to the mills and into Mount Calvary Baptist. Through Jamie, I discovered a world beyond our fenced-in yard and pool. The lessons I learned from him stayed with me. I have incorporated a bit of his swagger into my own personality. Faced with a challenge, I channel my inner Jamie.

For me, puberty came on like a creeping flu. I maintained some casual friendships, made good grades, dissected a frog in junior high, and dated a couple of girls in high school. (Two girls, to be exact, and one fewer than four times, but it still counts.) I had grown bored with my life in LaSalle by the time I reached college age. My mill-town home seemed almost unnecessary once I moved away, yet it pulled me back. At the beginning of my junior year in college up north, I received a call from my father. I remember holding the phone, looking out on a young maple beyond the window, its branches scarlet against a hard blue sky. He told me my mother had died of a sudden stroke. That news cauterized my childhood. In the decades since, I have selected my memories with care. The rest I have boxed up and tried to forget. I never agreed with the doctor's opinion that her headaches had no bearing on her fatal stroke. Every memory I allowed myself to have of her seemed to foretell an early death, and the rhythm of her headaches prefigured the permanent loss. I feel guilty that I never told her what she meant to me. Her sudden martyrdom made her, in my mind, more ideal than real, almost saintly. My guilt and grief closed off any chance of seeing her whole.

I sometimes hear Jamie's voice urging me out of my shell, but more often, my mother's. She resides within me. I harbor none of Allyn's resentment toward her. If my mother acted a bit reserved, then so do I. If she sometimes said less than what she was thinking, I do the same. In my attitudes and manners, my mouth, eyes, and gestures, I proudly resemble her. I admired my mother for acting on her sympathies. Too many other introverts seem simply to languish in vague feelings of goodwill. When Rob McAllister put a torch to his career, my mother defended him at church, gave shelter to his son, and rushed to help his traumatized wife.

I was emulating her when I left college and returned to LaSalle to look after my father. Allyn, who had been living in Atlanta, moved home as well. Back in the old house together, we found a life nothing like the one we had known. No one swam in the pool or played in the yard. We did not wake to the smell of frying bacon. We watered my mother's potted ferns, but they died anyway. Grief emptied every room.

It surprised Allyn and me that my father showed so little resilience in dealing with my mother's death. We all grieved, and we could appreciate that he had experienced a keener loss than our own, but he fell into a lethargy we could do nothing to alleviate. He said little, drank too much, and neglected the shop. Allyn diagnosed his condition as something other than grief, and she pestered him until he agreed to see a doctor. What he learned from the physician he shared with me, not her. He could not bring himself to admit to any female, even his own daughter, that cancer had lodged in his colon.

The operation weakened him, as did the radiation. His treatment seemed a torture, and we watched him wither away. He bore it stoically enough, knowing the cancer would win. Each evening, I parked him in a soft chair, sorted out his pills, and turned on Huntley-Brinkley, because he didn't trust Walter Cronkite. We argued about Vietnam until bedtime, each scoring points here and there, no one ever winning. As we debated the domino theory, our last opportunity to speak frankly to one another slipped away. I wouldn't change that. Any expression of "true feeling" embarrassed my father. He shied from the confessional, detested the maudlin. Had I spoken to him in the honest way a psychologist would advise, attempting to put into words my complicated feelings of love and respect, my father would have recoiled. In his world, expressions of love diminished a trust that needed no acknowledgment. When the day came for me to return to school, he shook my hand, thanked me for coming home, and asked about my connecting flight. I returned to Boston, resumed my classes, smoked pot, and marched against the war. I left Allyn alone to care for him. A succession of maids came and went, none for more than several weeks in that oppressive house. His condition worsened, and my father's soiled pajamas required constant changing. As these well-meaning women struggled to pull his wasting arms through the baggy sleeves, he laced into them with words from a different era. Times had changed, and Allyn's profuse apologies could not make his language acceptable.

To my surprise, those endless months with my father inspired Allyn to become a nurse. She faced what I fled, and she discovered in herself a genuine capacity for caring. Allyn does not come across as a particularly warm person. Hallmark cards and Christmas movies do not bring her to tears, nor do kittens or babies, but she calls me often and still sends a present on my birthday. I have watched her practice a utilitarian kindness. Her tough personality conceals a good heart.

I regret that I never had an adult conversation with either of my parents. I like to think that, once I had established my own identity, I would have grown closer to my father. Certainly, I'd like to know more about his childhood on the farm, his relationship with his own parents, and his friendship with Brother. I wish also that he'd lived to witness my success, to see that his sensitive child turned out better than he expected. He would have seen that, through the agency of people like Jamie McAllister and Dermot Bogue, I found a way to thrive.

I knew my mother only as a boy does, not as one adult knows another. The fact that her image has faded seems like a failing. If she meant so much to me, shouldn't I remember more about her? Lately, I've tested myself and tried to recall the sound of her laugh or to recreate a specific conversation that does not belong to the vortex of that rushing summer. Inevitably, I slip back to the familiar. I have managed to preserve a few memories well-worn with grief, smooth as skipping stones.

After my father's funeral, I closed the cabinet shop, paid off the workers, and sold the table saws for pennies on the dollar. Allyn and I cleaned out the house together. We bagged my mother's clothes and took them to Goodwill. We found Bit's shoebox above the maid's toilet off the laundry room. The box held a comb, a couple of pins, a yellow ribbon, a hand mirror, and a tin of snuff. Until that discovery, neither of us had known that Bit dipped snuff. We found nothing profound in her box, but each item serves as a reminder: a pin that once held her hair, a mirror that once held her image. Even the box feels old, the cardboard soft at the corners. It holds only relics now, worthless but for what we remember.

CHAPTER 31

D RIVING into LaSalle for the first time in thirty years, I get lost. I should be the last to complain, but these big box stores and restaurant chains have ruined the place. I barely recognize the shopping plaza near where I grew up. With a Wendy's at one corner and a Colonel Sanders at the next, developers have substituted generic Sunbelt retail for the little bit of character this commercial district once possessed.

Downtown looks familiar but run-down. The same gray columns command the courthouse portico, and Sweet Papa still stands watch in the square, his musket at-the-ready, though his days are numbered. No great work of art, the statute's face could represent any one of the thousands of great grandfathers who fought in gray. I now know that the town erected this memorial in 1927, not after the Civil War, as I had once believed. Five soulless stories of brick and glass have replaced the old bank building where we stood to watch the marchers. Empty sidewalks and storefronts line Broadway, the little shop owners stamped out by Big Commerce. I remember Winn Prather complaining that the demonstrators would scare away the tailor, the clerk, and the shoeshine man. Well, they've left all right, but not because a civil rights march drove them out.

Mt. Calvary remains much the same, though the neighborhood has improved. Still nothing grand. Crabgrass sprouts through cracks in the sidewalk, and the cheap public housing shows its age. They have leveled Bit's neighborhood, closed the ditches, paved the road, and planted rows of spindly trees that look under-watered. I arrive early to the church, contented to watch the hall fill. A Black girl in a fuchsia dress greets me with a bright smile. She hands me a program and points me down the red carpeted aisle. I surprise her by stating my preference for the balcony. Climbing the stairs, I experience, for the first time, a genuine sense of return. I can remember following McAllister's long legs up these very steps.

I can't be sure that the pew I choose is the one McAllister selected, but close enough. The balcony, smaller than I remember, retains its pleasing horseshoe shape, and the pews and floorboards still moan with their same sad music. I have barely had time to settle in when a white woman enters the balcony. She ignores the empty pews and heads straight toward me, as if, in all this empty church, I have stolen her spot. My age or older, tall with good bones, she wears chic sunglasses. She stands at the end of the pew and studies me.

"Well, if it isn't little Little," she says.

"Julia?" I say, and we embrace, laughing.

She joins me in the pew and faces me, our knees nearly touching. The loose folds at the corners of her mouth and an age spot on her cheek do little to diminish her regal looks. Without her sunglasses, those blue McAllister eyes remain spectacular. She exudes the confidence of a woman who has looked beautiful all her life.

She tells me her father brought her to this church once, and they sat in the balcony, in the very pew I have claimed. "My father would take me places, show me things. He wouldn't tell me where we were going. All he said was, *there is something I want you to see.* We sat up here and watched Tim Butters preach." She looks down to the pulpit. "I'll never forget it."

"And now you're back," I say.

"Now I'm back," she says, turning to smile at me.

I ask about Jamie, and she tells me he lives in Ohio, in Wooster, where he has retired from teaching college students about Emerson and Thoreau. He enjoyed immense popularity with the students, and some of them, now alumni, have begun a movement to name a library for him.

I laugh at that. "The James T. McAllister Library! I love it! And he's an Emerson scholar? That means he must have come to Massachusetts."

Lots of times, Julia tells me. It pains me to realize Jamie came so close, and I never knew it. I catch a fleeting glimpse of a relationship that might have continued, childhood friends from Georgia getting together on the scholar's regular pilgrimages to Concord. I should have stayed in touch. Julia tells me she is widowed, but she lives close to her daughter in San Francisco and has grandchildren to keep her company.

"San Francisco is a long way from LaSalle," I say.

"It is," she says. Below us, the church is slowly filling.

"You came all this way just to hear Emma G?"

Julia laughs. "I think it is Emogene now, Little. Better yet, Dr. Emogene Harrison. And yes, I came all this way just to hear her. My father would have come. He would have been so proud of her and so happy to see Tim Butters remembered. Proud of LaSalle for its progress."

"Progress," I say. "I read about it before I came. The town council voted six to five in favor of taking down the Confederate memorial. The four African Americans were joined by a Ms. Wu and a Mr. Mugheri. The five whites voted no."

Julia shrugs and says nothing. "What do you remember about Emogene?" I ask.

"Nothing from LaSalle. I don't know that I ever met her when we were living here, but my father kept in touch with Bit after she and Emogene moved to Newark. When Emogene received her master's degree from Columbia, my father and I attended the ceremony." Julia laughs. "You should have seen Bit, decked out in yellow head-to-toe, the proudest mother hen in the flock."

"You saw Bit?" I ask, incredulous. I try to picture Bit in New York, attending her daughter's graduation from Columbia, but I can't do it. The incongruous image refuses to form. When Bit left us in the McAllister drive, she fell off the edge of the earth. Now I learn that she kept in touch with the reverend and even invited him to Emma's G graduation. I'll admit to feeling betrayed, as if her invitation revealed a preference for his family over ours.

"The transformation struck me," Julia says. "Not just hers. Seeing my father next to Bit, I realized how he had diminished. When the church kicked us out of town, I think my father recognized that if he was going to remain married to my mother, he would have to take care of her. That became his primary job. He spent less time in his study and more time with her. He even recycled a few sermons, which he never would have done in LaSalle. It disappointed me to watch him become so domestic, but his decision saved their marriage. He chose how to live. How many people do that?

"Bit seemed like a different person. You can imagine what graduation at Columbia looked like back in those days, all the students with shoulder-length hair and peace signs on their mortarboards, and all the mothers in their tasteful pearls, and there stands Bit, dressed like a buttercup! She pulled us over and introduced us to her brother as 'her old friends from home.' It touched me that she would describe us in such a sweet and utterly ridiculous way. You would have thought we all went to church together, which, I suppose, we did, though not in a way anyone outside of LaSalle could have imagined."

"I loved Bit," I say, and it feels like an old truth, one of the few permanent features of my time on earth.

"Bit changed my life," Julia says. She is looking away from me and down, watching people find their seats. "She rescued me when I was young and not very smart."

"I seem to remember some connection between you two," I say, as if I don't know exactly what she's talking about.

"I adored her. Everyone in my family did, except my mother. Bit doted on Jamie, and we could all see how much she admired my father. As for me, I was a girl in trouble, and Bit acted as my savior." Julia touches my hand. "Can I share a secret with an old friend? That summer, when my father's article was published and my mother was institutionalized and our family seemed to be falling apart, I managed to get myself pregnant. Pure genius, don't you think? I was determined to rebel, and my little insurrection blew up right in my face. I had no one to turn to. My mother couldn't manage her own life; as for my father, he had thundered off on his high horse to save the world. I felt utterly trapped and alone. To my good fortune, Bit just happened to show up in our house at exactly the right moment."

"Bit helped?" I say, continuing to play dumb. Then, feeling bold, I add, "I'm guessing that Bit would have taken you to a Dr. Amos Swift, and that he... performed the procedure?"

Julia looks puzzled. "I don't think I remember an Amos Smith," she says. "Was he a friend of your mother's?"

"The doctor, the ob-gyn. Isn't that who Bit took you to see?"

"I told Bit I needed help, that if she didn't help me, Tucker Gran had found someone across the river, in Alabama, who would do it. God knows who that was or whether I would have gone through with it, but I told Bit that if she didn't help me, I'd have to rely on Tucker. The idea horrified her. I really put her in an awful spot, I see that now. But she didn't take me to a doctor. She took me to your mother."

This can't be right. "My mother?"

"Your mother took me to a doctor. She waited for me outside his office during the— what did you call it?—procedure, and then she drove me home. Everyone was focused on my father's last sermon. I told my parents I was going to a friend's house for a farewell party, and your mother drove me straight from the church to the doctor. Not a soul in sight on a Sunday. The doctor met us behind his office because he didn't want anyone to see the car in the parking lot. I remember how terrified I felt watching him unlock the door and turn on the office lights."

I cannot imagine any version of my mother that would arrange an abortion or even know how. She had headaches. She stayed home. How had Allyn put it? For our mother, filling the birdfeeder amounted to all the excitement she could stand. "Are you sure you're remembering this right?"

"It's not the sort of thing one forgets. Your mother told my father she was sending Bit over to fix our dinner, but in fact, Bit went there to look after me. Your mother dropped me at the corner and watched until I ·

walked through the door of our house, and Bit met me inside. She put me to bed and told my parents some fib about me not feeling well. Only three people knew: me, Bit, and your mother. We formed a little cabal."

My mother did not form cabals. The person I remember would have talked some sense into Julia. She would never have engaged in some surreptitious "procedure."

"Of course, they both tried to talk me out of it," Julia continues, "but your mother knew we were moving away, and she worried that if she didn't arrange something right away, something safe, I would have done something foolish. I don't know if you ever noticed—you were young for your years—but your mother had feelings for my father. Nothing inappropriate, you know, just this ardent sympathy. I think she understood that my parents couldn't handle another crisis, so she handled this one for them. He never knew. He wrote to your mother several times after we left LaSalle, but he said she never answered. I've always wondered whether she was protecting my secret."

Then what Julia is telling me begins to make sense. My mother didn't act for Julia's sake or for the good of the McAllister family. She did it for him. I remember the two of them standing in the door of his house, her smaller hand clasped in his, how she looked up at him. She never would have helped Julia but for him. An illegal abortion. The very words sound dangerous and vulgar, the morality tortuous, and yet my mother arranged it, for his sake.

Below us, Dr. Emogene Harrison has taken a seat in front of the altar. Gray dreadlocks spread across her shoulders. I would not have recognized her but for the prominent cheekbones. A much younger woman takes the chair next to her, slighter of build, with close-cropped hair and looping earrings. She introduces herself as a professor from the University of Georgia and begins her introduction of Dr. Harrison, but thoughts of my mother crowd out her words.

I have watered down my mother's memory to just a few images, all domestic and routine. I remember how she stretched out on her bed with a book, tilting her head to read through her bifocals, how she leaned over the sink in pink dishwashing gloves. But then I remember how her pale feet looked beneath the spring water on my uncle's farm, like the feet of a young girl, and I recall how she stood in the McAllister's kitchen, tipsy from her gin and tonic, waving the air horn, ready to blast the next caller. I remember how her face changed at the sound of the reverend's voice on the line, how his words moved through her body like a shockwave, the sudden relief nearly bringing her to her knees.

Dr. Harrison has begun to speak, saying something about white apartheid, something about scraps from the master's table, but I'm untangling a different history. "I don't know if you ever noticed," Julia had said. Noticed what? Noticed how? "You were very young." Twelve years old, young for my age, but I saw what I saw, noticed what I noticed. "Your mother had feelings." Her father. My mother. After the McAllisters moved to Ohio, I begged my mother to drive me there for a visit. She always promised, but never did. She put me off.

Because she knew she could not follow him.

Because she owed it to her family to let this man go out of her life, this tall man of words with his quick blue eyes, dark brow, and ironic smile. A man of books and ideas, a dreamer like her, a man who was willing to give up his livelihood just to do the right thing. A man she first admired, then loved. Because love does not require consummation. Her "boycott" of Patterson's amounted to a protest so private no one noticed. Just so, she harbored a passion she never revealed. I saw it without seeing, knew it without knowing.

Beneath me, an old woman with dreadlocks sits before an altar, a microphone pinned to her lapel, but her words cannot catch up to my racing thoughts.

Did my father ever guess? He was adept at missing cues. But that image may represent another convenient figment in the myth of my family. I remember my mother saying, *Don't listen to what he says. Watch what he does.* What if he saw how she responded to McAllister? What if he confronted her? She must have known that, for whatever hurt or fury he expressed, he would stay devoted to our family. He had no choice but to trust her. He relied on her to act as a good wife and mother, full of common sense, and he remained loyal to the bone.

None of this will send any mountains crashing into the sea, but it's enough to shake me. Allyn would never consider this version of our family life because she's entrenched in her own ideas of our shared childhood. Julia has opened a crack for me, just wide enough to see a truer version, a person conflicted but decent, tortured not in any grand sense, but with longings painful and real. A housewife who belonged to the PTA and served on the session of elders. My mother watched *The Ed Sullivan Show*, shopped at Piggly Wiggly, and suffered from migraines. And she felt something more than admiration for our minister.

My father used to fold the church program into an airplane, and, to amuse me, pretend that he was about to launch it over the pews. Once, mid-sermon, I saw her take the plane from his hand and smooth it. Beneath the list of hymns, she wrote the name *Yeats*, then slipped the program into her purse. She wanted to learn, had a heart that sometimes ached, and she wished for what she could not have. There she is. I can almost feel as she felt, think as she thought. Incredible that I, a man in his seventies, could remain blinded by a boy's simple love for his mother.

Then I hear the professor ask Dr. Harrison about growing up in LaSalle. "I had a happy childhood," she tells us. "I know that sounds ironic after all I've just said, but I was an only child of a single mother, and I received all her attention. In the material sense, we had nothing. When I spoke earlier about living off scraps from the master's table, I was not speaking metaphorically. We literally ate what was left over from their meals, and the clothes I wore were clothes they had thrown away. But I had a good mama."

Bit used the same words that day in the drive, as I clung to her and begged her not to leave. "You have a good mama," she said. "She won't never leave this family." Bit knew her as I never did, as one woman knows another. She saw how my mother looked at Rob McAllister and understood what I, a child, did not.

"My mother worked long and hard to get me out of LaSalle," Dr. Harrison says. "Every parent-teacher conference, she was asking about scholarships. She saved every nickel and worked every angle to make enough money for us to leave. At one point," Dr. Harrison laughs as she says this, "she even had two white boys selling baked goods for her down at the mill! I wasn't sure I wanted to leave LaSalle. I had friends here, but my mother never wavered.'"

It would have pained my mother to hear Emogene speak of living off scraps. What my mother thought of as a charity, Emogene remembers as an insult. And it must have hurt my mother to realize that Bit schemed to leave without ever confiding in her. She failed to see herself as Bit saw her, indeed, saw all of us. We never knew Bit's mind, though she came into our house almost every day.

I have not given Dr. Harrison my full attention, but I have seen and heard enough to understand that I cannot restore any meager connection that may have existed long ago. To place in her hands a shoebox of her mother's odds and ends will only confuse, embarrass, or insult her. No, I'll take the box home and protect it. Clearly, anyone else would have thrown it out long ago.

The relentless Georgia sun waits outside the church. I will escape to the river and walk in the shade of the now dormant mill. Before I catch my flight, I'll drive again past Courthouse Square, then I'll climb the hill to where our house still stands. I used to bike down that hill balancing a watermelon, an ordinary boy in what seemed an ordinary place. Infamous now, this town where I grew up. I lived in LaSalle.

ACKNOWLEDGMENTS

I'm grateful to Michelle Wildgen for her professional support and the invaluable guidance she provided on structure and character; to David Thomas, who delivered a welcome jolt to my prose; to Najah Webb and Kayla Dunigan, who helped me see this story from a different perspective; to Peter Alson, who generously agreed to edit and publish my novel; and to Rachel Kuech, for designing the striking cover.

Thanks also to Catherine Armsden, who combined friendly support with a novelist's perspective; to Skip Smart, Jerry Oyama, Walter Littell, and Don McLaren, who read earlier versions and encouraged me; and to my children, William, Henry, and Amelia, who agreed to read my story even though it addresses prehistoric times.

I'd also like to thank my siblings, Gwynn Polidoro, Hasty Johnson, and Lloyd Johnston, who remember those ancient times. They provided helpful perspectives, as did Sis Johnson and Roger Polidoro. Allyn Hart didn't complain when I borrowed her first name.

Peggy Greenough read every word more than once, then sat on the porch with me for hours, helping me to imagine another world.

About the Author

After growing up in Columbus, Georgia, Joel F. Johnson graduated from Harvard and made stops in Alta, Utah, Boulder, and Manhattan, before settling in Concord, Massachusetts. His collection of poems, *Where Inches Seem Miles*, was selected by *Kirkus Reviews* as one of the best independent books of 2014. *Never* is his first novel.

CPSIA information can be obtained
at www.ICGtesting.com
Printed in the USA
LVHW050942280523
748221LV00007B/195

9 781958 762073